A PERILOUS POSITION

Annie maneuvered down the stairs from the piquet room, rounded the corner in the entry hall, and drew up short as she saw a gentleman loitering in the back hallway. She gasped, her heart pounding, only to look up into the smiling eyes of Mr. Frake. She let out her breath on a shaky sigh.

His brow creased in a slight frown. "Did I give you a start?"

"No, sir." She tried to push past.

He remained in her way. "I have a few more questions for you, when you have a chance."

"You're always havin' questions for me, sir. And I don't have no chance. Please, sir," she added, as he still showed no sign of moving. "I got my duties, and we're ever so busy tonight. There's all them in the rooms askin' me about what happened last night, and they ain't none of them happy when I says I don't know."

"Tell them I've ordered you not to say nothing. That should set them all a-gog." His expression remained solemn, but his eyes twinkled. He stepped aside. "I'll be here, whenever you get the time."

She bobbed him a quick curtsy and rushed past, vowing it would be a long while indeed before she'd find that kind of time. Why did he keep wanting to talk to her, anyway? It would be best if she avoided him completely.

She retrieved another load of bottles, then started once more up the steps. She neared the top, stepped on the next stair, and her foot slid out from under her. The tray fell from her hands, the bottles crashed to the carpeted floor, and she grabbed wildly for the banister as she toppled backward . . .

ZEBRA'S REGENCY ROMANCES DAZZLE AND DELIGHT

A BEGUILING INTRIGUE (4441, $3.99)
by Olivia Sumner

Pretty as a picture Justine Riggs cared nothing for propriety. She dressed as a boy, sat on her horse like a jockey, and pondered the stars like a scientist. But when she tried to best the handsome Quenton Fletcher, Marquess of Devon, by proving that she was the better equestrian, he would try to prove Justine's antics were pure folly. The game he had in mind was seduction — never imagining that he might lose his heart in the process!

AN INCONVENIENT ENGAGEMENT (4442, $3.99)
by Joy Reed

Rebecca Wentworth was furious when she saw her betrothed waltzing with another. So she decides to make him jealous by flirting with the handsomest man at the ball, John Collinwood, Earl of Stanford. The "wicked" nobleman knew exactly what the enticing miss was up to — and he was only too happy to play along. But as Rebecca gazed into his magnificent eyes, her errant fiancé was soon utterly forgotten!

SCANDAL'S LADY (4472, $3.99)
by Mary Kingsley

Cassandra was shocked to learn that the new Earl of Lynton was her childhood friend, Nicholas St. John. After years at sea and mixed feelings Nicholas had come home to take the family title. And although Cassandra knew her place as a governess, she could not help the thrill that went through her each time he was near. Nicholas was pleased to find that his old friend Cassandra was his new next door neighbor, but after being near her, he wondered if mere friendship would be enough . . .

HIS LORDSHIP'S REWARD (4473, $3.99)
by Carola Dunn

As the daughter of a seasoned soldier, Fanny Ingram was accustomed to the vagaries of military life and cared not a whit about matters of rank and social standing. So she certainly never foresaw her *tendre* for handsome Viscount Roworth of Kent with whom she was forced to share lodgings, while he carried out his clandestine activities on behalf of the British Army. And though good sense told Roworth to keep his distance, he couldn't stop from taking Fanny in his arms for a kiss that made all hearts equal!

Available wherever paperbacks are sold, or order direct from the Publisher. Send cover price plus 50¢ per copy for mailing and handling to Penguin USA, P.O. Box 999, c/o Dept. 17109, Bergenfield, NJ 07621. Residents of New York and Tennessee must include sales tax. DO NOT SEND CASH.

A Desperate Gamble
Janice Bennett

ZEBRA BOOKS
KENSINGTON PUBLISHING CORP.

For Adele and Jennifer—
about time, isn't it?

One

The furtiveness of the movement caught Annie Gooden's attention. She spun about, seeking the source, then focused on the burgundy velvet curtain that closed off the doorway leading to the servants corridor. Around her, the rumble of animated voices in the gaming hell rose and fell, but she ceased to hear them, even the ones calling her name, crying for the wine bottles she carried on her laden tray.

Where—?

The drapery swayed, then a wiry figure slipped between the heavy folds. Without so much as a glance about, he darted across the room's open space and went to earth behind the lush foliage of a huge potted palm. Samuel. She'd been right.

Anxiety flickered through Annie, to be swept away the next moment beneath a tide of irritation. She thrust her tray onto the edge of the nearest table, then darted a searching look around to make sure no one else had glimpsed her elder brother. No one, at least, who might take umbrage at his daring to venture into the rooms. Mrs. Wickham, the proprietress of the private gaming establishment, was nowhere in sight. She must be upstairs, circulating among the rooms. Mr. Henry Wickham, her nephew, would be up there too, hovering over the tables devoted to the games of faro and deep basset which drew such large crowds. As for Captain Palfrey, he stood at his accustomed post on the far side of the dicing room, overseeing the hazard tables, intent on his players and paying her no heed. He never so much as glanced her way.

Safe. So far.

Trying not to attract attention, she slipped off on an intercept course as her brother sidled toward a curtained alcove on the far side of the dicing room. "Samuel Gooden," she hissed as she caught his arm.

He started, spinning to face her, then fixed her with a reproving eye.

Before he could protest, she propelled him into the sheltering cover of the alcove and dragged the drapery partly closed behind them. "Just what game are you playin' at?" she whispered. "What ever are you doin' up here? You know what Mrs. Wickham would say."

With the back of his hand, he swiped at the shock of unruly hair, so dark as to be almost black, that hung over his wide-set brown eyes. "Some greetin' that is, I must say." He sounded more indignant than he looked. "Here I goes to all this trouble, just to have a look-in at you, mind, an—"

"Oh, is that what you're doin', is it? You slip in here, bold as brass—"

He straightened. "I ain't bein' bold. I'm bein' what ol' Rumguts'd call—"

"Samuel!" Annie protested.

"—the very picture of discretion," Samuel finished, ignoring her interruption.

She sniffed. "You ain't to go callin' Sir Joshua that. What'd happen if he heard you? And you've been at the bottle, too, I'll wager."

He grinned. "Now, Annie, m'girl—"

"You just slip right back out, you hear? I'll not have you lookin' over the customers. If you so much as put a finger towards one of them gents' pockets—"

"As if I would!" He drew himself up to his full five foot two inches and regarded her down the bridge of a long nose, crooked from having been broken more than once during the course of his twenty-three years.

"A groom's got no business in the rooms," she informed him loftily. "What're you plannin' to say if Sir Joshua sees you?"

He grinned. "I got me a good excuse if that cheese-paring old trout casts his daylights this way. Just comin' to check with his honor to see what time he wants me to walk him home. He'll never remember if he told me or not. Beetle-headed, he is."

"I—" Annie broke off as a strident voice shouted her name. She turned and, through the wide gap in the alcove's curtain, saw Viscount Daylesford, a slim young gentleman of moderate height, bearing down on her from the direction of the doorway into the entry hall. As he drew nearer, she saw the bleary expression of his green eyes as they regarded her from above the straight, broad nose.

Jug-bitten, he was. He had unbuttoned his coat of deep green velvet, which hung open to reveal a startling waistcoat in a brightly colored floral pattern. Within the intricate folds of his neckcloth gleamed an emerald stickpin, now slightly askew. He waved at her. Captain Palfrey would notice if she didn't tend to him, and right fast at that.

"Go away," she hissed at her brother. "Get back to the kitchens and your Ruby."

She slipped out, hoping for once her elder brother would do as he was told. Not much chance of it, she supposed. With one hand she smoothed the black bombazine of the apron she wore over her burgundy merino round gown, and with the other she tucked an errant dark curl back under her ruffled black mobcap.

Viscount Daylesford ambled forward, grinned at her, and swept a bottle from her abandoned tray as she reached it. With an owlish smile, he departed the room, making his way toward the stairs. Probably returning to the piquet room. He seemed to spend most of his time there.

She glanced over her shoulder in time to see her brother emerge none too steadily from his temporary shelter and stroll casually along the back wall—away from the majority of the players and the blazing candelabra, thank heavens. She delivered her bottles, then looked around for him again. He'd drawn just a little too close for her taste to one of the dicing tables where several gentlemen and two ladies—not that they deserved the term, of course—kept their unwavering attention fixed on the casting of the ivories.

Except for one man, who stood back a pace—just far enough to make a tempting target. Captain Thomas Bevis watched the play, his figure tall, elegant, and sophisticated. The full lips beneath the aquiline nose twitched in tolerant amusement as one of the gamesters swore. A pair of deep-set gray eyes dominated the classical lines of his face, and his artlessly tumbled brown hair curled back from a high forehead. His coat, cut to perfection, must have cost him more than five years' wages for Annie, and his neckcloth was a right treat to see. He held a chased silver snuff box loosely in one hand. Samuel's gaze remained riveted on that expensive little trifle.

Annie wove her way through the crowded room, as straight toward Samuel as she could manage, and caught him by the arm. Ignoring his muffled yelp of protest, she thrust him out the door of the dicing room and into the entry hall with its red and gold wallpaper and gilded mirrors. The door to the salon opposite stood closed, as did the one to the dining room. For the moment no one was climbing the broad staircase to the more elaborate rooms above.

"Now, Annie—" Samuel began, his tone wheedling.

"Now Annie, nothin'," she snapped, keeping her voice low. "Don't you never go thinkin' of stealin' anythin' from Captain Bevis, or you'll land yourself in the suds for sure. Oh, Sammy, can't you use your head for once? You ain't bacon-brained. You know how often the captain visits Sir Joshua. What would happen if he called in the Runners on you?"

Samuel snorted. "I ain't afraid of no Redbreasts."

"Then you're a fool, Samuel Gooden. Runners are trouble. They look right inside you and know what you're thinkin'." At least the last one she'd encountered had done that, fixing her with the penetrating stare of his impossibly innocent blue eyes . . .

Samuel snorted. "Now, if you ain't bein' Miss Prunes and Prisms. Hen-hearted, that's what you are, as if you was nine and not nineteen. You wouldn't see me runnin' from a little rough and tumble with a nabbing-cull."

"No, he'd have you pinched afore you could get away." She glared at her brother, arms akimbo. "Now, you get. We don't want Sir Joshua cuttin' up stiff if he sees you. We need him in a good mood. You know that."

Samuel's brow lowered, giving him a stubborn, bull-like countenance. "What we need is for him to do what's right and proper."

"Well, he hasn't, has he? Not so far, leastways. And if we want him to do anythin' other than give you the sack, which will only make everythin' so much the worse, you just leave it to me."

Samuel's lip curled. "You've been here nigh on five weeks already, Annie, and he's come here upwards of a dozen times. When're you goin' to have it out with him?"

Annie swallowed. "Tonight."

Tonight. She watched her brother swagger down the back hall toward the servants stair leading below to the kitchen as a small group of gamesters descended from above. She turned back into the dicing room.

Tonight, somehow, she was going to make the opportunity to confront her former employer. She couldn't let her nerve fail her. Matters had grown too desperate.

She scanned the crowded chamber, but couldn't see Sir Joshua anywhere among the hazard players. Probably upstairs. He, like Lord Daylesford, favored cards. She returned to the hall, collected the last of the bottles that stood waiting on the sideboard in the short corridor leading to the back of the house, and started up the narrow servants stair.

This let her out on the next floor into a small, dark passageway which ran the width of the establishment. She made her way first to the farthest room to her right, the library with its shelves of books and musty smell of leather, lemon oil, and beeswax. Comfortable chairs stood in groups before a blazing hearth, and a small writing table stood on either end of the room. Mrs. Wickham varied between proclaiming her house to be nothing more than the location of private evening parties, and a club along the lines of a miniature Watiers or White's. Annie knew it for what it was, a hell where the gaming was a trifle more honest than at other such establishments.

She checked the brandy decanters and found them untouched. Next she crossed the hall to the series of interconnected rooms at the front of the house which were given over to players with no taste for deep doings; silver loo tended to be the game of choice. The level of voices rose in a crescendoing rumble, for here conversation as much as gaming held sway.

She collected only a few empty bottles, replacing them as she went, then emerged through the main door. A number of people milled about in the corridor by the great oak staircase, some going down to the hazard tables, others coming up to join in one of the various card games offered on this floor. Sir Joshua wasn't among them.

Nor did she find him in the large double drawing rooms opposite, where every conceivable game of chance with cards took place. She circled this massive chamber, delivering bottles to those who dragged their attention from the games long enough to notice her, then moved on. He'd be in the smaller room at the back, she supposed, the one given over to piquet.

As soon as she entered that chamber, she saw him, her gaze drawn by the sheer force of the man. Tall and slender, with a hawk-like nose and wild mane of silvering hair, he sat stiffly erect at a small table against the wall. An aura of power and determination seemed to emanate from him. He had always made her uncomfortable, though he had mesmerized the other maids at Templeton Grange. Her sister Violet, among them.

Tonight he was dressed in the somber black he had adopted seven months ago, upon the death of his only son, Captain Oliver Templeton. Annie shivered. There seemed to be more vengeance than grief in the man. He made the skin prickle along her arms.

Yet she had to approach him, beg a word with him in private. Only her desperation, her fears for her sister, kept her from turning tail.

Right now, though, she could see no chance of carrying out her purpose; he was not alone. Viscount Daylesford sat across the table from him, the bottle he had taken from her not long ago already less than half full, judging from the angle at which he held it as he poured more of the heady red wine into his glass.

Annie pursed her lips in disapproval. Where Sir Joshua displayed the concentration of a seasoned and dedicated gamester, the viscount leaned forward, his brow creased, his expression clearly betraying his uncertainty in his discards. His sandy hair, so artfully tousled when he arrived, now hung disordered and limp, his valet's painstaking efforts with the curling iron ruined by agitated fingers. His neckcloth was rumpled, and the pin—Annie vividly remembered the square-cut emerald set in gold that had nestled among the folds—was nowhere to be seen.

Yes, it was. There, on the table. The silly sapskull had wagered it. He and Sir Joshua must have been playing for some time.

A touch on her arm recalled her attention, and she stepped hastily aside before turning. Mrs. Wickham, her plump figure swathed in yards of pale green silk, bent her head toward Annie, causing her three ostrich plumes to slide askew from where they were fastened in her fuzz of impossibly yellow ringlets. The proprietress's brow creased in concern.

"There, if someone should not warn dear Viscount Daylesford about playing with skilled gamesters." The woman had to raise her voice to be heard over the hum of conversation. "I do so hate to see one of my guests so distressed."

Annie sniffed. "Someone ought to give Sir Joshua a good scold about takin' advantage of a mere lad," she said, then flushed at her temerity.

Mrs. Wickham's close-set eyes widened. "I'll not have you say anything of the kind, my girl. Sir Joshua—Sir Joshua makes his own rules, and they have nothing to do with you. Have you carried wine to the other rooms recently?"

"Yes, mum." Annie's cheeks burned. "I'm that sorry, mum. The gamin'—"

"—is not for the likes of you," Mrs. Wickham finished for her. "Or is it young Daylesford you're watching?" Her gaze narrowed as she studied Annie. "It's all to the good it's that Mrs. Leeds he's been casting sheep eyes at, for you may be certain she's up to snuff, which you, I'll warrant, are not. Now, you mind your step, girl, and have nothing to do with the gentleman, or you'll find yourself with more trouble than you know what to do with."

"Yes, mum." Meekly, Annie scooted away to retrieve more bottles from the cellars.

As she descended the second flight of stairs toward the kitchen, redolent odors wafted out, welcoming her. Lamb, beef, potatoes, something with a cheese sauce. . . . Each individual aroma separated from the rest, then blended once more, tantalizing her with promises. Onion, oregano, a subtle touch of garlic. . . . Her stomach responded, and for a moment she allowed herself to breathe deeply. Later, there'd be leftovers, scraps she could have, perhaps some Cook would actually allow her to take home with her, to her sister.

And maybe—just maybe—after she confronted Sir Joshua, they would no longer need to depend on such largesse.

She entered the cavernous chamber of the kitchen, only to be brought up short by the sight of Samuel, idly shelling peas as if he belonged there. The kitchen maid Ruby stood by the hearth, turning a joint of beef on the spit. The heat flushed her creamy complexion, and her soft brown ringlets clung damply to her forehead. Her generous figure filled out her burgundy round gown with its begrimed muslin apron. The girl turned and fluttered her lashes over her shoulder at Samuel, spotted Annie, and returned hastily to her task. For the next minute, the joint spun industriously.

Cook looked up from his labors with an incurious glance, then returned to his exacting arrangement of a garnish on a plate of small cakes and pastries. Annie forced her eyes from the sugary concoctions and made her way to the pantry where she refilled her tray with more of the burgundies, canaries, and champagne that had been set out for the night. At least for the time being, her brother wasn't upstairs planning any mischief.

Once more she made the rounds of the rooms. Intensity filled the air, mirrored on almost every face. Why did they come? They didn't look as if they enjoyed themselves. Except those who had left the tables, of course. They stood in small knots, talking, laughing, or staring blankly into space. Those last must be the losers, she reflected, and set another bottle next to a gentleman's elbow. Two empty ones lay on their sides near him and she cleared them away.

And how was Sir Joshua doing? Not that she wished Viscount Daylesford ill, but she hoped Sir Joshua was winning. She needed the old gent feeling well-disposed and generous tonight.

She crossed the hall to the back salon where the devotees of piquet gathered. Sir Joshua still sat where he had been before; he might not have moved at all. Only the pile of paper before him indicated hand after hand had succeeded one another—and he had continued to win.

Daylesford slumped over the table across from him, both hands gripping his cards as if he could wring the needed one from their midst. The poor cawker was losing badly. It was good for her, though.

She sidled about, still holding one last bottle, and positioned herself where she could see Sir Joshua's face. He betrayed no sign of pleasure at his impressive winning streak, except that the very blankness of his expression indicated his immense satisfaction. Even the mildest of displeasures, as she had reason to know, brought down his thunderous brow.

Daylesford, with a strangled sound that could have been a whimper, played the last card. Sir Joshua gathered them up with a careless sweep of his arm, along with the viscount's scribbled vowel. This he cast on the pile with the others, then squared the cards and began to shuffle.

"No—no more." Daylesford rose from the table, his face haggard. Even by the flickering light of the candles, he looked pale.

No, drained. As if his very life ebbed away. His hands trembled where they rested fleetingly on the back of his abandoned chair. A pang of compassion shot through Annie

Behind her, above the subdued background rumble, a woman's carrying voice said: "Daylesford seems to be having a run of ill luck."

Annie turned and recognized Mrs. Cornelia Leeds. The young widow leaned forward toward her companion, one slender white arm on the table, the pale blue silk of her low-cut gown setting off her fair complexion. A riot of blond curls framed a delicate face in which Annie could detect a frowning concern, yet no trace of real sympathy.

Her companion, an aging gentleman of ample girth, raised his quizzing glass and snorted. "Silly nodcock. Looks like he may have rolled himself up. You have yet to play to my lead, m'dear."

Mrs. Leeds's gaze lingered on Daylesford, then with a fatalistic shrug, she turned the full play of her flirtatious lashes on the gentleman opposite her. "I like to take the time to study the moves of a clever player," she said, and drew a beaming smile from him.

Daylesford, his expression stricken, stumbled away from the table. He brushed against Annie and stead-

ied himself with a hand on her shoulder. Not sure
what to do but wanting to help, she pressed her last
bottle into his hands. He grasped it, cradling it in
his arm as if in its possession he found his sole
measure of comfort. He made his half-blind, erratic
way out the door.

Sir Joshua hadn't so much as looked at his departing opponent. With infinite precision, he squared the
deck of cards again, tapped them absently with one
finger, then looked around. Probably seeking another
opponent, Annie reflected. Didn't the fortune he'd
just won satisfy him? But with him it wasn't the
money so much as the game. And the winning.

She studied his expression and detected a slight
upward curl to his lips. A good sign, she remembered
from the days when she'd been an under housemaid
at Templeton Grange. He must be feeling satisfied—
perhaps smug enough to be generous. If no one
joined him, she could beg a word with him. He'd
hardly create a scene in here by refusing to talk to
her. She'd just get him another bottle, then—

Sir Joshua stood, and before Annie could react, he
wended his way among the tables, exchanging an occasional nod of greeting with acquaintances, and exited the salon. Annie scrambled after him. By the
time she reached the doorway, he'd already crossed
the main hall and started into the refuge offered by
the small library, the one quiet room in the gaming
establishment.

Annie drew a steadying breath. He'd be alone. Hope
and nerves jostling within her, she started across the

hall. Now, after months of bringing herself up to the
sticking point—

Samuel ambled into the hallway from the corridor
leading to the servants stair. Dismayed, Annie turned
to waylay him. "Now you get—" she began.

He held up a hand. "I'm here all official-like, I am,
so don't you go gettin' on your high ropes, Annie.
Sent, I was, by Ruby. T'fetch you."

Annie's heart sank. Time to carry up the multitude
of dishes to the dining room. Sir Joshua—and all her
hopes—would have to wait. With reluctant steps, she
started down the stairs. "Ain't you comin'?" she
asked over her shoulder.

"In a minute," came his blithe response. "You
hurry ahead. They're waitin' on you."

Below her, on the next floor, she could see Ruby
beckoning to her. The girl's gleaming dark hair still
clung about her face from the heat of the kitchen, but
she had changed out of her work apron into the lace-
trimmed black she used for serving the elaborate supper offered nightly by Mrs. Wickham's establishment.

" 'E's ever so cross tonight," the girl announced
as Annie reached her.

"Who? Oh, Cook?" Annie grimaced. There went
any hope of his holding back any choice pieces for
the servants. "Why?"

Ruby wrinkled her short nose. " 'E caught Samuel
eyein' the pastries. As if 'e'd of taken one!"

"He would of," Annie retorted.

Ruby pouted. "You're just sayin' that 'cause you're

'is sister. Samuel wouldn't go stealin' nothin' that wasn't rightfully 'is."

Annie rolled her eyes but otherwise made no response. If that were true, then Samuel held a rather loose definition of "his." She moved ahead, descending the next flight as quickly as the steep, dark stairs allowed, and emerged at last into the kitchen to be met by the glaring Cook.

The next twenty minutes she spent ferrying platters from the basement to the dining room on the ground floor, and inhaling the most heavenly odors. How, she wondered, could Ruby and Cook stand behind the table serving without ever helping themselves to even a morsel? Annie could only be glad her willpower wasn't put to the test by her having to join them. She'd be needed pouring wine, fetching cards—and perhaps slipping away for just a few minutes to talk to Sir Joshua.

She set down her last dish and ducked out of the room before Cook could command her aid in rearranging everything one more time. For a moment she stood in the entry hall, drawing a deep breath, preparing herself for the confrontation. It wasn't easy. The noise of the place washed over her, deafening, distracting. Champagne corks popped at random intervals, loud even over the rumble of talk and shrill laughter.

She hurried up the back steps, then paused to smooth her apron and tuck stray curls under her mobcap. To present a sloppy appearance would only turn him against her from the start. She took a determined step toward the library, only to be brought up short by a woman's deep voice.

"You, girl." A middle-aged lady, considerably the worse for drink, leaned against the wall beside the main gaming room, her shawl drooping from her elbows. Her elaborate head of plumes had slipped over her startlingly red curls, her lace cap hung askew over one eye.

Perforce, Annie crossed the main hall. "Yes, mum?"

"Fresh cards. And be quick about it." The woman turned and made her dignified way back into the room, weaving only a little.

Annie bobbed a curtsy to the retreating figure, then promptly relegated the matter to the back of her mind. Her own business, just this once, would come first. With renewed determination she turned again to the library, in time to see Viscount Daylesford, his shoulders squared, but his gait weaving, amble out of the loo rooms and enter ahead of her. She was too late.

She waited, but a full minute passed and still the viscount didn't hurry out. Mayhap Sir Joshua had already left—except she hadn't seen him anywhere else. Well, since she couldn't launch at once into her speech, she would use the time to rehearse it again. She did so as she ran up to the next floor, to Mrs. Wickham's office, to fetch the wanted cards.

These she delivered to the woman, who received them with a surprised indifference and apparently no memory of having demanded them. Annie bobbed her another curtsy and began a tour of the rooms, searching for either Sir Joshua or Lord Daylesford. Apparently, neither gentleman had emerged from the library. She might as well deliver more bottles while she waited.

The company had begun to thin out of the gaming rooms, and the stairway filled with those making their way down to the supper. She couldn't blame them, for the wonderful aromas filled the hall, reminding her that her own meager meal had been hours before. The noise level increased toward deafening as everyone seemed to talk at once, shouting to be heard over everyone else, all but drowning out even the muffled explosion of the occasional champagne cork. Annie positioned herself near the door to the library and tried to look as if she were supposed to be manning this station.

At last, the door opened and Viscount Daylesford emerged. His countenance remained pale, but relief emanated from him, so strong as to be a palpable force. His eyes glittered with triumph. He paused on the threshold, straightened his coat and neckcloth—in which his emerald once more glinted—then strode forward with a jaunty step to catch the first person who passed. "I just won my fortune back from Sir Joshua," he announced, his voice loud and carrying even over the ever-present din.

The man eyed him blearily. "Well done," he muttered, and moved on.

"And a great deal more, on top of it," Daylesford shouted after his uninterested listener.

Still with that carefree gait, the viscount crossed

the hall into the loo rooms, leaving the door ajar behind him. He went straight to the hearth where a small fire crackled. From his pocket he drew a handful of papers which he proceeded to feed into the flames, one after another.

As if his happiness were too great to be contained, he looked over his shoulder. "I beat Sir Joshua," he announced to the occupants of the table behind him.

"You?" an aging gentleman demanded, and snorted.

Daylesford straightened. "Of course, me. Must say, though, he didn't take it well. Looked absolutely despondent." He shook his head and fed the last of the papers to the flames. "Bad loser, Sir Joshua."

"Doesn't get much practice at it," another elderly man said with a short laugh. "Good for you, Daylesford." He returned his attention to his cards.

Sir Joshua despondent. He'd be wanting a few minutes alone to recover his composure.

Annie's heart sank as she turned back toward the card room to clear more empty bottles. Why couldn't she have beaten Daylesford to Sir Joshua, talked to him first? She could pity the poor viscount, but she needed Sir Joshua feeling rich and in an expansive mood. Little hope remained of that now.

Daylesford, whistling a lively tune between his teeth, joined the flow of people headed down the stairs to the dining hall. The aromas beckoned to Annie, as well, but she steadfastly thrust them from her mind. None of this changed the desperate straits to which she and her sister Violet had been reduced. She still had Sir Joshua to confront, and the hour grew later all the time. She couldn't give him much longer.

She rubbed her gritty eyes. Exhaustion crept over her, despite—or maybe because of—her nerves. She never liked late nights. She'd be glad once she'd conducted this long overdue interview with Sir Joshua. Then she could leave here, find another position, one where she could make some sort of a life for herself and her family.

The bleakness of that possibility stiffened her resolve. She had to make Sir Joshua listen. Perhaps he'd be in a receptive mood now that he'd had a chance to reflect on the emptiness and fleetingness of material possessions. Perhaps he'd take a sympathetic interest in the plight of the natural daughter he'd fathered, be moved to remorse over the failing health of the infant's mother.

Buoyed by that thought, and before her nerve could waver, Annie strode up to the library and shoved wide the door, her opening lines on the tip of her tongue.

All was still inside. Only a single candelabrum flickered at the far end of the room, throwing the rest of the chamber into deep shadows. A high-backed chair, facing away from the door, stood a little apart from one of the writing tables. A man sat in it, his right arm hanging over the side, his head slumped slightly to the left.

Had Sir Joshua fallen asleep? Surely he wasn't jug-bitten; he hadn't been drinking heavily. She took a cautious step into the room, not wanting to disturb him, yet too desperate to put off this confrontation any longer.

A wadded handkerchief lay on the floor beneath his dangling fingers. Would gentlemen never learn to be neat about anything? Abandoning her circumspect approach, she strode forward and stooped. She scooped it up, then stopped, straightening slowly.

Something lay inside of it, something heavy and metallic.

She moved the stained cloth, and at once she became aware of the odor of burning over the blending of lemon oil and old leather. In her hands, still wrapped in the soiled, muffling white muslin, lay a tiny carriage pistol. For a puzzled moment she stared at it, then with dawning dread she swiveled to face Sir Joshua.

A small, neat hole seeped blood from his right temple, just below his hairline. A thin trickle of deep scarlet ran down the side of his head and neck, to be absorbed in the intricate folds of his neckcloth. Annie stared, numb, her mind reeling.

Two

Behind Annie, the latch clicked on the door, and it swung open. Still gripping the pistol, she raised her gaze to encounter the taken-aback expression on the face of the gaming hell's proprietress. Annie opened her mouth, but no words came out. She could only shake her head as her employer paused in the doorway.

Mrs. Wickham frowned at Annie. "What are you doing in here, girl?" she demanded. With a visible effort, she pulled herself together. "I am quite certain if Sir Joshua—" She broke off as her gaze came to rest on that gentleman for the first time. "Is he sleeping?" Her voice dropped in volume. "Let him be, girl. You have no call to disturb his rest."

Annie shook her head. "He—he's dead."

"Sir Joshua—" Mrs. Wickham stared at the body for the length of several breaths, then transferred her shocked gaze to Annie.

Annie met it for a long moment, and the impact of it staggered her. She looked down at the pistol she still held in the powder-burned handkerchief and shook her head. "I—" she began, and broke off.

Mrs. Wickham took an unsteady step backward. "You—you've—"

"I didn't never!" Annie broke in. "I found him like this. He shot himself."

"Shot himself," Mrs. Wickham repeated numbly, staring once more at the body. "Shot— Oh, how dreadful, and the house in such terrible straights as it is. How ever shall we manage? We will be shunned for certain, and just when I had almost dragged us out from our mountain of debts."

She approached Sir Joshua's body, peered at him, and her mouth tightened into a thin line. "How dare he do this to me? After all we had been to one another, and now to serve me such a backhanded turn."

Annie almost choked. Mrs. Wickham? Could she have been Sir Joshua's mistress at one time? That thought shocked her almost more than his taking his own life.

Mrs. Wickham folded her arms, hugging herself, glaring at the body. "Of all the vile things! He has done this on purpose, to ruin me, you mark my words. Oh, I shall never forgive him. I suppose I should have expected this of the old skin-flint, though. Annie," she turned to her. "You had best bring my nephew. And don't say a word to anyone else! Well, go on, girl, what are you waiting for? This is no time for just standing about gaping."

Annie, still stunned, hurried out the door, then hesitated. Mr. Henry would probably still be in the dicing room where he'd taken over managing the hazard. She hurried down the stairs, and found him presiding over a table still crowded in spite of the presence of the dinner only a few steps away. She touched his sleeve, then waited.

He cast her a harassed glance, which faded at once as he studied her face. "What is it?" he demanded.

She swallowed. "If you please, sir, Mrs. Wickham is wishful of havin' a word with you. In the library, sir."

"The devil," he muttered. "Very well." He looked about, then handed the dice box to the gentleman who stood at his side. "I'll just be a moment."

"Longer, sir," Annie murmured.

He cast her a shrewd glance. "Indeed. Very well, then." He led the way.

They entered the library a few minutes later. Mrs. Wickham stood where Annie had left her, still hugging herself as she glared down at the body. The woman looked up at once, and her tension faded into relief.

"There you are, Henry. Thank heavens. Sir Joshua has killed himself, and I want you to get rid of his body at once."

"He—" Her nephew stared at her, bewildered, then his gaze transferred to the body. "He's dead, you say?" He stepped quickly to Sir Joshua's side and reached for the pulse at his neck, only to pull back almost at once. "This—this is dreadful."

"It doesn't have to be," his aunt said. "I've been thinking about it, and the best thing to do will be to get rid of him."

"Get—" Mr. Henry blinked at her. "You mean—"

"Move him," his aunt explained with a touch of impatience. "Really, it's such a simple thing, I fail to understand why you cannot grasp it. I will not permit my house to be ruined by his spiteful action, so the only thing to be done is take him someplace else."

Her nephew stared at her, fascinated. "Move him," he repeated.

"That's what I've been saying. Dump him outside somewhere, where someone else can find him and suffer the consequences. I don't want him here."

"My dear aunt—" Henry Wickham began.

"What are you waiting for?" the proprietress interrupted. "At any moment someone might come in here. Go on, carry him out through the servants door."

Mr. Henry straightened, his eye kindling. "I'm not going to move him. My dear aunt—"

"Not going to—" The woman broke off as if too shocked to continue. "Do you mean to refuse to help me, your own flesh-and-blood, in my hour of need?"

"I am merely trying to point out—"

"You are," she declared in tragic accents. "I never would have believed it possible. Your dear father would be mortified by this lack of family feeling you display. It makes me quite glad he is dead and cannot see it for himself."

"My dear aunt—" Henry began once more.

"No," she protested. "You are no nephew of mine. Changeling, that's what you are. Unfeeling." She sniffed, and her face crumpled as if she were about to dissolve into tears. She fumbled in her reticule, drew out a handkerchief, and sought refuge in its lacy depths.

"You're not getting around me that way, ma'am," he declared, harassed.

A muffled sniff was his only answer.

"I admit this is disturbing—"

Her head shot up and she glared at him. "Disturbing? *Disturbing?* Is that all you have to say about it? Do you want to see my livelihood—and yours!—vanish from beneath us? Callous, unsympathetic boy."

He held up his hand. "I am not in the least unsympathetic, I assure you. But you aren't thinking clearly. Far too many people know he gamed here this night, and there's young Daylesford downstairs, shouting it about that he has won Templeton's fortune. This," he gestured to Sir Joshua, "will attract less comment than if we try to move him. Believe me," he added, "the *ton* will make little enough of this. It might even bestow a *conge* upon us. Lend us an air of distinction, you know."

Mrs. Wickham looked up, her expression arrested. "Do you really think so? It's quite true that no one could hold us to blame. He did not lose his fortune to us, more's the pity." She tilted her head to one side, considering. "I suppose you are right," she said at last. "Well, then. We had best do everything of the most proper. We don't want to be the least bit backward in any attention."

She studied the body, apparently wondering how to get the most out of this situation. Annie and Henry Wickham waited, neither saying anything.

"We should call someone in," Mrs. Wickham announced at last. "Someone in authority, of course, but very discrete."

Mr. Henry frowned, then his expression cleared. "What about that Runner fellow who was here over the Tavistock affair? No scandal ever came of that."

His aunt sniffed. "The earl didn't die in our house," she reminded him tartly.

"No, but it was a murder," he pointed out, "and it touched on us quite closely."

Annie, still standing by the door, felt her stomach clench. They were going to call *him*. Any Runner would have been bad enough, but this particular one. . . . A chill crept up her spine. She'd seen him just once, briefly, when she'd opened the door to him on that previous visit of his, but that had been more than enough. And now she'd have to face him . . .

"Send for him," Mrs. Wickham commanded. "Only have him come by the servants' entrance."

Benjamin Frake paused as he stepped over the threshold of Mrs. Wickham's gaming establishment off Jermyn Street. Young Mr. Henry Wickham moved past him, but for the moment Frake paid him no heed. The din from the gaming rooms just beyond this vestibule blocked out even the noise of the closing front door.

The place dazzled by night, he noted, but he remembered it very well from his previous daytime visit. Morning light hadn't been as kind. Now, the flames of upwards of a dozen candles flickered in the gilt-framed mirrors, setting a glow dancing off the multi-branched candelabra. The deep red wallpaper with its gold *fleurs-de-lis* appeared elegant rather than worn and faded. Even the sprays of flowers covered the cracks in their china bowls.

There was something—or rather someone—else he remembered very well from that last visit, too. An enchanting little maid, all great frightened eyes and a halo of dusky ringlets. He couldn't help but wonder if she still worked here. It had only been a little over a month.

He looked up, saw Henry Wickham waiting impatiently just ahead, and followed him up the stairs. In the hallway above he glanced through an open doorway, where the serious business at hand seemed to grip everyone. The bustle of activity created a hushed rumble. Apparently no one yet knew of the suicide within the library.

Mrs. Wickham hurried out of the card room, her expression distracted. "So many people . . . You will be discrete, will you not?" She cast a troubled glance over her shoulder. "Though to be sure, it is very good of you to come. You were the only person we could think of, you see. I had no idea whom to call in a case such as this. Silly of me, I suppose, never to have anticipated the need, when one thinks about it. So many men game recklessly, and Sir Joshua was not one to take losing well. I'm rattling on, aren't I?" she added naively. "But I'm that upset."

Her eyes certainly held a glazed appearance, and

she wrung her hands continually. Frake was mildly surprised her demeanor hadn't alerted everyone present that something was amiss. But the gaming seemed to occupy everyone's full attention, and the distraught behavior of the proprietress might indicate nothing more to them than that the house suffered a losing streak.

Mrs. Wickham cast an uneasy glance at the room across the corridor, toward the back of the house. "I suppose you'll want to see him, now. We've locked the library, of course." She drew a key from her reticule and, fumbling only a little, let them into the somber, ill-lit apartment.

The situation looked much as he'd been led to expect. A gentleman sat slumped at a writing desk, a hole from a small-size ball in his temple. No glass to indicate he'd been drinking, no notes or rewritten wills to explain his actions.

"Have you touched anything?" Frake strolled forward and made a rapid examination of the body.

"Annie—she's our maid—picked up the pistol, of course," Mrs. Wickham said. "Such a tidy little thing, but then she hadn't realized yet that Sir Joshua had shot himself."

Annie. So his little maid was still here. His spirits lifted. If this situation involved interviewing her, he wouldn't mind so much looking into a case that more rightly belonged in the province of the Watch.

He returned his attention to Sir Joshua for a moment, then drew out the Occurrence Book that rested in his breast pocket and began jotting down notes.

The gentleman appeared to be well into middle age, he decided, tall and lean with only the beginnings of a paunch. Frake frowned and touched the dark mahogany stain on the hair at the temple. A powder burn surrounded the vicious little hole. The man's right arm dangled over the side of the chair.

Frake took more notes, then frowned at the body. Apparently this Sir Joshua lost heavily and chose the so-called honorable way out. More like the coward's way out. His gaze ran over the black satin knee breeches and the dove gray brocade waistcoat with the silver thread shot through. A fob crossed this, from which hung a seal and several small rubies. A heavy gold signet ring with a square-cut ruby encircled the middle finger of his left hand. How much money did a man really need?

His gaze moved on to the intricately tied cravat where another deep red stone nestled among the disordered folds. It looked like he'd clutched the cloth. Frake's eyes narrowed as he studied the position of the shoulders, then how the man sat. He'd been slumped, Frake realized, before he'd fired the gun. Dejection? Or something else?

Frowning, he examined the wound once more. The pistol had certainly been pressed against the temple when fired, and at an angle that indicated he had held it in his own hand. But that didn't necessarily mean Sir Joshua had provided the force that pulled the trigger. If he found other signs, as of a struggle . . .

A smudge of something dark stood out against the floral pattern of the carpet near the chair. Frake bent to touch it, then sat back on his heels, frowning. Mud. And from a stable, by the smell. Well, well, well.

Looking about, he spotted the pistol on a side table. He picked it up by the barrel and gave it a tentative swing. The butt connected with the palm of his hand with an authoritative thud. The weapon might be small, but it seemed thoroughly effective in more ways than one.

Thoughtful, he replaced it and returned his attention to Sir Joshua. He rotated the lifeless head forward, and his experienced fingers ran through the hair, examining the skull. There, on the left side, a softer spot, which had had no time to swell. Sir Joshua hadn't been hit hard enough to break the skin, but the blow would have been sufficient to render him unconscious for long enough to stage his suicide.

Frake straightened and gently eased the head back to its original position. Well, well, well, indeed.

From the doorway, Henry Wickham coughed. "Are you done? If you want to break the news to his family, his nephew—his heir, I believe—is in one of our rooms. Playing faro when I saw him last."

Frake studied the young man for a moment. "Actually," he said at last, "I'd like a word with your aunt, and with the maid—Annie, I think?—who found him."

Mr. Wickham shrugged and slipped out the door.

A few moments later, his aunt entered. "I don't know where Annie is," she informed Frake as she bustled in, trailing a paisley shawl in her wake. "She is very conscientious about her duties. My nephew has gone to search for her. Are there more formalities?" She sounded daunted by the prospect.

Frake rocked back on his heels, his steady gaze studying every nuance of her expression. "I'm afraid so. I'm very much afraid so. Sir Joshua didn't kill himself."

"But—" The woman stared at him blankly. "He *is* dead, isn't he? Then do you mean it was an accident? How—"

"Murder." He said the word bluntly.

Mrs. Wickham's countenance paled, then flushed. "Oh, how dare he! Of all the inconsiderate—! If that isn't just like him, to get himself murdered here. The scandal! I vow we shall never recover." She drew her handkerchief from her reticule and mopped at her eyes.

They appeared remarkably dry, to Frake.

The door opened again, and he looked up quickly to see Mr. Henry Wickham enter, followed closely by a small, slender young maid all huge wide-set eyes in a pale face surrounded by a thick fluff of dusky ringlets. Little Annie, in her burgundy gown, black apron, and mobcap. A warm glow seeped through him, a comfortable satisfaction mingled with pleasurable anticipation.

She sidled into the room, then stood near the door, her back to the wall, as if keeping her distance. She watched him, her expression guarded, her soft brown eyes filled with suspicion. Or perhaps fear?

He smiled at her, but no answering light flickered in her piquant countenance. Instead, she edged back a step until she collided with a bookcase. Her fingers twisted in the black bombazine of her apron.

"Won't you have a seat, Annie?" Frake gestured toward one of the comfortable armchairs.

She remained where she stood, rigidly erect, only her hands betraying her agitation.

"I'd like you to help me, if you will," Frake tried again.

She looked up briefly, then returned her attention to her hands. "Yes, sir."

A response, at least. Frake opened his Occurrence Book once more, but tried to keep it as much out of the way as possible. No use terrifying the girl with all the trappings of his authority. She seemed to be feeling it enough all ready. Aloud, he asked: "Now, what brought you into the library when you found him?"

She bristled. "I was just doin' my job, sir. Ain't nothin' wrong with that. A girl has her duties to look after."

"And which duty in particular brought you in here?" He found her antagonism a touch disconcerting.

"Go on, girl, answer him," Mrs. Wickham prompted.

Annie hunched a shoulder. "I just come to see if anyone wanted anythin'."

Something about the defensiveness of her response piqued his curiosity. "Had you reason to think someone was in here?"

Color touched her cheeks—quite becomingly, he noted. Her gaze slid from him, touched on Sir Joshua's body, and she looked quickly away, down at the floor.

She bore every appearance of someone rapidly concocting a lie.

"His lordship, Viscount Daylesford, come out, tellin' everyone as how he just won Sir Joshua's money. I thought mayhap Sir Joshua would be wantin' a glass of wine."

"So you brought him one, did you?" His rapid gaze scanned the room. Only the untouched brandy decanter stood on the far side of the chamber on an occasional table, with its arrangement of glasses on the tray beside it. No other stemware or bottles.

Annie hesitated, her eyes wide. Haunted. She reminded Frake of a wild creature, trapped. Not used to prevarication, he decided. So why did she feel the need now? He fought back an urge to help her out of this tangle. Instead, he drew out a chair for her, placing its back to the table where the body still slumped.

Annie threw a frantic glance at Mrs. Wickham.

"Go ahead, girl." The proprietress waved her toward it. "You just tell Mr. Frake the truth. You've got nothing to hide."

Annie's color deepened. "No, mum," she murmured, and perched primly on the edge of the wingback chair.

Was it her employer she was afraid of? Frake cleared his throat. "Why don't you and your nephew return to the other rooms," he suggested genially. "Folks might be wondering where you've got to. But don't go saying nothing about what's happened in here. And don't let anyone leave, neither."

Mr. Henry Wickham, who had settled on the edge of a table near his aunt, raised his eyebrows. "Do you want us to place a guard on the front door?" The beginnings of a rueful smile tugged at the corners of his mouth.

"Aye, that's the ticket." Frake beamed at him. "You just go take care of that, and mind, don't you go alarming folks none. Just ask them to wait a few minutes. Say there's going to be an important announcement." He crossed to the door and held it open.

Mrs. Wickham hesitated. "If you really think—"

"I do." Frake ushered her out, then her nephew after her. "You keep people from guessing what's gone on in here until I've had a chance to ask a few questions." He closed the door behind them.

"Should have asked for the key," he muttered, and turned back to find Annie watching him with veiled hostility. Apparently, any charm he might possess utterly failed to affect her. With an inward sigh, he drew another chair up before her. He, too, sat on the edge and leaned forward in a confiding manner. Annie drew back.

"You know he was murdered, don't you?" he said, making it a statement.

Her head jerked up, horror in her huge eyes. "I didn't never!" she cried. "I never touched him, I just found him like that. I never wanted him dead. And now what is to become of—" She broke off on a gasp, and her hands clenched convulsively in her lap.

She didn't, he guessed shrewdly, worry about the

fate of the gaming house. Something else lay behind that stifled utterance, something of which she was afraid to speak. He drew his briarwood pipe from the depths of his pocket and tapped the gnarled bowl thoughtfully in the palm of his hand. "Well, you may tell me more about that later." He offered his best avuncular smile.

It failed miserably. She sniffed and eyed him with unease.

"Were you watching this room?" he asked bluntly.

She hesitated, then gave a tentative nod.

"Good. That should make all this a whole sight more easy." He beamed at her, to no good effect that he could see. "When did Sir Joshua come in?"

"About one-thirty," she said, grudgingly.

"Very good. Now, did anyone come in here after he did?"

"I wasn't watchin' it all the time," she temporized. "I had my duties."

"No," he agreed, "you wouldn't go neglecting those, would you? Not even if they went and conflicted with what you'd rather be doing."

That hit home, he noted, watching as the wariness crept once more into her expression. She leaned back in her chair, more an attempt to put some distance between them than any seeking of a more comfortable position.

"Who *did* you see come in here?" he pursued.

"Lord Daylesford," she responded readily, then fell silent.

"And when was that? Right afterwards?"

She shook her head, setting her ringlets swaying about her cheeks. "No, sir. I'd gone to help carry the platters up to the dinin' room for supper. That took twenty minutes or so. It wasn't 'til I come back up here that Lord Daylesford went in."

Twenty minutes or more, during which time any number of people might have come and gone. But Sir Joshua hadn't been dead when Viscount Daylesford entered, or he would have reported it to someone. Or would he? Frake tapped a finger on the stem of the pipe. "Did anyone else go in along with Daylesford?"

"Not with him. There might of been someone else in there already. I wasn't around the whole time."

Still, unless Daylesford had murdered Sir Joshua, it didn't matter. He jotted the times into his Occurrence Book. "And how long was Daylesford in here?"

Annie studied her hands. "Maybe fifteen minutes," she said at last.

"And did you hear any noises from in here? Perhaps a champagne cork popping?"

"I heard them," she admitted, "but not as I could say for sure as how one of them come from in here."

No help there. "Did anyone else come in after Daylesford left?"

She didn't look up. "Not as I could say for certain, sir. I had my duties."

Unfortunately, he reflected. "And what of the other door?" He nodded toward the small entry way at the far corner of the room. "Could someone have come in through that?"

She glanced at it. "Yes, sir."

He jotted that down. "And when did you find Sir Joshua?"

Annie closed her eyes. "Just goin' on two-fifteen, it was, sir."

So about forty-five minutes total, with Daylesford the critical element. If he left Sir Joshua alive, then the murder happened between five after two and two-fifteen. If he lied about the card game and found him dead when he went in, then Sir Joshua was killed between one-thirty and one-fifty. Or Daylesford himself could have killed him during those fifteen minutes.

Or if Annie killed him—

He would speak with the viscount next, he decided.

He looked up and found Annie watching him with trepidation. He smiled at her, trying to insert as much confidence and reassurance as he could into this simple gesture. "Now," he said with gentle firmness, "you will tell me why you needed Sir Joshua alive."

Three

The blood drained from Annie's cheeks, leaving her chilled and clammy. "It—it ain't got nothin' to do with this." She lowered her gaze, not daring to meet the penetrating regard of the Runner's candid blue eyes. Still, they drew her back.

A flicker of triumph lit their depths, and Annie's heart sank. She'd betrayed herself to him again, let him know his guess had been right. She wished he'd go away, far away. He sat there so calm and steady as if he had never destroyed a person's life. Maybe he never thought of the damage Runners like him did to the families of their victims. She looked up and added deliberately: "Nor it ain't got nothin' to do with you."

Still he watched her, his expression neither accusing nor patronizing. "Hasn't it?" he asked in a tone that invited confidences.

"I just said as how it hasn't," she snapped, more harshly than she'd intended. What was it about him that set her nerves all on end? He was a Runner, of course, and so to be scorned. But there was more. Something that both called to her and frightened her.

She slid as far back in the chair as she could manage and wished she could just slide right out the door.

As if in answer to her hopes, the door swung open. But instead of offering her escape, it was filled by a tall, slender gentleman silhouetted against the brilliant lights of the hall. Mr. William Templeton squinted into the dimmer light; then he spotted them and stormed forward, mincing slightly as he did so. A wasp-waisted coat of deepest blue, worn over black satin knee breeches, set off his dandified figure. Only the faintest touches of gray streaked his black hair, styled *à la Brutus* by an expert hand. He stopped, eyeing them with a frown creasing the brow above his hawk-like nose.

He glanced at Annie, then his gaze settled on the Runner. "I demand to know what is going on here. Henry Wickham has actually had the impertinence to tell me I cannot leave, that I must see you! What," he added, his lip curling into a sneer, "have you to say to anything in this house?"

Mr. Frake turned in his chair, then rose slowly to face Templeton. "Your name, sir?"

"I fail to see where that is any of your business," Templeton snapped, sounding very much like a spoiled child. "What I want to know, is—" He broke off and peered into the shadowy recesses of the library, toward the writing desk where Sir Joshua's body remained slumped in the chair. His petulance evaporated and an expression of ghoulish fascination settled on his countenance. "I say, has there been a spot of trouble?"

"You might say as how there has, sir." Mr. Frake

rocked back on his heels, his gaze intent on the new-comer's face.

"Shot himself?" Templeton craned forward, as eager as any little boy for a glimpse of something gruesome.

"If you don't mind, sir?" The Runner edged him back toward the door.

"I'm not hurting anything," Templeton complained, still trying to see past Mr. Frake. "Who is it? What happened?"

"All in good time, sir. Just a few formalities to take care of first. If you'd just be so good as not to mention this? That's right, we don't want to cause any unnecessary distress to no one."

"Just don't take all night about it." Templeton backed out the door, retreating before the Runner's determination. "No, no point trying," he said to someone in the hall as Mr. Frake began to close the door behind him. "They won't let you go in there. They're being devilish close about it. Looks like some foolish fellow must have rolled himself up and decided to end it all."

"Keep your voice down," the other responded shortly. "They can't want that spread about yet. Here, perhaps we'd best keep people away."

Mr. Frake nodded in approval, then returned to An-nie and raised his eyebrows. "Who were they?"

"That was Mr. William Templeton who come in here. Sir Joshua's nephew. And heir," she added, re-membering what Mrs. Wickham had said earlier. She derived considerable satisfaction from the way the Runner's brow snapped down at her words.

"Well and well and well," he murmured. "And the other gent? The one who told him to hold his tongue?"

"That was Captain Bevis. He—" She broke off as a commotion arose outside the door.

With a muttered oath, Mr. Frake crossed to it and threw it open. Curious, Annie followed. Outside stood several men, including William Templeton, Captain Bevis, Mr. Henry Wickham, Captain Palfrey, and Lord Daylesford.

"I said, where the devil is my uncle, and I will raise my voice if I want to." William Templeton glared at the others. "I know he hasn't left, for I found his things in the front salon, yet he isn't in any of the rooms." He rounded on Viscount Daylesford. "You! Word's all over the house you lost a fortune to him, then won it back. Where did you leave him?"

Daylesford cast an uncertain glance toward the library, and his eyes widened as he seemed to take in the presence of Annie and the Runner. "In there," he said. "Though I don't see why—"

Mr. Templeton paled, and the hand he held out trembled. "No," he breathed. "He wouldn't. He couldn't have lost all his money. He—" He spun about, his expression haggard. "Who is that in there?" he demanded. With three long strides he reached the Runner and clutched him by the lapels of his coat. *"Who is it?"*

Captain Bevis thrust his way between the others who stood immobile, grabbed the distraught man by the shoulder, and dragged him back a few paces. "Easy there, Templeton. I'm sure our good Captain

Palfrey or Mr. Wickham will explain everything in a moment?" He made it a question as he cast a glance over his shoulder at the two men who helped manage the gaming house.

Mr. Henry tore his fascinated gaze from Mr. Templeton and looked to his companion, as if for guidance. "I fear the matter has been taken out of our hands. Any questions you may have should be directed to Mr. Frake, there. Ah, of Bow Street."

"Bow Street!" Bevis's gray eyes narrowed. "Bow Street, is it? What the devil has been going on here tonight?"

"That is precisely what I'm trying to figure out." The Runner faced the gathering crowd with an expression of bland imperturbability.

"Is it my uncle?" Mr. William Templeton shook himself free of Bevis's hold and pushed forward. His gaze swept from the Runner to Annie, and apparently read the confirmation in her face. "It is! He— No, he couldn't have lost his fortune. There'll be enough left."

Mr. Frake rocked back on his heels, his innocent blue eyes never wavering in their regard. "That's as may be, sir. Now, if you don't mind?" He looked over Mr. Templeton's shoulder and caught Captain Palfrey's eye. "Perhaps everyone might be more comfortable in the dining room, sir?"

"I'll see to it." Leaning heavily on his cane, Captain Palfrey limped forward and took Mr. Templeton by the arm. "This way, old fellow. I'm sure everything will be explained in a very short while. We all want this settled every bit as quickly as you do."

Templeton shook himself free. "There is no need to lay hands on me. No matter how much my uncle lost tonight, there will still be enough left to cover my debts here. And a great deal more besides, I should wager."

"I'm sure there will be. Henry?" With a jerk of his head, Captain Palfrey indicated his request for help in rounding up the crowd and herding them downstairs.

Mr. Frake watched for a minute, then drew back into the room, closing the door.

Annie, grasping her chance, caught it and started to ease it open again. "I've got to go, sir. They'll be needin' me down there, what with so many people all that upset."

"I need you more." He offered her another of his gentle smiles.

Almost, she could believe him. A touch of warmth lit the blue depths of his eyes, encouraging her trust. But she knew better than that. No Runner was to be trusted. She wrinkled her nose. "What was you wishful to know?"

"Why did you want to see Sir Joshua? There's no use denying it. I'll only keep asking until you break down and answer." His smile never wavered, and his voice maintained only the most reasonable of tones. "So why don't you just make it much simpler for us both and tell me everything? I'll find out from someone in short order, that you can count on."

She glared at him. He probably would discover everything. It wouldn't be that hard, and he possessed an air of quiet determination that warned her he probably got most anything he wanted, and right quickly, at that. She sniffed. "It's my sister."

Frake's eyebrows rose ever so slightly. "Why don't we sit down again?" was all he said.

She did so, then eyed him with resentment.

"Now," he went on as he resumed his own seat. "What has your sister to do with Sir Joshua?"

"Too much," she said before she could stop herself. She drew a steadying breath. "She was assistant to his cook at Templeton Grange, she was, until six months ago."

"That's his country seat? I see." He jotted more notes in his Occurrence Book. "She'd be older than you then."

"By two years," she agreed.

"And why did she leave?"

Annie braced herself. "She had his daughter two months ago. Seduced her, he did, then cast her out to fend for herself, and her that sick she can barely feed the poor little mite." To her horror, she found herself trembling with repressed emotion. "And now he's gone and gotten himself killed, and I can't even afford to bring a proper doctor to see her, and I'm that scared she'll die, and—" She broke off, biting her lower lip, aghast at all she had blurted out. Those deceitful, gentle eyes of his, lulling her like that. "So you see," she said, her voice muffled by her efforts to keep it steady, "I had every reason for wantin' him alive."

"Unless he refused to help," Mr. Frake murmured as if to himself.

Annie sprang to her feet, fists clenched, her cheeks blazing. "How dare you say that! Though it's nothin' more than I should have expected from the likes of you. Runners! You ain't interested in truth or fairness, only in makin' your arrest or killin' your suspect afore he can defend himself. What does the likes of you know of the troubles of the poor?"

Mr. Frake made no attempt to answer. He merely watched her with his eyebrows slightly elevated.

She subsided back into her chair, the resentment of her glare growing. He held out a handkerchief toward her. Her chin thrust forward. "I got my own." She searched through the slit in the side of her gown, found the pocket tied there, and retrieved the serviceable square of muslin.

After resolutely blowing her nose, she crumpled the handkerchief in her lap. "You're so busy tryin' to blame me for what's happened to Sir Joshua, you ain't even thinkin' of anyone else. What about Lord Daylesford? He's far more likely than me to of shot him. But no, he's a nobleman. You don't never go suspectin' the rich and important folk."

"As a matter of fact," the Runner remarked mildly, "I find him highly suspicious. If all I've heard is true, I'd say as how he has the greatest motive of all." He once more produced the briarwood pipe from the pocket of his coat and idly twisted the stem between his fingers. "His lordship lost a vast amount of money to Sir Joshua, he was the only person seen to enter the library after him, and," he held up the pipe for emphasis, "he came out announcing how he'd won all his fortune back and more—enough, maybe, to drive Sir Joshua into taking his life. He might've simply killed Sir Joshua, stolen his vowels back, then left him a seeming suicide."

Annie's suspicious gaze narrowed on the Runner. "Do you really think as how that's possible?"

"I think it'll be very interesting to see if his lordship has any proof of his story." He chewed on the pipe's stem. "What will you do about your sister now?" he asked abruptly.

She shrugged. "It don't matter none to you."

"To this case, perhaps it doesn't." He studied her for a moment, and an odd expression flickered across his face. "To me, it does. What will you do?"

Annie tugged at her handkerchief. "See Mr. Templeton. Or I suppose he's Sir William, now. Mayhap since he knows what it's like not to have no money, he'll take pity on poor Violet and the baby."

"*Sir* William," the Runner mused, his expression arrested. "Now, that there title might be thought worth a murder. Especially if there's a fortune as goes with it." He cocked an inviting eyebrow at Annie. "Is there?"

Her chin rose. "I wouldn't know as how great a fortune it is." Nor would she tell him if she did. Let him do his own dirty grubbing for information. As long as he hadn't simply decided on her as the guilty party, she'd take no more part in casting aspersions.

He jotted down more notes. "Now, then—"

A faint creak caused him to break off, and he spun to face the back corner of the room where the door to the servants corridor had eased open. A dark mop of hair popped in, then vanished at once. The door slammed closed.

Mr. Frake surged from his chair and crossed the library in a sprint. The next moment, he, too, disappeared into the dark corridor beyond. The thudding of footsteps carried back to Annie as she also sprang to her feet. She reached the door in time to see the Runner lay hands on her brother.

"Here, you let him go!" She hurried toward them, bristling with indignation.

Samuel slumped against the wall, his shoulder firmly under the Runner's hand, and grinned at his sister. "Nabbed fair and square. Light on his feet, he is."

Mr. Frake looked from his captive to Annie. "Who is this?" he demanded.

Annie glowered at the Runner. "My brother."

"Well, well, well," Mr. Frake murmured. "Now, what would he be doing in this house?"

Annie opened her mouth, then closed it with a snap. After a moment she said, through gritted teeth: "I might of known as how you'd put the blame on some poor cove who ain't got no one to stand up for him." She sniffed, just to show her disdain. "Much easier than tryin' to confront a nobleman like his lordship Viscount Daylesford."

Samuel wagged an amiably drunken finger at her. "Now, no need you gettin' so het up about it, Annie m'girl." He straightened and addressed himself to the Runner. "I," he pronounced in pretentious accents, "am groom to Sir Joshua. I come in as I always does, to have a word with m'sister and steal a kiss from the kitchen maid." With that, he collapsed against the wall again and began humming off key.

"Sir Joshua's groom?" Frake looked at Annie. "And your sister was assistant to his cook?"

Annie dragged her despairing gaze from her brother, who launched into a bawdy ballad. "We was all born on his estate." Exhaustion crept over her, a combination of the late hour, reaction to finding Sir Joshua, and the presence of this man with his endless questions. But she wouldn't break down.

"So you've always served Sir Joshua?" Frake pursued.

"Rightly speakin', my brother served Mr. Oliver, Sir Joshua's son. Went with him to the Continent when Mr. Oliver bought his colors, but Samuel, he wouldn't take the King's shillin'. Said bein' a groom was what he knew and what he'd remain."

Samuel broke off his singing long enough to say: "Tha's right."

"It was Samuel," Annie went on with determination, "who brought Mr. Oliver home after he'd been wounded so bad. He died of it seven months ago, and Samuel has been servin' as undergroom for Sir Joshua since."

Mr. Frake regarded Samuel with a thoughtful expression as his gaze ran over him. "You've got a touch of mud on your boots."

Annie eyed the Runner with renewed hostility. "And what if he has? He's a groom, ain't he? It'd be a strange thing for sure if he didn't have no mud somewheres about him."

"Mud," the Runner repeated. "You just come along with me now, lad, and let's have ourselves a little look-see at something."

With no apparent effort, he dragged Samuel erect and propelled him down the hall. Annie followed, her uneasiness growing. She was accustomed to receiving orders, accusations, and blame with no sense of logic or fairness behind them. This Runner's calm reasonableness unnerved her.

They re-entered the library, and Mr. Frake picked up the candelabrum as they passed. Much to Annie's further discomfort, they approached Sir Joshua's body. She wanted to hang back, not look at it again—remain as far from it as possible—yet she needed to know what this dangerous man was about with her brother.

Instead of touching Sir Joshua, Mr. Frake knelt at his side, examining the carpet. Annie, from several feet back, peered at the area illuminated by the three candles. A dark spot. But what—?

The Runner drew a small knife from his pocket and scraped a bit of the mud from Samuel's boots. This he held next to the spot on the rug. After a moment, he let out a deep sigh and rose. "They're one and the same, they are, my lad. Now, why don't you tell me what you was doing in here earlier. Did you kill Sir Joshua?"

Four

Frake watched the groom's fuzzed amiability change to a snarl. So, when really cornered, this one could turn fighter, not whiner. Pity. Bullying usually worked quite well with the latter, dragging the truth, and right quickly, out of a good number of young care-for-naughts. This kind, though, took more careful handling.

Samuel Gooden straightened his slumped shoulders and enunciated with careful precision: "Go t'Hell."

"Sammy!" Annie shot Frake a frightened glance.

Frake returned it with a smile, which seemed only to disconcert her all the more. So, the lad would show his hackles. Careful handling it would be. He folded his arms and arranged his features into their blandest, least threatening expression.

"Bloody China street pig," Samuel spat out. "He ain't got no call to go about castin' accusations at inner—innocent grooms. Don't have a leg to stand on, so's he's talkin' wild nonsense."

Frake toyed with the stem of his pipe. "I merely asked a question, is all."

"And a right rum one, at that." Samuel thrust out

a belligerent jaw. "Ain't no one goin' to accuse me
o' somethin' I didn't never do."

"You've got a lot to learn." Frake shook his head
in his best avuncular manner. "Accusations there'll
be a-plenty, my lad. What you need to learn is how
to counter them." He gestured toward the chair recently occupied by Annie. "Sit down and let's get
this here matter all sorted out, shall we? You just tell
me what you've been about this night."

Samuel sat, then darted a challenging glance at
Frake. "I ain't sayin' nothin'." He folded his arms
before him, leaned back, and closed his mouth with
a pointed snap. The next moment he ruined the effect
by winking at Annie, then starting to hum tunelessly
once more.

"That's right, don't you trust that Runner none." Annie paced several restless steps. "He's tryin' to trick
you."

Samuel snorted. "Ain't no one as can trick Samuel
Gooden." He gave an emphatic nod, which action
seemed to please him. He continued to bob his head
up and down.

"That's right." Frake beamed on him and settled
in his former chair. "A right leery cove, that's you.
Just the type of lad I need to help me in this here
investigation. We'll have this business straightened
out in two shakes of a lamb's tail."

A crafty glint entered Samuel's dark eyes. "Well,
now, that's just as what I can't go and do for you."
He shook his head with exaggerated regret. "I wasn't
never in here, you see. That there mud, it must of

come from someone else's boot. Me, I've been in the kitchen all night. Didn't never leave it, not even once."

Frake's gaze flitted to Annie and caught the primming of her mouth. "Is that right, is it? Well, that's easy enough to prove, I'll wager. I'll just have me a chat with the cook, and—"

"Hey, now." Samuel sat up, alarmed even through his alcohol-induced haze. "There ain't no call to go doin' that, is there? I might of stepped out for a moment or two, like, but I didn't never come up here."

"Then what brought you in the servants door just a bit ago?"

Samuel considered for a minute, then brightened. "A right regular hubbub there was. Wondered what was goin' on. Thought as how I'd just have myself a little look-see."

"I see." Frake nodded in approval. "And what made you think to check in here? I gather this room isn't much in use."

Samuel frowned as if in an effort of concentration. "Heard as how it was in here," he muttered at last.

"Did you, now?" Frake cast Annie a quelling glance as she opened her mouth, "And what was it you heard?"

"As how ol' Rumguts went and shot himself in here," the groom announced proudly.

A vexed exclamation escaped Annie.

Her brother glanced at her in mild surprise. "What, you still here, Annie? Be a good girl and fetch me that decanter on the table over there."

"You've already had too much to drink." She sank into the nearest chair. "Oh, Sammy—"

"Now, don't you go interrupting," Frake admonished. "This here conversation is just getting real interesting, like. Now, Gooden, who told you as how it was old—er—Rumguts up here?"

Samuel shot him a suddenly sobered look. "Don't remember."

Frake shook his head. "Sorry, lad. That won't fadge. Word couldn't have been carried to the kitchens that fast. And if you'd heard about Sir Joshua, you'd have also heard as how I was in here. And that you didn't know."

"I—" Samuel began, then broke off. He cast a haunted glance at Annie.

Frake straightened in his chair. "Enough of this argle-bargle, now. You just up and tell me what really happened."

"Do, Samuel," Annie urged. "You're only makin' it sound as if you've got somethin' to hide."

The groom hunched a shoulder. "All right, so I come in here to have a go at the brandy. There's nothin' wrong with that, is there?"

Frake held up his hand, cutting off Annie's retort. "Nothing in the least," he said smoothly, drawing an indignant snort from the girl. "Now, you just tell me what happened."

Samuel roused himself from an inspection of his fingernails. "Didn't nothin' happen. I come in here, I seen him, and I left. That's all there is to it." He gave another of his short nods for emphasis.

Frake clutched at his rapidly slipping patience. "Let's see if we can find a little more, shall we? Which door did you come in by?"

"That one." Samuel jerked his head toward the entrance leading to the servants corridor.

"All right." Frake nodded approval of this cooperation, earning a cocky smile from the drunken groom. "Now, was anyone else in here?"

"Well, o'course there was." Samuel regarded him with disdain. "Ol' Rumguts, which you'd know if you'd been listenin' to me."

Frake clenched his teeth but kept his smile firmly in place. "I meant besides him."

Samuel considered for a moment, then said brightly: "Me."

There were days, Frake reflected, when the thought of retirement to some quiet village held out considerable allure. Keeping that reflection to himself, he asked: "Was there anyone else?"

Samuel subjected this to a moment's consideration, then shook his head.

"Can you tell me what you saw?" Frake tried, knowing full well he might be letting himself in for a wearying and probably nonsensical answer.

"Just what you seen," Samuel said with unexpected directness.

Frake pulled out his Occurrence Book and jotted down a note, then looked steadily across at Samuel. "He was dead?"

Samuel beamed. "As dead as a door post."

"Did you touch anything?"

Samuel straightened with righteous indignation. "O'course not. As if I'd do any such a thing. Least-ways," he added with a wink, "not until I had myself a chance to think on it a bit. Muddled, you know," he added, tapping the side of his head for emphasis. "Not used to wine like they got here."

"You come over to look at him?" Frake pursued.

Samuel nodded, apparently feeling himself once more on safe ground. "That's right. Couldn't believe it, at first. Well, who would? Ol' Rumguts." He said the name with relish.

"So you come in, saw him sitting there—"

"Gave me a right shock, I can tell you," Samuel stuck in. "That relieved I was when he didn't move."

Frake tapped the bowl of his pipe in his palm. "So you went to have a look at him? And then what?"

"Left. Told you. Wanted to think about it."

"And you didn't tell anyone what you'd found in here?"

The look Samuel directed at him held pure scorn. "Not," he pronounced slowly, as if explaining to a dull-witted audience, "until I had myself a chance to think on it." He gave him an owlish wink. "See if there weren't some way to turn this here to my advantage."

"And how long ago did you find him?"

Samuel tilted his head to one side and considered. "A while," he pronounced at last. "Been thinkin' on it a good bit."

No hope of establishing an exact time, Frake reflected with regret. "And what brought you back now?" He sat back in his chair and fingered the stem of his pipe. "Did you think of something?"

Samuel hung his head, and a foolish, if somewhat sheepish, smile played about the corners of his mouth. "More I thought about it, the more it didn't seem likely. Had to make sure he was really dead."

Frake regarded him, keeping his expression blank. On the whole, the story held a ring of truth. But then the lad had had some time to concoct a good tale and could be feigning the drunkenness. Best let him be for awhile, then question him again.

He rose, smiling amiably on the couple. "I'd best be getting on with talking to all those folks down in the dining room."

Annie thrust out her chin. "About time, too. Never did see why you was so set on talkin' to us."

He awarded her the slightest bow. "A spot of pleasure before business." And unfortunately, in her case, that contained an element of truth. He would be quite willing to talk to her some more. "Why don't you take your brother back to the kitchens and sober him up a bit?"

Annie opened her large eyes to their widest. "Why, I never would of thought of such an idea for myself," she said, her voice heavy with sarcasm. "Amazin', you Runners, that's what you are." She hoisted Samuel to his feet, and he ambled at her side out the door into the servants corridor.

Frake's gaze lingered on her departing figure, with more amused assessment than cool calculation. He liked what he saw, he decided. Young and inexperienced, yet a tigress for those she loved. He could only hope she had nothing to do with this mess.

Unfortunately, she had sufficient reason to be angry with Sir Joshua. If he'd laughed at—or insulted—her, she might have struck out at him in anger, then panicked and staged the suicide which killed him. He'd have to find out where that pistol came from, if she could have gotten hold of it. Judging from the obvious, little Annie Gooden certainly appeared the most likely murderer.

Only there was very little of the obvious about Annie Gooden. Unexpected, that's what she was. A surprising mixture of loyalties, humor, and determination. And, he was forced to admit, he'd fallen for her the first time he saw her. He'd spent a good part of the last month trying to get her out of his mind, but it hadn't worked. He'd actually considered finding some excuse to call here, to make her acquaintance, and envisioned seeing her nervous shyness melt. Well, it had melted all right, but not into what he'd hoped. She didn't have time to be nervous around him. She was too busy distrusting him.

He slammed the gnarled bowl of his pipe into the palm of his hand. He didn't want her to be guilty. Not for her sake, not for her brother's, not for her sister's or the poor little fatherless babe's. And especially not for his own sake.

This didn't accomplish anything. It looked like he was in for a very long night, so he might as well get on with it. A great number of people awaited his coming.

He strode out of the library, only to stop short as he almost collided with Mrs. Wickham, who paced back and forth before the door. She steadied herself on his arm, one hand going automatically to protect her quivering lace cap with its clutch of swaying plumes. Stillness surrounded them, a startling quiet after the din he'd encountered on his arrival.

"Captain Palfrey and Henry—they've been such a support to me this night," she exclaimed, her hand still resting on his elbow. "They have brought everyone together in the dining room, though I vow I don't know how much longer they'll be able to keep them there. They are all talking about it now, even those who didn't know, before, and it is quite dreadful, and I fear they will never come back—but to be sure, I mustn't run on, so."

He disentangled himself from her grip. "The first thing to be done is find those who couldn't possibly have had anything to do with this affair so they can go home."

She beamed on him as if he were a prize pupil who had just given her a correct answer to a difficult question. "They will be so glad."

Not as glad as he would be to cut down the number of people with whom he must talk that night. He allowed her to lead the way down the stairs. "Can we be certain of any who never came up here tonight?"

"Those playing hazard. Dear me, the dicers so often scorn the games with cards. Captain Palfrey will know, of course. Who played all night, I mean.

He keeps ever so sharp an eye on goings on. I vow, I don't know how he does it, and when I compliment him, which you must know I do, of course, he just smiles as if it were the easiest thing in the world. Watching, I mean. Not smiling. Though to be sure, that comes quite easily for him as well. Come, we must ask him."

But Captain Palfrey, it turned out, had anticipated this question. He had already begun the process of gathering the names and directions of those who had not stirred from the dicing tables. This included a considerable number of people, all of whom, when Frake asked them, denied having heard or seen anything in the least bit unusual. Had eyes for nothing but their gambling, Frake guessed, and dismissed them to take their leave.

Next he turned his attention to the upper rooms. To his relief, he found one very large party that, having talked one of their members into starting a faro bank, had remained at that table the entire time. These people he was able to send home, as well, along with a party of older gentlemen who had been indulging, during an evening of loo, in an animated and lengthy discussion on the relative merits of several pugilists for an upcoming bout. All had been oblivious to anything else.

Mr. Henry Wickham next brought to him several young gentlemen who also had been intent upon their games, aware of nothing but the turn of the cards. As Frake finished taking down their names, he felt a touch on his arm.

"Please." A catch sounded in a woman's voice just behind him.

Frake turned to see a slender young woman just above medium height, gowned in the height of fashion in a pale blue silk evening dress with a very revealing décolletage. A lace cap boasting three plumes that curled down about her cheek set off ringlets of the purest guinea-gold. Most of her face remained obscured behind a delicate lace handkerchief.

"This is Mrs. Cornelia Leeds," Mr. Wickham told him.

"Indeed?" Frake regarded her with mild interest. In his experience, ladies of quality had as little to do with Runners as they could possibly manage. Unless, of course, she wanted to go home.

With a corner of the handkerchief she dabbed at her eyes. Green, Frake noted, with not a single trace of redness or puffiness marring their brilliance. Nor did the lace-trimmed linen show any signs of dampness.

"I—I should very much like to get this over with," she declared, managing an almost convincing sniff. "It—it's all so very dreadful. I knew him, you see. We—we were much more than just friends. In fact," and she managed a coy look through her supposed sorrow, "he had been on the verge of making me a—a very flattering offer. I—this is so very difficult for me."

"My condolences," Frake said with only the mildest touch of sarcasm as he led her outside into the corridor. He closed the door firmly behind them. "Were you going to accept? His offer, I mean?"

She fluttered long, flirtatious lashes. "Viscount Daylesford has paid me very flattering attentions of late, as well. Quite jealous, the pair of them."

"Are they?" Frake watched her closely. "Might his lordship have been jealous enough to have up and killed Sir Joshua?"

Mrs. Leeds hesitated and a guarded look of quick calculation flashed in her eyes. "What a dreadful thing to suggest. My good man, the days of fighting duels over a lady's eyes are quite passed, more's the pity. And as for murdering someone in cold blood—! No, dear Daylesford would never do such a terrible thing."

Except, Frake reflected, Viscount Daylesford happened to possess another and far more compelling motive than the undoubtedly lustrous eyes of this fair charmer. He had lost a considerable fortune to Sir Joshua. That one reason alone might have been compelling enough; add to that the rivalry for the favor of this lady, and the issue might well be decided.

He studied her slightly averted face for a moment. To whom had she been showing the greatest favor? Abruptly, he asked: "Did you come with either of the two gentlemen tonight?"

For a very long moment, she said nothing. A slight flush touched her cheeks, betraying—what? Embarrassment? Or merely her distress?

"I—I came alone," she admitted. "But I knew I should meet with both of them here this night."

"Don't it bother you none that neither of them escorted you?"

She opened her eyes wide. "Why should it?"

She seemed to regard it as being of no importance that neither of her supposed gallants chose to squire her. Well, well, well. From his pocket, he drew out the little pistol with its elegantly carved ivory handle. "Ever seen this before?"

She peered at it and wrinkled her nose. "A carriage pistol, is it not? Forgive me, but I positively loathe pistols. But . . . Do you know, it looks rather like the one Mr. William Templeton was trying to show us earlier in the evening."

"Us?" Frake asked. "Who did he show it to?"

Mrs. Leeds's brow puckered in thought. "I'm so sorry, I can't remember," she said at last. "There were several of us. Viscount Daylesford, I know. I remember, because Mrs. Wickham joined us just then and suggested he form a faro bank. One of them might remember who else was present. Not that I think it matters, though."

"Oh?" Frake's graphite pencil stopped its scratching. "And why is that?"

She leaned forward in a confiding manner. "If you really want to find the person who killed Sir Joshua," she said, "you should have a talk with that maid. You've seen her, I'm sure. The one who plays off those innocent airs?"

"What about her?" Frake tried to keep his voice neutral.

"I heard her a few days ago." Mrs. Leeds nodded in satisfaction. "Right in that library, too."

He gritted his teeth. "What did you hear?"

"She was threatening him. She said she'd expose him if he didn't do as she demanded. As bold a hussy as I've ever encountered!"

"And what did she demand?" Though he rather fancied he knew.

Mrs. Leeds lowered her lashes. "That, I'm afraid I didn't hear. And when I asked Sir Joshua about it later that night, he denied having any such conversation with her. I suppose that was natural, though, wanting to keep it hushed up, even from me, since she'd threaten to expose something about him. But I heard what I heard, and if he'd only told me the whole, he might be—be alive right now." She buried her face in her handkerchief. "If—if you have any sense of justice, you'll go and arrest that maid at once."

Annie stood, arms akimbo, beside the great brick hearth in the kitchen. A kettle hung over the low-burning flames, the water just coming on to simmer. A little more coffee, she reckoned, and Samuel just might think a little clearer. If that would be any help. She had her doubts.

He regarded her through bleary eyes from where he sprawled in a wooden chair before her. Cook had retired to the opposite corner where he inspected the copper bowls Ruby polished and repolished in a vain attempt to meet his ill-tempered demands.

"Now," Annie said, taking the empty cup from her brother's slack hand, "what have you been about, Samuel? You tell me the truth, now."

"I did." He essayed an attempt at his usual engaging grin. It slipped awry as he winced. "My head," he muttered, and lowered it gingerly into his hands.

"You know better than to drink when you ain't finished work yet. And you can stop playin' off them airs, 'cause I'll tell you to your face, Samuel Gooden, they ain't goin' to work on me."

He glared at her. "Unfeelin', that's what you are."

"And you're avoidin' my question. Now, you up and tell me straight. What have you been about?"

"I haven't been doin' nothin' wrong." He slid easily into his wheedling tone. "Just wanderin' about the place, keepin' an eye out, like."

She sighed. "Seein' what you could steal, you mean. Can't you behave yourself? With poor Violet in such straights—"

"How the devil else am I to raise the ready to help?" he demanded, sobering at last. "One snuff box, just one, and we could pay for a right proper doctor for her, we could. *And* for little Rose."

Annie turned away, fighting back the sudden emptiness in her heart. "You seem to be forgettin' what happened to Papa when he tried just such a trick and for just such a reason." Only one unwary and desperate venture into dishonesty . . .

Samuel slumped deeper in his chair. "I ain't becomin' no bridle cull, no matter how sick Violet is."

"Hush!" She glanced over her shoulder, her stomach clenching in alarm, afraid someone might hear. But Cook once more berated Ruby for some supposed failing in her duties, and the poor girl hung her head, oblivious to all but the tyrannical scolding she received.

Samuel ignored her. "A lifetime of honest work, and what did it get Papa?" he demanded. "Nothin' but nothin', that's what. Poorer than church mice, we was, and Mama dyin' of consumption and not a thing he could do to help her, not even buy medicine!"

"And his one time takin' to the High Toby," Annie reminded him, "got him shot by a Runner."

"A plague on all Redbreasts," Samuel muttered, and slumped back in his chair.

"Samuel." She kept her gaze fixed on him until he looked up once more. "I got to know. Did you talk to Sir Joshua about Violet tonight?"

"O'course not."

"There's no 'o'course' about it. You said as how—"

"And you said to leave it to you. So I did. Don't want to be turned off without my character, which is what he'd do, more than like."

Still, Annie reflected, unconvinced, her brother had been wandering about the house. He had entered the library. She had only Samuel's word for it Sir Joshua was already dead. What if they'd argued, if Sir Joshua had turned him off? Samuel's temper was none too steady. But she wouldn't—couldn't—believe her brother, ramshackle as he was, guilty of murder.

With a sinking heart, she regarded the belligerent set of his jaw. Getting the truth out of him when he was in one of these moods was nigh on impossible. With a fatalistic sigh, she gave up her attempts to extract more information and settled in another chair. It would be a long night of waiting, she guessed.

She must have dozed off, sitting before the glowing fire, for a noise nearby caused her to stir. She rubbed gritty eyes and yawned, then looked up to find Mr. Frake standing a few feet away, gazing down at her. She drew back, nerves bringing her fully awake. The gentleness of his expression didn't fool her one bit. There wasn't anything gentle about Runners.

"What do you want?" She straightened, tugging her apron back into position.

"Just to clear up a little point." He rocked back on his heels, waiting.

Giving her time to recover? How did that benefit him? She tucked several curls back under her mobcap and started to rise. He waved for her to stay where she was and drew up the other chair. The one in which Samuel had sat.

Samuel. She looked quickly about, but there was no sign of her brother in the kitchen. She could only hope he hadn't gone back upstairs to see what valuable objects might be lying about, unwatched.

"This shouldn't take long." He drew out his Occurrence Book and offered her a bland smile. "It's been reported to me as how you were overheard a couple of days ago threatening Sir Joshua with exposure of some kind if he didn't do what you wanted. Now," he added, fixing her with a look reminiscent of a betrayed puppy, "why didn't you tell me you'd already spoken with him?"

The blood drained from Annie's cheeks, leaving her chilled. For a moment she couldn't command her voice. She swallowed, then looked down at the hands she clenched in her lap. "I didn't, sir," she managed. "Leastways, he wasn't there."

"I see." He nodded encouragement. "You talked to him, but he wasn't there?"

"I know it sounds strange-like, but it's the truth. Practicin', I was, tryin' to get up my nerve. I went through everythin' he might say, and what I'd say back at him, tryin' to make him help poor Violet and little Rose. I was that afraid I'd go all tongue-tied when it come to the point. I—I don't like confrontin' folks."

"Like you're doing now?" A sudden twinkle glinted in his eyes.

She peeped up at him, wary. Did he believe her? Or did he think she confronted Sir Joshua on a previous visit, then planned his murder?

Abruptly he nodded, stood, and made his way up the kitchen steps. Annie remained where she sat, too weak-kneed to move if her life depended on it. What if he hadn't believed her? What if he'd gone to fetch his patrol and arrest her? Then what would become of Violet and Rose?

And where was Samuel? He could be anywhere in

the house by now, doing who knew what—though she could guess. With that sharp-eyed Runner about, he'd be caught for sure. She doubted anyone escaped the clutches of that Mr. Frake.

She hurried up the kitchen steps. He wouldn't be on the ground floor; too many people moving about, in and out of the dining room. The next floor, perhaps? She mounted the dark stair, hurrying, her uneasiness growing.

As she neared the top, something sharp and thin bit into her ankle, tripping her, and she pitched forward. With a cry she grabbed for the banister, but already she slid on the steep, shallow steps. She banged her knee, overbalanced as she tried to catch herself, and tumbled backward down the stairs.

Five

Frake strode up the stairs, resolutely refusing to think about Annie Gooden, yet utterly failing. His tendency was to believe her. His hunches frequently proved correct, but this time he had to admit his judgment was seriously clouded by her huge eyes and the fluff of errant curls he wanted to smooth back from her forehead.

Her uneasiness in his presence gave him pause. Lots of people became resentful and nervous when finding themselves face to face with the law, but there was usually some underlying reason for it. It bothered him that she might have such a reason.

A muffled scream, accompanied by a series of dull thuds, brought Frake up short. From above? No, somewhere behind him. He turned from the dining room and sprinted down the corridor leading to the servants stair.

A soft moan greeted him. He peered through the dim light to see someone lying in a crumpled heap halfway up the steps. Annie.

He reached her without realizing he'd moved. She remained still, her slight body wedged sideways, the very narrowness of the staircase probably all that saved her from tumbling to the bottom. Fear clutched at him as he stooped over her, finding her hand, checking her pulse. The rapid, strong beat reassured him. By a stroke of great good fortune, there would not be another death in the house this night.

"Annie?" For one moment his fingers lingered on her wrist as awareness of her, of the softness of her skin, flooded through him. She lay so still. . . . He set to work chafing the wrist he held.

She opened her eyes and winced.

"Annie?" He reached out to touch her cheek, realized what he did, and drew back his hand. "You just stay right there. I'm going to fetch you a brandy."

He descended the few steps to the hall, perturbed by the feelings that had surged through him at seeing her like that, at touching her. He needed his thinking clear, not tangled by emotions. And Annie needed brandy.

He considered a minute, then tried the front salon. Right his first try. He poured a generous amount from the decanter that rested on a side table and carried it back to where Annie now sat on the step.

Her hand trembled as she reached for the glass. He gave it to her, then guided her hand with his own, far too aware of her fingers pressed beneath his. She took a tentative sip and flinched back, her nose wrinkling, but a touch of color seeped back into her ashen cheeks. She shook her head when he tried to give her more. She returned the glass to him, then set about straightening her mobcap, shoving ringlets beneath it at random.

"Feeling better?" he asked, and knew it must sound inane. "That could have been a right nasty fall."

She looked at him for the first time, her eyes wide. "Somethin' tripped me."

His brow snapped down. "Did it, now? What?"

She turned her head with care and peered up the steps. "I—I don't see nothin'. But I felt it. Caught my ankle, it did, as I was goin' up."

Up. If she'd been going down, the fall would have been much worse, quite possibly fatal. He straightened. By pressing himself against the wall he managed to ease by her. He mounted slowly, testing with each step. Nothing. He knelt on the landing, leaning over to run his hands along the treads of the first three steps. Still nothing.

He sat back, troubled. *Had* there been something set here to catch her feet? Or did she seek, for whatever reason, to turn a simple accident into a mystery? If she'd hoped to distract his thoughts from Sir Joshua's murder, she was succeeding admirably.

Annie rose shakily and caught the banister for support. "It—there *was* somethin' there," she said as if reading his thoughts.

He stood. "That's as may be. But there isn't now."

"There *was*. I—" She broke off and leaned heavily on the railing.

He joined her, but she rejected his offered aid. He followed her down the steps, his gaze resting on the back of her head while he wished he could see into her mind. At the ground floor, he took her elbow and escorted her, over her stammered protest, to the front salon.

"Now," he said as he closed the door behind them. "You're sure there was something there for you to trip over?" Gently, he pressed her into a chair.

She glared at him. "I should of known you wouldn't believe me."

She must be feeling better; that one statement held a wealth of antagonism. He sighed and settled across from her. "I didn't find nothing." He held up his hand, breaking off her indignant exclamation. "Can you think of any reason why someone might set a trip wire for you, then get rid of it afore it could be seen?"

Her eyes widened. "The person who murdered Sir Joshua?"

Frake leaned back, his gaze remaining fixed on her face. "You were loitering near the library. Mayhap our murderer thinks you saw him. Or her." Or Annie had taken advantage of a simple accident to make him think just that.

"But I—I didn't! Not so as I'd know."

And if she told the truth? What if the murderer *had* tried to silence her? That possibility haunted him. He rose, unable to remain still, and paced across the room.

"I'll make an announcement," he said at last. "I'll tell everyone as how I've talked with you, and you couldn't help me none. But you take care, mind. Do you live here? No? Then get that brother of yours to walk you home."

She stood, very much on her dignity. "I ain't one

to be caught unawares twice," she informed him, and left the room.

He watched her go with an unpleasant—and unfamiliar—sensation of worry. She'd accepted the possibility that someone might want to kill her rather calmly. Was it because she knew it wasn't true? Or because she was used to shouldering burdens too heavy to bear?

Short of standing guard over her, his best chance to keep her safe would be to solve the murder, and right quickly.

Frake crossed the hall to the dining room. As he entered, a sudden hush fell over those gathered there. Tension vibrated in the air as everyone turned to look at him; it set his nerves on edge. He made his announcement concerning Annie, but though he searched the faces of his audience, he could detect no betraying signs of relief.

Had he accomplished his purpose? For that matter, had this precaution even been necessary? He'd give a great deal to know for certain.

He returned to the front salon to continue the seemingly endless task of conducting his interviews. Very few of the numerous people brought in to him appeared to have anything of importance to say whatsoever, though some tried. Several claimed to have heard shots at hours inconsistent with the times Annie had provided. That these times were substantially correct, he felt fairly sure. Several gentlemen had seen Sir Joshua leave the piquet room when his game with Daylesford had ended. And as for the time the body was found, Mrs. Wickham verified that.

Annie. . . . With a determined effort, he dragged his thoughts from her. She'd be careful. Intelligence as well as pride shone in those lovely brown eyes. She wouldn't take chances. He'd have to content himself with trusting in that.

The door opened once more, and Mr. William Templeton strode in, a picture of calm control with only his bloodshot eyes to betray how much wine he had consumed earlier in the evening. He directed a petulant glare at Frake. "Well, have you learned anything, yet?"

"First things first." Frake turned to a fresh page in his Occurrence Book and made a show of preparing himself to take notes. "Now, your name and direction, please?"

Templeton straightened. "My good man, you already know my name. And as for my direction, I have rooms in Duke Street." Only the slightest slur marred his words.

Frake drew out his pipe and twisted the stem. "You are Sir Joshua's nephew?"

The merest suggestion of smugness touched his thin mouth. "His only blood relative, since Oliver got himself killed."

Frake jotted a quick note. "Oliver. That would be his son? Captain Oliver Templeton?"

"I am pleased to see you have gained at least a grasp on the pertinent facts," Templeton drawled. "Indeed, I do mean his son."

"And you are now Sir Joshua's heir?" Frake rocked back on his heels. "Would it be more appropriate to address you as Sir William?"

A very satisfied smile flickered across Templeton's face, to disappear at once beneath an expression of infinite—and calculated—sadness. "Now hardly seems the time, my good man, with my uncle but barely departed from this earth." His tone held gentle reproof. "Please, Templeton will do for now."

"Templeton, then." And a masterly handling that was, Frake admitted to himself. Far better than his earlier blunders about his relief in inheriting the old man's money. Templeton must have recovered his wits and had time to consider what he would say. It would be interesting to see if he could shake him. Frake regarded him through half-lidded eyes. "Perhaps you could tell me where you were this night, from about one-thirty on?"

Templeton appeared to give this matter his undivided attention. "Do you know," he said at last, "I don't think I can. I'd finished my second bottle by then, you see. I don't believe I went near the library, though. I'm sorry," he added, his tone pure condescension, "I'm afraid I didn't see anything that might be of any help to you."

"Just your own whereabouts will do for now."

Very slowly, Templeton raised the quizzing glass that hung about his neck on a black silk riband. He regarded Frake through it for a full ten seconds, then allowed it to drop. "My good man," he enunciated with care, "are you actually asking me—me!—to prove to you," he made the last pronoun sound like something mildly unpleasant, "that I could not have killed my dear uncle?"

"Aye, that's the ticket." Frake beamed on him, not the least put out by the air of hauteur.

Templeton's lip curled. "The idea is preposterous."

"That's as may be, but I still need to know. Just to make my report complete, you understand."

"Ah, your superiors, to be sure." Some of the rigidity left Templeton's demeanor.

"Aye. My superiors. So if you'll just humor me along?"

Templeton cast him a suspicious glance, but apparently saw nothing but the bland innocence of Frake's deceptive blue eyes. "Very well, but I don't really remember. I was always with some person or other. A devilish amount of gaming going on, and I circulated among a number of tables. I remember being with any number of people. They'll be only too happy to assure you I'm telling the truth—if you're inclined to believe them." He provided several names.

Frake finished jotting them down. "I'm sure they'll vouch for what you've said, sir. And now, if you'll just have a look at this?" From his pocket he once more drew forth the carriage pistol. "Recognize it?"

Templeton took it and turned it over, nodding as he did. For the first time, he seemed to relax and take an interest in the proceedings. "I've got one just like it," he announced. "Beautiful, isn't it? I only bought mine a week ago. A gentleman needs something to carry with him when he goes about London at night. Lot of unsavory types hanging about in the streets. My uncle took to having one of his grooms accompany him, you know. I'm surprised the Watch doesn't take stronger measures. Mine—" He broke off as he reached into his coat pocket. A moment later he pulled out his hand and searched the other side of his coat. A puzzled frown settled on his countenance. "Odd," he muttered. "I know I had it earlier. Now, where—" He stopped abruptly and stared at the gun in his lap. "Where did you get this?"

"This," Frake said mildly, "was the weapon used to kill your uncle."

Templeton's mouth dropped open. "I—I showed it to several people," he muttered, then looked up, his hazel eyes blazing. "That Leeds woman! She saw it. Devilish keen she's been to get her talons into my uncle. And he'd finally caught on to her. He'd been avoiding her all evening. She must have realized she'd queered her suit with him."

"She'd hardly kill him for that," Frake pointed out.

"Woman scorned, do you mean? Of course not, not the Leeds female. But if Uncle had found out something about her—enough to make him give her the cut direct tonight, which I vow he did—she might have been afraid he'd pass the word to Daylesford."

"Daylesford?" Frake's tone held only the mildest interest.

Templeton gave a sharp laugh. "It's no secret she was out to snare one or the other of them. Uncle was richer, but a canny old goat. Daylesford's the sort of silly young chub ripe to make a fool of himself with a widow on the catch for a title and fortune."

"Indeed," Frake murmured politely as he scribbled more information into his Occurrence Book. This was turning into quite an evening for accusations. How many more would he be privileged to receive before the night's interviews ended?

He cast a surreptitious glance at the clock. Almost dawn. He fought back a yawn. He'd have to draw a halt to the questioning soon, before his brain refused to function. Besides, Sylvester—the aging marmalade tom that deigned to honor him with its presence in his home—would be expecting his breakfast soon. The last time Frake was late for that meal, Sylvester ate the leaves off the potted peppermint presented to Frake by Nanny Gossett, who lived down the hall. At the moment, he reflected, he possessed a pot of chamomile of which he was particularly fond, and another of meadowsweet. He'd rather the cat didn't make a meal of either of them.

He looked up from his book. "That will be all for now, I think. I don't want to keep everyone up all night. I'll visit you on the morrow, if you don't mind, when we've all had some sleep and might be thinking a mite clearer."

Templeton rose languidly. "Tomorrow," he repeated.

Despite his drawling tone, there was nothing slow about the manner in which he exited the room. Relieved to escape? For any reason other than exhaustion, perhaps?

And where was Annie? Safe in the kitchen?

The door had no sooner closed behind Templeton than it opened once more. Henry Wickham looked in. "Captain Thomas Bevis," he announced, and ushered in the gentleman who had helped keep people away from the library earlier.

Frake looked him over, noting first the deep-set eyes of smokey gray. They dominated the handsome face with its fair complexion. The cut of his clothes bespoke a very exclusive and expensive tailor. He strolled in, as if assured of his importance in any setting.

"I really don't think I can help you much." Captain Bevis arranged his lanky form in one of the comfortable chairs, leaned back, and stretched his long legs out before him, crossing his ankles. He folded his hands in his lap and regarded the Runner with an assessing scrutiny. "I only wish I could. I'd like to see this matter settled as quickly as possible."

"Would you, sir?" Frake refrained from mentioning that it was somewhat of an ambition with him, as well. "And why is that?"

"I happen to be a friend of the family." Bevis drew his snuff box from his pocket and studied the chased silver lid. "His son was my closest friend. We entered the same regiment."

"His death must have been a blow to you." Frake opened a new page of his Occurrence Book and made some quick notes on the gentleman. "Why did you sell out?"

Bevis leaned his head against the cushioned back of the chair. "Does it matter? Oh, very well. Joining

up was something of a lark for us. Adventuring, you
know." He sighed. "Peacocking about the Continent
in our Hussar's uniforms, charging on the enemy,
showing off our courage. It was all a big game." A
frown set a deep crease in his brow. "Without Oliver—
I found I'd lost my taste for campaigning. It's a dead
bore, you know, sitting in some sodden tent in the middle of some cursed forest, slogging about in the mud
for weeks on end, with narry a sight of the enemy. No
glorious charges into battle, no heady call to arms. Just
that endless rain and tedium. No life for an active man.
So I came home."

Frake scribbled quickly. "And you've kept in close
touch with Sir Joshua, even after the death of his
son?"

"Somehow, it seemed the least I could do." Bevis
flicked open the box and helped himself to a pinch.
"I've spent many an evening with the old man, remi-
niscing about Oliver. Stout fellow, he was. One of
the best." He lapsed into brooding silence.

"Now, about tonight," Frake began.

"That is why I am here," Bevis pointed out. "What
would you like to know? Where was I while Sir
Joshua was in the library?" He frowned. "About one-
thirty, I was playing cards. Piquet, for a while. With
Lord Harcourt. Then—yes, I went down to the dicing
tables for a bit. After that, I went back upstairs and
joined a faro table. I had just left there, as I recall,
when I encountered Templeton in the hall, babbling
about someone taking his life." His expression hard-

ened. "When I learned the truth—" He broke off, but his hands clenched convulsively in his lap.

"And did you see or hear anything during that time that might be construed as being suspicious?"

A sudden gleam lit Bevis's eyes, then his expression turned thoughtful. So, he was one who liked to throw the cat among the pigeons, Frake guessed. That should make for some interesting information.

"That story of Daylesford's." Bevis lounged back in his chair. "I might have believed the part of his winning his fortune back. Sir Joshua is—was—a reasonable man. If he'd guessed the young fool had ruined himself, he'd have given him a chance to break even again. But what I can't swallow is his claiming to have won a staggering portion of Sir Joshua's fortune. Sounds to me as if he were trying to create a reason for a suicide."

With that, Frake agreed, but he kept the reflection to himself. He merely nodded, jotted the information in his book, then resumed his expression of fascinated listener. "Anything else, sir?"

Bevis frowned. "This is going to sound odd," he said after a moment, "but I could have sworn I saw Oliver's groom, the lad Gooden, about the place. The dicing room, to be exact. Not very likely, though, is it? Even if he is serving Sir Joshua now. What would a groom be doing in the front rooms of a gaming house?" He met Frake's gaze with a steady stare. "No good, that much I'll warrant."

Frake hid his surprise under the guise of taking more notes. So, Samuel Gooden not only entered the library by the servants door, but he'd also been about the other rooms, as well. It dawned on him he'd accepted a little too readily Gooden's explanation that a search for brandy had brought the groom to the library in the first place, when he discovered the body. Could Gooden have a history of thieving? That might explain his sister's bad case of the jitters over having a lawman about. He'd talk to them both again, as soon as possible. He wanted to check on Annie, anyway.

Once more, he drew the pistol from his pocket. "Have you seen this before?"

Bevis examined it a moment, then shook his head. "Never. Almost a toy, isn't it? A carriage pistol. Not the sort of thing I'd choose for myself. I prefer a weapon with some authority. A lady, perhaps?"

Frake took it back. "Now, weren't you one of the ones young Templeton was showing it to earlier?"

Bevis raised his eyebrows. "Was that what he was waving about? I wondered. Good God, do you mean the man actually brought the pistol here and showed it to who knows how many people? Any one of them could have taken it from him! He was three parts disguised before the evening ever got rolling."

"That," Frake said, "was just what I was thinking. Were Mrs. Cornelia Leeds and Sir Joshua particularly close, by your way of thinking?"

Bevis straightened, and his eyes took on a dangerous glitter. "I have fought a duel with a man for such an aspersion against a lady. Ah—but that was on the Continent."

"And not with a lawman asking questions in pursuit of his duty," Frake pointed out, unruffled.

Bevis's stiff posture eased a trifle. "Very true. But my good man, just because I said a woman might have carried that coaching pistol, I had no intention of implying Mrs. Leeds had anything to do with this. As to how close they were, you will have to ask her."

A touch of jealousy there? Frake wondered. Captain Bevis had neither fortune nor title to recommend him, and if William Templeton were right, and the lady was on the catch for both, Bevis, undeniably handsome as he was, hadn't a chance of wedding her. But that didn't eliminate another form of liaison between the two.

"If you are searching for a woman who might wish Sir Joshua ill," Bevis went on, "I suggest you look no further than Mrs. Wickham. In case she has not so informed you, it was Sir Joshua's money that started this establishment. If he indeed lost heavily tonight, as Daylesford has claimed, it is a very good possibility he demanded repayment from her."

Frake considered, then shook his head. "What good would killing him do her? Templeton will demand the money as well, won't he?"

Bevis studied his exquisitely manicured nails. "It wasn't a formal loan. No papers to prove it. Oliver told me about it at the time. His father was besotted with the woman and offered to set her up, with her paying him back as she could. She never repaid so much as a shilling. And now, it appears she won't ever have to."

Six

Another hour passed before Frake finally dismissed the last of the gaming house patrons. Henry Wickham, fighting back a cavernous yawn, saw the gentleman to the door, then made his way down to the kitchen. Frake finished his notes and followed.

The pre-dawn glow seeped through the high basement windows, bathing the chamber in pale, cold light, highlighting the gleam of the copper and brass fixtures. A kettle simmered over the hearth, and the fragrance of fresh bread and strong coffee wafted out to greet him. Cook, it seemed, had been busy.

All seven occupants of the room sat in chairs drawn up about the fire. Mr. Henry Wickham and Captain Palfrey drank from steaming cups, while Cook, the kitchen maid Ruby, and Samuel munched on fresh rolls. Mrs. Wickham, her plumes abandoned next to a bowl of apples on the huge wooden table, lolled back in her seat, dozing. She stirred as he crossed the floor, and gave him a bleary-eyed look. Annie sat stiffly erect, cradling one wrist as if it pained her, her gaze coming to rest on Frake the moment he came down the stairs.

Henry Wickham gestured for Frake to help himself to coffee. Frake did so, adding a generous dollop of sweet-smelling cream and several spoonfuls of sugar. It had been a long night, and despite the approach of daybreak, it wasn't over for him yet.

He stirred the cup and closed his eyes. He wanted to go home. He wanted to sleep for two days, uninterrupted. He even, amazing as it seemed, wanted to have Sylvester purring in his lap. The one thing he didn't want was what he had: Annie's resentful, suspicious gaze following his every move.

He took a scalding sip and perched on the edge of the table. Since Annie already distrusted him he had nothing to lose; he might as well get on with it. "Now, then," he said, and drew his ever-present Occurrence Book from his breast pocket. "Would you mind telling me, Gooden, what you was doing in the library when you discovered Sir Joshua's body?"

Mrs. Wickham gasped. "In the library? Him?"

Samuel Gooden cast Frake a resentful glare. "Just lookin' about a mite." He straightened his shoulders and fixed his expression into one of rapt appreciation. "Grand place, this is. A real eyeful. Fine as five pence. I loves to just stroll about, I does, seein' the gentry in all their fine togs. Never meant no harm by it."

"Pricing the candelabra?" Frake hazarded.

Betraying color shot up from Samuel's neck, and a shifty, cornered look entered his bloodshot eyes.

"There ain't no call to go accusin' him." Annie bristled with indignation for her brother. "He ain't done nothin' wrong."

"That's right," Gooden stuck in with an exaggerated air of virtue. "Nor never has."

"Nor can you go sayin' he has," Annie added with a quelling glance at Samuel. "You're just tryin' to blame it on servants, who ain't got no one to stand up for them. Much easier than blamin' the nobs."

Frake repressed a sigh. "Seems as if you've mentioned that before."

She cast him a furious look. "The thatch-gallows who murdered Sir Joshua has probably gone home by now," she informed him, "and all you can think of doin' is sittin' in here all comfortable-like, drinkin' coffee, and accusin' decent folk of crimes they'd never think of turnin' their hands to."

Gooden cast his sister a sideways, admiring glance. She steadfastly refused to meet it. She was blustering, trying to turn his attention, Frake realized with a sinking heart. But from her brother's involvement with Sir Joshua's death—or from his general predilection toward crime? Tomorrow—or rather, today, after he'd had a brief nap—he'd ask around Sir Joshua's stables. If Gooden had ever indulged in petty thievery, one of his comrades would be bound to know. But getting that comrade to admit it might not be so easy.

Of one thing, though, he could be certain. As long as he suspected her brother, he would never get more than scowls out of Annie. Certainly no information or help. Or could that be her plan? To keep him suspicious of the wrong one of them? That possibility put the perfect cap on a completely unpleasant night.

* * *

Annie dragged off her apron and hung it on the peg behind the pantry door. She'd thought that Runner would never get around to giving his permission for them to leave. Thorough, that's what he was. Too thorough. He hadn't missed anything, so far as she could tell. And he looked like he had a heap of guesses and suspicions. Most of them directed at her or Samuel.

She threw her cloak about her shoulders and fastened it at her neck. The dawn air, in spite of the arrival of summer, had been chill of late. She hurried out to the kitchen and stopped. The room stood empty. Samuel had vanished.

He'd promised to walk her home! At least, she'd asked him and he'd agreed. He'd probably forgotten again the next minute. Unreliable, that was Samuel. She should know better than to count on him.

Well, she wasn't afraid to walk alone. It wasn't even really dark out there any more, and the light grew brighter every minute. So why did she hesitate? Violet would be waking soon, and be alarmed at her absence. Still, she stood in the center of the chamber, reluctant to leave the safety of the kitchen.

Samuel was right, she was nothing but a pudding heart. Just because Sir Joshua had been murdered, she was turning everything into a Cheltenham tragedy. One little stumble on the stairs, and she'd made it out in her own mind to be an attempt on her life. Yet the sensation of a wire pressing into her ankle returned. Could she, in her unease, have imagined that detail?

The door above opened and she spun about, biting back a startled cry. But no evil villain grasping a pistol or knife came into view. In a way, it was much worse. Mr. Frake descended the stairs, his frowning gaze resting on her. Annie hugged her cloak closer about her and eyed him warily.

He paused on the fourth step as his gaze swept the cavernous chamber. "Where's your brother?" he demanded.

"What are you wantin' with him, now?" she countered. "Ain't you talked with him enough for one night?"

He continued to the bottom of the stairs, where he remained. "I thought as how he was going to see you home safe."

So had she. She hunched a shoulder. "There ain't no need. I can look after myself."

Mr. Frake straightened. "Do you mean to tell me he's up and left without you?"

"I told him to," she lied. The Runner had a low enough opinion of Samuel already. They didn't need this to make it worse.

Mr. Frake's mouth tightened. "Someone should be having a care for you. That could have been a very nasty fall you had earlier."

"No, could it?" She opened her eyes to their widest. "And here was me thinkin' as how I'd bounce if I hit the bottom. Anyway, weren't you the one who said as how I didn't trip over nothin' at all?"

"I said as how I couldn't find anything. That doesn't mean it couldn't have been removed between the time you fell and the time I got there. And," he forged on, "all things being equal, I don't think we should take any chances. Do you?"

No, she didn't. But at the moment she didn't feel like agreeing with him. Why was he acting so concerned about her? What did he hope to gain by it?

"We've been kept here so late," she said pointedly, "I'd best be gettin' off home if I want any sleep at all afore I have to come back."

He gave a short nod. "All right, then. I'll come with you."

"You'll what? You'll do nothin' of the kind!" She drew back, alarmed by the sudden race of nerves up her spine. She didn't want to be with him a moment longer than necessary. The fact that his solid presence would afford her protection didn't matter. He was a Runner. She'd be happier without him.

"You ain't worried that someone might try another trick on you?" He watched her closely.

"O'course I am. But didn't you say as how you was goin' to tell everyone I didn't know nothin'?" She tilted her head to one side. "Besides, it ain't dark out there, and I don't have much more than a few blocks to go. It'd be plain foolish to be afraid, it would."

"Plain sensible, you mean."

She thrust out her chin. "I don't need no one to see me home. You just get along and leave me be."

She turned on her heel and headed for the door.

She listened, expecting him to protest, to try to stop her. It was with some surprise at still being alone that she mounted the area steps.

She was glad. A little nonplussed, too. He'd had the unexpected decency to believe she meant what she said. Now, all she had to do was believe it herself.

She cast an uneasy glance over her shoulder, but at this dawn hour, very few people moved about the street. Only folk like her, heading home from long nights of work—or the gentry, leaving their parties to seek their beds. It didn't seem natural, people living this way. Daylight was for being awake and doing things; the dark of night should be for sleep.

Some day, she promised herself. Some day she'd live like that again. She'd have a real home, with Violet and little Rose—and maybe even a husband and children of her own. Some day.

An eerie sensation crept over her, as if someone watched her. She shivered and looked quickly about. No one. Unless—

She spun around and peered down through the dimness into the area before the kitchen door. A shadowy shape stood there, almost invisible in the dark. A scream welled in her throat, and she took an unsteady step backward.

The figure moved, separating from the wall. Mr. Frake put his foot on the first of the iron steps, and Annie's knees threatened to give way. She hadn't even heard him leave the kitchen.

"What do you think you're doin', creepin' up on a person like that?" she demanded.

"Was I creeping? And here was me thinking I'd only come out a door." He mounted to the street. "If we're walking the same way—"

"I don't need no one to walk with me." Reaction to her fright made her words sharper than she'd intended. With a defiant toss of her head, she set off for Haymarket.

After a few steps she glanced back; he hadn't moved. Good, she told herself, and fought off the lingering desire to accept his protection. She didn't want to be beholden to a Runner. Before her courage could fail her, she quickened her pace.

She knew these streets. She'd walked them every day since she started working at Mrs. Wickham's. Nothing terrible had ever happened to her. So nothing would today, either.

The uncomfortable sensation of eyes boring into her back assailed her once more. She turned quickly, searching through the pale dawn light, but saw no one. Not even Mr. Frake.

Had he taken to hiding so she wouldn't know he followed her? Yet this feeling was different from the last. Before, she'd simply known there'd been someone watching. Now—now, her skin crawled. With an effort, she fought back the wave of fear that surged through her.

She walked on as fast as she could without breaking into a run. Probably her imagination working too hard, creating these hobgoblins. After all, it wasn't every day she found someone who'd been murdered—and someone she knew, at that. It ought to surprise her if she *didn't* develop a case of the high fidgets.

Well, no worry about that; she had them now. A good case of them, in fact. No matter how sternly she told herself she was being foolish, she couldn't get rid of the feeling that someone followed her.

Yet she had no reason to really suspect it. When she looked back—which she did more and more often—she didn't see anyone ducking out of sight. She didn't hear anything, either. She only felt it.

On impulse, she dodged down a dark alley and into the welcome shelter of a doorway. If someone really trailed after her, they'd turn, too. And then what would she do, if she found herself face to face with a murderer?

She drew back into the darkness, pressing against the door, and peered back the way she'd come. Here, in the narrow confines between the tall buildings, the frail dawn light barely penetrated. She could see nothing more than shadows.

One moved across the alley's entrance, slowly, as if it searched through the gloom for something—or someone. Annie's fingers clutched at the wood as she willed herself to blend into her surroundings, to be invisible. Why hadn't she let that Runner come with her?

Face to face with a murderer. The phrase repeated in her mind. Face to face with a murderer.

That prospect proved too much for her. Exhaustion and nerves overcame the last shreds of her courage, and she took to her heels. She could feel as foolish as she wanted later, once she was in the safe shelter of her own room.

She raced blindly on until she burst out into a wider street. For a moment she allowed herself to slow, to listen. Was that the pounding of feet she heard behind her? She didn't wait to analyze; she raced on, dodging laden carts on their way to the markets.

She became aware of the cries of street vendors, and slowed to see a number of men trundling barrows or bearing their wares on trays suspended around their necks. People, at last. She fell in beside two stout men bearing a barrel of ale suspended from a yoke that rested on a shoulder of each. When they reached Compton Street, she turned off, joining a dustman who swaggered along with his basket while talking to a young rabbit-woman who carried her wares hanging from a long pole.

If she hadn't been such a coward, she might have discovered the identity of the murderer. But would it have been at the cost of her own life? For that matter, she didn't even know if the person she'd glimpsed in that alley had been following her, or had merely been some chance passerby.

Yet that feeling of being watched still sent shivers down her spine. She increased her pace, every step faster as she neared her own familiar alley. With a last glance behind her, she ran down it as fast as she could, finally reaching the steps of the house where she had her room.

And still that eerie sensation persisted.

Seven

The lusty squall of little Rose's crying dragged Annie out of her brief slumbers. Beside her in the narrow bed, Violet tossed, moaning softly, once more in the throes of the fever the last medicine had failed to bring down. Annie dragged herself free of the patched covers, stumbled sleepily over the chair that had one leg shorter than the others, and picked up the baby.

Rose had her mama's pretty eyes, Annie decided as she laid her down on the foot of the bed to change her into dry things. And her papa's vociferous demands. Poor little thing, fatherless before ever she had a father to acknowledge her.

"I'll not let you down, Rose," Annie vowed as she hoisted her to her shoulder. "Those Templetons will admit as you're one of their own, don't you worry none."

"Annie?" Violet raised herself up on her elbow. "I'm ever that sorry. I'd meant to tend Rose myself this mornin' and let you get what sleep you could. You was ever so late." Sudden hope lit her glassy eyes. "Did you talk to Sir Joshua?"

Annie drew a deep breath. "That—" Suddenly, she couldn't keep up the pretense, the false hope that buoyed them. "Oh, Violet. He's dead."

"He's—" Violet brushed the lank dark hair back from her forehead. "Dead? Annie, how? He—" Tears filled her eyes, and she gave a violent sniff as she dashed them away. "And don't you go tellin' me as how I shouldn't cry." She sniffed again and sought a handkerchief on the bedside table. "I know he treated me bad, but Annie, I did love him so."

Annie sat beside her, the baby still held against her shoulder, and stroked Violet's hair with her free hand. "He had that way with him, he did, and that careless how he went and ruined a good, sweet girl."

Violet dried her eyes. "Was—was he taken with a fever?"

"No. Here, you lie back and get comfortable, and I'll tell you about it. Just let me get some water boilin' for your herbs." She handed Rose to her eager mother, who began to feed her. They'd had to hire a wet nurse, for despite the infusion of goat's rue, cabbage, and marigold recommended by the midwife, Violet's persistent fever kept her from producing sufficient milk.

Annie busied herself at their tiny hearth, all the while relating the events of the previous evening—though omitting any reference to Samuel, her own tumble down the stairs, and the fright she'd had thinking she was being followed. She shivered. No need worrying poor Violet any more than necessary. She was worried enough for them both. When she ended her tale, she turned back to find her sister watching her, wide-eyed.

"Murdered," Violet breathed. She hugged Rose to her and murmured soothing words.

Annie poured the boiling water over the herbs, and the pungent odor filled their tiny room. She'd have to buy more honey today. More chamomile, too. The pottery jar held barely a spoonful of the dried flowers.

"And you say that Runner don't know who done it?" Violet dabbed at her tear-filled eyes. "Oh, Annie, I know you never saw the good in Sir Joshua—"

"And now you see I'm not the only one." She poured the infusion into their best cup—the one with only two chips in the rim—and carried it to her sister. "Here, you give me Rose and drink this up."

"Will you be goin' to the gamin' hall today?" Violet took a tentative sip and wrinkled her nose.

Annie replaced the baby in her makeshift cradle and took her daytime uniform from its peg. "That Runner, he didn't say nothin' about closin' the place. I'd best get hoppin' if I don't want to be late."

Some twenty minutes later, she ran down the three dingy flights of stairs leading to the alley. Mrs. Appleby, the wetnurse who lived in the next building, had arrived with her own little boy and settled down for a nice chat with Violet. Violet would undoubtedly tell Mrs. Appleby of Sir Joshua's fate, and the young woman would exclaim and bless herself, and Violet would cry while the woman fussed over her, and then she'd feel much better. If only her continuing fever would heal as easily.

And if only Annie might make sure Samuel were safely out of this business, before Violet thought of that possibility.

She hesitated in the street, peering around, but didn't see any lurking shadows. Had it all been her imagination last night? She couldn't quite convince herself of that. The feeling of being watched had been too strong. She didn't have it now, though.

She had hurried nearly four blocks before her steps slowed once more. She'd never be able to concentrate on work today, not with so many questions about her brother's involvement in the murder belaboring her mind. And how could she continue to look that Runner direct in the face and lie to him about what Samuel might have been doing in the gaming rooms? He'd know. He saw way too much. She needed to find out the truth about her brother.

She slipped her hand through the slit in her gown and felt for the pocket that hung from her chemise. She'd picked up a few coins last night for fetching one of the gentlemen a bottle of burgundy. She'd meant them to pay Mrs. Appleby, or buy more herbs. But perhaps peace of mind—hers and Violet's both—was worth a little more.

As she weighed them in her hand, torn, she caught a flicker of movement out of the corner of her eye. Every nerve alert, she spun to face it, in time to see a shadowy shape disappear through a doorway. A prickling of fear raced along her spine, then settled in a cold lump in the pit of her stomach.

Had that person been following her? Or did she

see phantoms and hobgoblins where none existed? At least it helped make up her mind. She hailed the first hackney that passed, and gave the jarvey the direction of the mews where Sir Joshua kept his horses stabled while in London.

She sat forward on the seat, one hand clutching the door, too overcome by jitters from thinking herself followed and by guilt at this expense, to enjoy the novelty of the ride. She had to find out about Samuel, and she could think of no other way. He should be out exercising the prads now. Her one fear was that the normal schedule would be interrupted by the death of the master. Yet animals needed to be tended, no matter what. She'd take that chance.

Her fingers tightened on the window. Maybe it wasn't Samuel's being arrested she should be so worried about. It was she who the Runner kept watching in that unnerving way of his, she whose movements his gaze followed, she whose tale of tripping on the stairs he didn't believe. And he'd let her go home alone last night. If he'd really believed her to be in danger, she had a shrewd suspicion that nothing would have kept him from accompanying her.

She was his prime suspect—and she couldn't blame him in the least, not if she were honest. It looked pretty bad for her.

Unless, of course, Sir Joshua's murderer got to her first.

If something happened to her, what would become of Violet and Rose? They had Samuel, of course, but she knew better than to count on him. He'd taken to drinking since his return from the Continent with the dying Captain Oliver Templeton. Once he got hold of a bottle, he forgot everything and everybody. At the rate he went, she didn't know how much longer he'd be able to hold onto a job. Then there'd be nothing left for Violet and Rose but the Workhouse in St. James's Parish.

The hackney drew to a halt, and she started from her unhappy reverie. Enough of this fruitless worry. She had a job to do right now.

The parting with the coins caused her a severe pang, but it had been a necessary expense. She never could have walked here and back in time to get to work without a severe reprimand—and possibly even the loss of her own job. So she'd better get on with it.

Still, she found herself loath to walk along the mews, and not just because the area offered so many places for someone to hide or jump out at her. She felt herself a traitor to her brother with every step. Or perhaps Samuel would be there—or worse, she might find no one. Then the trip—and the coins— would be wasted.

She hesitated at the partly open double doorway leading into the barn-like structure with its loose boxes and tack area. To the far side beyond the row of stalls a rickety stairway led to the loft above, where the grooms had their sleeping quarters. The sound of a rake scratching over cobbled stones reached her, and relieved at this sign of life, she stepped inside.

The darkness within made it difficult to see. She hesitated just over the threshold, peering through the gloom, trying very hard not to imagine lurking shadows. For once, she succeeded. She didn't see anyone.

"Now, what would you be wantin'?" came a creaky voice from the depths of the interior. An elderly man emerged from one of the boxes, a pitchfork in one hand.

"Loomis, is that you?" Annie took a step forward.

He peered at her. "Annie, me girl. Now, what would you be doin' 'ere? Young Sammy's off on 'is exercisin'. But you just come on in, m'girl. A sight for sore eyes, you is."

Annie clasped his hand. "It's ever so good to see you, Loomis. Is anyone else about?"

"That they ain't, lass. Gone to the park, they 'ave. Don't make no difference who's master 'ere. Them prads need their mornin' workout." He leaned on the pitchfork, both massive hands wrapped about the handle, and showed her a grin that boasted two missing teeth.

"I've got a question for you." She gathered her courage, then forged ahead. "How hard would it be to nick a small pistol out of someone's pocket without them knowin' nothin' about it?"

"Why?" he asked in mild interest. "Is you wantin' to?"

She ignored that. "How hard would it be?" she repeated.

He raised an eyebrow. "Now, Annie, me girl, what makes you think as 'ow I'd know a thing like that?"

"Cut line, Loomis." She fixed him with a compelling eye. "I know perfectly well as how it was you who went and taught Samuel the finer points of the forkin' lay."

He beamed. "And I've seen the results, I 'ave. Aye, I've seen 'em." He shook his head in pleasurable contemplation. "Never know'd such a talent. 'E could make 'is livin' that a-way, 'e could, and a much finer one it would be than could be found 'ere." He gestured around the stalls. " 'Is fingers could be in and out o' your pocket, and you'd never know." He sounded a touch envious at this greater ability.

Annie closed her eyes. Had Sir Joshua seen Samuel stealing from someone? If her brother feared he'd been caught, might he have slipped that pistol out of Mr. William Templeton's pocket? Samuel must have seen it, the way the gentleman had been waving it about. Maybe Samuel, in his wine-stupefied mind, had decided better a dead employer than being turned over to the Watch.

She shivered, wishing she could be certain of Samuel's innocence. "Would takin' a pistol be easy?" she pursued. "Could someone as had less practice do it?"

Loomis tilted his grizzled head to one side and wrinkled his brow in earnest consideration. "Depends," he said at last. "On the circumstances. 'Ow many people around the cully, if the cully's got 'is mind set on other matters, if 'e's been at the bottle. And," he added judiciously, " 'ow clever your friend is."

"Well, now." Mr. Frake emerged from around the corner of the doorway. "It's right glad I am to have that cleared up. Right glad indeed. That question has been exercising my mind quite a bit."

Annie spun about, staring at him in horror.

Mr. Frake merely gave her his bland smile. "Wondered how easy it might be," he explained. "Don't have enough experience with the matter myself to be a judge."

Didn't he? Annie narrowed her gaze on him. He seemed capable of just about anything—and she didn't, she realized, mean that in an altogether negative way. He still smiled at her, but somehow he looked different this morning—and not the least bit tired, in spite of the fact he couldn't have had more than an hour or two of sleep.

He looked more approachable, somehow. His clothes, that was it. He wasn't so dapper-looking as she'd seen him before. More comfortable-like. Dressed to go among the servants and grooms—which he did every bit as well as he fit in among the gentry at the gaming house. He blended into any surrounding, all with a change of garments.

Admiring his abilities, though, wasn't what she had in mind. "You followed me," she accused, finding her voice at last.

He shook his head, a disturbing smile playing about the corners of his mouth as if he were unaware of her antagonism. "We were both bound to see your brother. Or *was* it a desire to see your brother that brought you here?"

She glared at him. "There ain't nothin' wrong with visitin' my brother."

"Nothing at all," he agreed. "And we both learned some useful information, we did. Templeton's attention was on his gaming, and he consumed more than one bottle of burgundy. Offhand, I'd say as how anyone at all might have taken the pistol from him without need of your brother's skill."

She felt her cheeks warm. "He don't mean no harm," she said, and knew it must sound lame.

Mr. Frake didn't answer. Instead, he thanked Loomis for his invaluable contribution, then offered to escort Annie to the gaming house.

Her distrust of this Runner vied with the cost of a hackney, and won. She sniffed and raised her chin. "I can get there on my own, thank you." With a flounce, she started away from the stalls.

Mr. Frake fell into step beside her. "Seems quite a waste of the ready, us paying for two hackneys when we're both bound for the same place."

She ignored him, which was beginning to be somewhat difficult. There was something about him. The gentle humor in his innocent blue eyes begged for confiding and offered understanding. The set of his shoulders spoke of quiet power, his easy gait of confidence. She wanted to trust him.

But Runners weren't to be trusted. They led you on to say more than you meant, then pounced on you when you were all unawares. She edged away.

At the street corner they waited for several minutes, not speaking, before a soft exclamation of satisfaction escaped Mr. Frake. He strode forward a pace, raising his arm, and a hackney pulled up before him. Annie sniffed in determined disdain. No jarvey had ever stopped for her so easily. Of course, she had never had a chance to summon more than just a couple of them since coming to London.

Mr. Frake opened the door and simply waited, his expression unreadable. Annie hesitated, worrying her lower lip with her teeth. Those few coins it would cost her to take her own would pay Mary Appleby for a little longer. Was her pride worth more than little Rose?

And what if someone *had* been following her last night and this morning? If she'd lost that person when she'd taken the hackney to the mews, perhaps he—or she—would be lying in wait for her somewhere near Mrs. Wickham's. Would it be so terrible for her to take this one precaution and allow the Runner to see her safely to the door of the gaming house? With her chin held high, and her glance steadfastly avoiding his, she climbed in.

Sinking back against the squabs, she allowed herself a guilty little shiver at the luxury of it. And it didn't even cost her a penny! She peeked sideways at the Runner and said, with as much cool politeness as she could muster: "Thank you."

"My pleasure." This time, a touch of warmth crept into his voice. "How does your sister go on? And the baby?"

She blinked. He sounded sincerely interested. She weighed his question, trying to find a trap, but it seemed innocent enough. "Violet's no better," she admitted. "But little Rose—" She broke off, and a slow smile tugged at her lips at the memory of holding her niece that morning, of being able to still her cries. "She's our joy."

A minute passed, then he said: "You look right nervous and upset. Is sitting in here with me as bad as all that?"

She shook her head, but studied her hands in her lap rather than look up at him. She didn't want to tell him about her experiences of last night and this morning. She had no proof; he'd probably think she was lying, trying to make herself look like a victim rather than a villain. "It's just as how I'm that late for work," she said.

"We'll be there shortly."

And they were. It amazed Annie how quickly a carriage could get one about London. As soon as it pulled to a stop, she jumped down. Mr. Frake paid the jarvey, then followed her down the area steps. As he reached over her shoulder to open the door, it swung wide.

Mrs. Wickham, attired this morning in her startling dressing gown of puce and gold, stood on the kitchen threshold. Her brilliant yellow ringlets emerged from a lavish lace cap, and her lips boasted their bright red tinge. The lines about her close-set hazel eyes, though, showed her lack of sleep. Her gaze came to rest on Mr. Frake, and a deep sigh escaped her. "We hoped you would come back soon. What progress have you made?"

Annie tried to ease by her, but found her way blocked. "I'm that sorry I'm late, mum."

"It doesn't matter in the least. If you've been helping Mr. Frake, then you have been serving us all. Run along, now."

Annie held her breath and waited for Mr. Frake to make it clear they had only recently met up, and she had not been helping so much as trying to hinder him.

He merely smiled. "Annie has been most helpful. You are lucky, indeed, Mrs. Wickham, to have such a maid."

Annie cast him a curious look, then scuttled off to the pantry to don her apron and collect her feather duster.

There seemed to be more clutter than usual littered about the dicing room. She loaded dirtied glasses and empty bottles onto trays, then carried them down to the kitchen where they would become Ruby's problem. A quick dusting, the rearrangement of the chairs, the collection of stray dice she found on the floor, and she was ready for her broom.

Next came the card rooms upstairs. The small salon devoted to piquet showed the same clutter as the dicing chamber, along with several articles forgotten by their owners in the shocked aftermath of finding Sir Joshua. Annie set her teeth and concentrated on her work. The less she thought about last night, the better. And the less she thought about Mr. Frake, the happier she'd be.

Finished at last, she hesitated. Next she usually did the library. For a long minute she considered doing one of the other rooms first, instead, but knew from long experience the inadvisability of altering her routine. It threw her all off.

Still, she paused at the back hallway door, not

wanting to turn the handle and go inside. Sir Joshua's body surely must be gone. Nothing lingered in there, especially not his ghost. And she needed to make certain all traces of the tragedy were gone. If one of the patrons found some lingering evidence, there'd be a regular dust-up, with her all to blame. Collecting her wavering courage, she threw open the door and stepped inside.

Someone— She gasped, her hand trembling at her mouth, before she realized that not one but several people, all very much alive, occupied the room. Mrs. Wickham sat on the sofa beside her nephew, and Captain Palfrey and Mr. Frake sat on the chairs facing them. As one, they all turned to look at her.

"I—I'm ever that sorry," she stammered and ducked out the door.

The next moment it opened again, and Mr. Frake's deep voice called: "Come back."

She'd reached the end of the hall, but at his command she stopped. Slowly she turned to face him, her hands gripping her duster.

"You should be in here," he said. "Everyone's trying to remember details about last night. Little things that seem unimportant but might actually help. You could have something real useful to offer that you haven't realized yet."

"But my chores—" she began, loath to re-enter that room, and nervous of being in his company.

He didn't say a word, merely beckoning her with a gesture. Against her will, she moved toward him. Why did she respond? She couldn't actually let him have any power over her! Yet he had it over others. She'd seen it. It was amazing, the way folks did as he asked. Even the gentry up and told him the most amazing things. What chance did she have against him?

And she didn't like being at odds with him. He made her *want* to do his bidding. He always seemed so reasonable in his requests, so warm in his appreciation. Either he was a master of deception, or some shred of good lurked in the man.

He stood at the door, wearing that gentle smile of his, waiting. She joined him, but found she didn't have the nerve to look up into his face. What, she wondered, suddenly curious, would happen if she smiled back?

He ushered her within, just as if she were a lady and not a maid. She fought against the flicker of pleasure this little attention brought to her. Rather it should make her uneasy, she reminded herself with force. She should be wondering what he wanted from her.

They joined the others, and he drew up a chair for her. She took it, feeling uncomfortable. She shouldn't be sitting here, not with her employer. Yet none of the others seemed to mind her presence in the least—nor Mr. Frake's treating her so fine.

"So far," Mr. Frake said as he took the seat at her side, "we've gotten through the early part of the evening. Captain Palfrey here remembers Sir Joshua's arrival shortly after nine. In the devil's own temper, too, you said?"

"Everyone got the sharp side of his tongue," Palfrey confirmed. "He gave Captain Bevis the cut direct."

"Did he?" Mr. Henry Wickham stared at Palfrey

in amazement. "They've been so close since the death of Sir Joshua's son. You are quite certain the snub was intentional?"

"Well," Mrs. Wickham's smile was pure cattiness, "it was probably all due to that Leeds female. More than once I've seen her making up to Sir Joshua or that silly Daylesford in the most unconscionable way, then slipping off to meet with Captain Bevis." She nodded for emphasis. "Mind, he's as handsome as he can stare, but since she's set her cap at a title and fortune, she shouldn't continue an *affaire de coeure* with another."

"There's something between Bevis and Mrs. Leeds?" Mr. Frake added that to the growing amount of information contained in his Occurrence Book.

Captain Palfrey folded his arms. "Just gossip."

"It is not," Mrs. Wickham declared, heated. "They've been carrying on ever since Bevis came to town. Why, I've seen that Leeds female slip him gaming chips she's wheedled out of one of those suitors of hers. It's small wonder Sir Joshua finally caught her at it and realized she'd been taking him for a ride. Why, when I spoke with him—" she broke off, her expression aghast.

"When?" Mr. Frake's sharp eyes rested on her flushed countenance.

Mrs. Wickham threw her nephew a frantic look. He stared back blankly.

"So you entered the library while he was in here last night?" Mr. Frake hazarded.

Tears sprang to the woman's eyes. "I was in here

when he—when he entered," she admitted. "And you know he didn't die until much later, for young Daylesford came in after I'd left."

"And what did you talk about?" Mr. Frake held his pencil ready.

"I—" She broke off again.

"Mrs. Wickham was going to ask him for a little more money," Captain Palfrey put in. "No use trying to hide the fact, my dear Dorothea. He has only to check with your banker." He turned back to Mr. Frake. "They'd set up the meeting earlier in the evening."

Mrs. Wickham wailed softly.

"More money," Mr. Frake murmured. "What did Sir Joshua say?"

"So very unpleasant." Mrs. Wickham drew a handkerchief from her reticule and dabbed at her already bloodshot eyes. "I'd never seen him in such a mood. He—he said he wouldn't give me a penny more, and actually wanted me to begin repayment of what he'd already given me. And that had been a gift!" she added in indignation.

Annie peered over Mr. Frake's shoulder, struggling to make out the words, as he jotted down a surreptitious note. *Explains why no written proof of loan. Still, excellent motive.* She winced.

"So, Sir Joshua, Captain Bevis and Mrs. Leeds were all out of temper last night," Mr. Frake mused. "Anyone else?"

"Mr. William Templeton," Henry Wickham said. "He was losing all evening, and kept exclaiming about how he needed to bring himself about." He hesitated, an arrested look in his eyes.

Mr. Frake raised his eyebrows. "You've thought of something?"

Mr. Henry glanced down, the picture of embarrassment. "He blamed his uncle. Sir Joshua. They'd been playing at the same table, you see. He blamed— rather loudly, in fact—his uncle's phenomenal luck."

"Daylesford had a similar complaint." Mr. Frake tapped the end of his pencil on his book. "But then his lordship claims to have won it all back."

Henry Wickham looked skeptical, but held his tongue.

Annie watched Mr. Frake jot down a note to check on Daylesford's proof.

"Oh!" Mrs. Wickham looked from her nephew to the Runner. "I've just recalled something." She spun to face her nephew. "Do you remember the way Mr. Templeton looked?" She turned back to Mr. Frake. "We were both there when Mr. Templeton threw down his cards. It was just before he left the table. Sir Joshua gave that short laugh of his and refused him a loan, then apologized for not obliging him by cocking up his toes right then and there. And Mr. Templeton just turned and stared at him."

"By Jove," Mr. Henry breathed. "I do remember! That gleam in his eyes! Oh, Lord, you don't think Sir Joshua himself gave his nephew the idea to murder him, do you?"

Eight

Less than twenty minutes later, Frake left Mrs. Wickham's gaming rooms. After only a moment's consideration, he hailed a hackney and gave the jarvey the direction of Sir Joshua's bank in the City. The name of that establishment he had obtained from Mrs. Wickham, who had, upon more than one occasion, she admitted, received from him a draft drawn upon it.

The banker, a plump little man who peered at the world through a pair of thick spectacles, greeted Frake with a polite reserve. This, Frake quickly determined, was due more to distress at the death of his affluent client than any disinclination to be of help. Yes, the man admitted, Sir Joshua Templeton had indeed deposited his funds with them. The records would of course be turned over to Bow Street. In the interim, how could he be of assistance?

Frake settled in a slat-backed chair across from the massive desk with its litter of papers. Three other desks stood about the bustling office, along with six smaller ones at which industrious clerks copied columns of figures into thick ledger books.

The banker, who introduced himself as Mr. Phipps, adjusted the spectacles on the bridge of his nose. "It is truly a terrible thing that has happened to Sir Joshua. Now, what is it you were needing?"

Frake drew out his Occurrence Book. "Just to know if anything unusual has been happening to his account of late. Any large withdrawals or deposits? Anything that might surprise you or look suspicious in light of what's gone and happened to him?"

"Let me see . . . Templeton . . ." He picked up one of the books on his desk, glanced at the spine, then set it aside. He picked up the next, checked it, and nodded. "Here we are."

Frake raised his eyebrows, but forbore making any comment at the moment. The man was engrossed in his work, leafing through the pages, scanning the entries. Interesting, that he had the ledger already to hand.

"No." Mr. Phipps closed the hefty book, but continued to hold it before him. "Nothing significant at all. At least, not compared to this morning."

"This morning?" Frake swerved his scrutiny back to the little banker. "Was that why you had the book out? What was it about?"

Mr. Phipps wrinkled his short nose, causing his spectacles to slip askew. "Mr. William Templeton came in. Or rather I should call him Sir William." His voice held a note of disapproval. "He wished to draw upon his inheritance."

Frake's eyebrows rose. "Already?"

The banker drew a handkerchief from his pocket,

removed his spectacles, and began to polish them with vigor. "A sizable amount." He pursed his lips. "I must say, I cannot approve. To squander such a sum . . . And all for the sake of saving his cattle from being sent to Tattersall's."

"Is that a fact." Frake leaned back in his chair, tapping his book with the end of his pencil. "That much in debt, was he?"

Mr. Phipps fixed his earnest gaze on Frake. "Sadly improvident, I fear. I shall greatly miss my late client. Now, *there* was a gentleman who cared for his investments. One can only hope his heir, once he has grown accustomed to his new dignities, will begin to show his uncle's good sense in managing his income." Yet his tone held out little hope of such a happy event.

Frake asked several more questions, but learned nothing else that might be of help. He thanked Mr. Phipps for his time, restored his Occurrence Book to his breast pocket, and re-settled his curly beaver on his head. The banker escorted him outside into the brilliant midday sun, where Frake took his leave of him.

A fine day, Frake reflected, gazing up into the clear blue sky. Not a cloud anywhere, yet not sweltering like so many other June days. He might as well enjoy the fresh air while he could. He set off at a brisk walk, heading for the office of Sir Joshua's solicitor.

He was beginning to feel the heat when he at last arrived at the correct direction. He looked up at the tall gray building, then mounted the shallow steps leading to the front porch. He let himself in, then climbed a flight of stairs until he found himself outside the offices of Hamilton, Weybourne, and Hamilton, Solicitors. He entered the spacious receiving room, announced himself to the clerk, and settled in a chair to wait.

He didn't have long. The elder Mr. Hamilton erupted from his office, a large man with an imposing manner. He fixed Frake with a penetrating eye that must have sent his clerks scurrying on any number of occasions. "Frake?" he demanded in a carrying voice. "From Bow Street?"

Frake admitted he was, and Mr. Hamilton, after requesting his clerk to fetch Sir Joshua Templeton's will and be quick about it, ushered him into his comfortably appointed office. Frake had barely taken a seat when the clerk sidled in, set the document on the desk, then scurried out.

"Let's see." Mr. Hamilton spread the sheets across his desk. "You'll be wanting to read it, I suppose? Nothing unusual in it, if that's what you're hoping for. Quite a straightforward document, as they go."

"Glad to hear it." Frake picked up the first page and began to read. He found, as Mr. Hamilton had indicated, all the typical sorts of bequests a gentleman normally made to his family members and retainers. A number of people, Frake reflected, would be a good deal more comfortable in the near future.

Halfway through the list, he encountered the name of Samuel Gooden. He read the passage, then re-read it with considerable interest. Well and well and well.

So Sir Joshua left young Gooden the sum of five hundred pounds, in grateful recognition of the care given to his son Oliver during the journey home from the Continent.

Five hundred pounds. Frake drew his pipe from his pocket and twisted the stem between his fingers. That was a great deal of money, especially to a young man in the unenviable position of being head of his family with a younger sister as ill as Violet. And Sir Joshua was responsible for her predicament, at that. Might he have felt himself justified in killing Sir Joshua in order to obtain the money to help his sister? Did he have that much family feeling?

For that matter, did Gooden even know of the money?

He looked up to find Mr. Hamilton, his expression alert, watching him. "Would you know if a certain groom, Samuel Gooden, was aware of this here bequest?"

The solicitor spread his hands. "I have not shown this document to anyone, if that is what you mean. As to what Sir Joshua may have told his beneficiaries, I would have no way of knowing."

"Pity." Frake tapped the bowl of the pipe in his palm. He couldn't think of any way to find out for sure. Certainly Sir Joshua, in his first flush of gratitude at having his son restored to him, might have promised the largesse to the groom. Or he might never have mentioned it. It wouldn't be any good asking Annie if she'd heard of it, he supposed— though he just might try anyway. If nothing else it would provide a good excuse to talk to her—even if only to see her eyes light with anger.

That thought depressed him, and he returned to his reading.

After another few minutes, a second passage of considerable interest caught his eye. So, Sir Joshua forgave Mrs. Wickham's debt. Frake pursed his lips as he saw the named sum. Apparently, what he'd heard about Sir Joshua sponsoring her gaming house could easily be true. And she might well panic at the thought of having to come up with such an amount. Well, she needn't worry about repaying him now.

And that erasure of the debt gave Mrs. Dorothea Wickham an excellent motive for wanting Sir Joshua dead.

His next call was at Bow Street, to check on inquiries he had set afoot on each of his suspects. To his satisfaction, one of the clerks had the information neatly gathered for him. Most of it, as he expected, proved negative. Members of the *ton* rarely had records of criminal activity.

He turned a page, read Annie Gooden's name, and his brow shot down. A lengthy report. That he hadn't expected.

But it didn't concern Annie herself, he saw with considerable relief, or even her brother, but her father. Her mother ill, her father making one desperate venture on the High Toby, ill-luck brought a Runner on his path, he was shot and killed. Wife died of consumption a month later. Left three children. Frake didn't need to read their names to know them.

He set aside that report with a heavy heart. No wonder Annie regarded Runners with so much distrust and anger. And how could he ever overcome such a deep-rooted resentment? Her father—apparently a decent man driven to desperation.

Then there was her brother, whom he suspected had a healthy dose of larceny in him. It must be hard on Annie, seeing her brother slide so easily down the path of dishonesty. Now, he'd swear Annie herself hadn't a dishonest bone in her body. These were terrible burdens for a mere child to bear.

Annie stood on the walkway before the house in Duke Street, eyeing the front door with considerable trepidation. Such a bang-up neighborhood. The likes of her had no business walking right up to the front door here. She should be slinking down the area steps, the more appropriate entrance for the servants.

Only she hadn't come here today as a servant.

She drew a deep breath, and found she trembled with nerves. Before they got the better of her, she forced herself to march up the steps and apply the knocker. The hollow sound echoed back at her, mocking.

The aging man who opened the door to her bore all the appearance of a retired gentleman's gentleman. He looked down his supercilious nose at her, and the shrewd glance summed her up. He deigned to bestow a condescending smile on her. "What is it, girl?"

Annie straightened. "I've come to see Mr. William Templeton."

The man's eyebrows rose. *"Sir* William Templeton," he said in mild reproof. "If you have come with a message for him from your master—"

Her chin thrust out. "I'm here on my own business. Urgent, it is. And he'll be wantin' to see me, seein' as how it concerns his late uncle."

The man regarded her for a long, thoughtful moment, then showed her into a small sitting room. "I will bring him the message," he said, his tone holding out little hope of a happy result. "If you will give me your name?"

Annie provided it, and watched the man leave. Mr. Templeton—*Sir* William, she corrected herself— would probably think she'd come on business concerning his uncle's murder. At least that might bring him down to her.

She paced about the little room, feeling out of place, wishing necessity hadn't forced her to come. But Violet needed help, and Sir William, as Sir Joshua's heir, was the rightful person to provide it. That fact helped firm her resolve, which kept sagging.

William Templeton strode into the chamber some ten minutes later, attired in a velvet dressing gown over buckskin breeches. He stopped a few feet in front of her, eyeing her with considerable curiosity— and not a trace of friendliness. "I can give you five minutes," he said shortly. "I have pressing business to attend to."

Not quite the greeting she would have liked, but better than being refused permission to speak to him at all. She clutched her hands together and held herself erect. "If you please, sir, it's about your uncle and my sister, Violet Gooden."

Sir William stared at her. "What the devil are you talking about, girl? Violet? Who the devil is she—aside from your sister, of course."

Annie plunged on. "She was a great deal to your uncle, sir. She just bore his daughter, and that sick she is, and me not able to fetch a proper doctor to her."

"She just bore—" He broke off. "Good Lord," he said faintly. "Uncle? With a maid? The old dog."

"Please, sir, Violet is ever so sick. A fever, it is. And little Rose—the baby—she's such a dear little thing, but your uncle, he never gave Violet so much as a penny, and for all they weren't married nor never thought to be, Rose is his natural daughter, and I know he'd want you to do the right thing by her."

Sir William perched on the arm of a chair and fixed his unwavering regard on Annie. "What had my uncle to say to you?"

Annie felt the warmth rising in her cheeks. "I never got to talk to him, sir. I tried, but he didn't never take the time to see me. But if he'd known about Violet, how sick she is, I mean, I'm sure—"

Templeton raised his hand, silencing her. "And since my uncle is dead, you have come to me." He drew his watch from his pocket. "Your five minutes are up, and I must be going. I'll think about it." He gave her a dismissive nod and strode out of the apartment.

Annie stared after him, too shaken to think clearly. Had he just promised to help her? No, nothing that

definite. But he hadn't thrown her out, either. That
had to be good. He'd think about it, like he said, and
see how unfairly his uncle had treated poor Violet.
He'd give them something, she didn't dare hope it
would be much, but anything would help. Violet
would get better. She had to.

The retired valet who ran the lodging house ushered
her out. Annie went, barely noticing what she did.
She'd been that scared, having to build up her nerve.
But she'd done it. She'd confronted him and asked for
help. It was over. And now she felt shattered.

She was also, she feared, going to be late getting
back to the gaming house. But maybe they'd soon
get enough from Sir William so she could indulge
in a hackney when she needed one. But not yet. She
knew better than to count on anything. She set off
at a brisk walk.

She arrived at Mrs. Wickham's some ten minutes
later, out of breath. She hurried down the area steps
to the kitchen and let herself in. Ruby, already at
work setting out pots and pans for the evening, waved
a greeting. Cook looked up from the bread he was
about to put in the oven, but chose to ignore her.
Annie hurried past the great wooden table laden with
vegetables that still needed cleaning, and slipped into
the tiny chamber where she changed into her evening
uniform.

Hope did funny things to a person, she reflected
as she made her last check of the gaming rooms. It
made her want to believe everything would come out
all right. She had to fight the urge to feign illness

so she could take the night off, go home, and tell Violet that everything was well on the way to being settled. No, she'd rather wait. It would be so much fun to carry the money to her sister and toss it on the bed, just so she could see the joy and relief that would light up her face.

But that was all just a daydream, so far. And even if Sir William did help them out, not all her troubles were over, not by a long shot. She still had that Runner regarding both her and Samuel with too much suspicion. She sank onto a chair, returning to reality with a thud.

"Annie?" Mrs. Wickham strode into the room, her ample figure swathed in yards of pale green satin trimmed with blond lace. A tatted shawl drooped from her elbows, swinging with her every step. "Is something the matter, girl?"

Annie rose quickly and clutched her duster. "No, mum."

Mrs. Wickham patted at the net cap which held her plumes in place. "There may be quite a crowd here, tonight. Curiosity, you know. If Captain Palfrey forgets to do it, see that extra bottles are set out, will you?"

"Yes, mum." Annie sidled toward the door.

The proprietress crossed to a gilt-trimmed mirror that hung on the wall and inspected her reflection with a slight frown. "Well, go on, girl. There's no time to waste."

Annie spent the next hour and more ferrying bottles of wine from the cellars to the sideboard where she could retrieve them quickly as they were called for above stairs. Progress was slow, for she regarded every step with suspicion, unable to forget her fall of the previous night. She still had bruises. By the time she finished, the first of the patrons already moved about the rooms, finding partners and settling at tables. They were early, Annie noted; probably their morbid curiosity, and the thrill at being in the establishment where one of the gentry had been murdered in cold blood.

Very quickly, Annie discovered that information was going to be as much in demand as wine. To all the innumerable questions she murmured an unhelpful "Don't know, sir," and escaped as quickly as possible. It was going to be a very long evening.

She maneuvered down the stairs from the piquet room, rounded the corner in the entry hall, and drew up short as she saw a gentleman loitering in the back hallway. She gasped, her heart pounding, only to look up into the smiling eyes of Mr. Frake. She let out her breath on a shaky sigh.

His brow creased in a slight frown. "Did I give you a start?"

"No, sir." She tried to push past.

He remained in her way. "I have a few more questions for you, when you have a chance."

"You're always havin' questions for me, sir. And I don't have no chance. Please, sir," she added as he still showed no sign of moving. "I got my duties, and we're ever so busy tonight. There's all them in the rooms askin' me about what happened last night, and they ain't none of them happy when I says I don't know."

"Tell them I've ordered you not to say nothing. That should set them all a-gog." His expression remained solemn, but his eyes twinkled. He stepped aside. "I'll be here, whenever you get the time."

She bobbed him a quick curtsy and rushed past, vowing it would be a long while indeed before she'd find that time. Why did he keep wanting to talk to her, anyway? Hoping she'd slip up and say the wrong thing and land herself or her brother in a heap of trouble? Not if she could help it, she wouldn't. It would be best if she avoided him completely.

She retrieved another load of bottles, then started once more up the steps. She was getting behind, going so slow each time. She neared the top, stepped on the next stair, and her foot slid out from under her. The tray flew from her hands, the bottles crashed to the carpeted floor, and she grabbed wildly for the banister as she toppled backward.

Nine

Annie caught herself on the railing and clung, trembling, to it. That had been like stepping on ice! Or grease.

She pulled herself erect, then stooped to run her fingers over the stair. Grease, all right. But how? It hadn't been here on her last trip down, only a few minutes before.

She sat on the next step below, hugging her knees to her chest, shaken. No food had come up or down these stairs—at least, not that she knew of. And who else would be carrying it besides her? Not Ruby or Cook, not yet. They weren't done with the supper, yet. And even if they were, they wouldn't be bringing it to this floor.

As for the gentry, they stuck to the main staircase. No one in their right mind fumbled about back here in the near dark unless they had to.

In fact, anyone who wished her harm could be pretty sure no one else would pass this way.

She glared at the spot of grease. If she fetched Mr. Frake to have a look at it, would it still be here when she got back with him? And if it were, would he assume she put it there herself in an attempt to make him believe she was innocent because someone wanted to kill her?

And if she had been hurt or killed, it would have looked like an accident caused by her own carelessness.

She buried her face in her arms and drew in several deep, calming breaths. She could no longer doubt she was in serious danger. And from someone who acted in very subtle ways.

She returned to the kitchen, where the sheer normalcy of Cook's and Ruby's routines of arranging food on platters helped steady her. She fixed a bucket of soapy water, found a rag, and scrubbed the grease from the stair. What would her stalker try next? Another accident here on the dimly lit steps? From now on, she'd use the main staircase and stay out of dark corridors. If Mrs. Wickham objected, she'd—she'd just up and quit.

She shoved her pail and rag into a corner, rescued her tray, and collected the scattered wine. It had received a pretty bad shaking. She'd best return these to the cellar and fetch other bottles. She turned her back on the servants stair and headed for the one reserved for the gentry.

As she exchanged the wine at the sideboard in the lower hall, the unexpected sight of Sir William Templeton, emerging from the dicing room, greeted her. She stopped short, staring, then set off after him at a safe distance as he mounted the steps to the upper rooms. He couldn't have come for the gaming, not with his uncle dead less than a day. The possibility he had come to see her, to hand over a handsome sum, could not help but intrude into her thoughts. Why else would he venture to visit this establishment while he was in mourning?

And he was in mourning, no doubt of that. He was garbed in the severest of black, but still managed to look like a sulky little boy. Maybe it was the way he carried himself with that belligerent air of importance. His expression, when she caught a glimpse of his face, showed the faintest smirk of satisfaction.

He strode up to Mrs. Wickham, who broke off her conversation with an elderly gentleman to greet him with unfeigned pleasure. She held out both her hands, exclaiming: "What a delightful surprise."

He carried first one, then the other, to his lips for a gallant kiss. "I haven't come to play—the mere suggestion of such a thing would be the height of impropriety. I just wanted to assure myself that everything was all right here, that last night's tragic occurrence has not harmed your charming establishment."

"As you see." Mrs. Wickham gestured toward the crowded tables.

A hush fell over the room as the gamesters began to turn and look at him. Sir William drew to the side, taking Mrs. Wickham with him, into a corner where they would be less noticeable. Annie crept a little closer to hear what he would say.

"I have also come to find out if anyone has learned anything new from the Runner," he said.

"Of course." She patted his hands. "It must be so

very distressing for you. Your uncle. But that Mr. Frake hasn't said a word to any of us. He is somewhere about, but I vow, I have no more knowledge of what he does than you do."

Sir William withdrew his wistful gaze from the faro table near them. "I suppose he is competent?"

Mrs. Wickham sighed. "Completely, I make no doubt. He just doesn't give anything away."

His gaze traveled about the room. "There is Bevis," he said abruptly. "Perhaps he will bear me company when I return home." He started across the room.

Annie, seizing her chance, hurried after him then managed to step in his way. "Good evenin', sir."

He looked at her, his expression distracted. "Good evening." He pushed past.

She caught his arm. "If you please, sir? There's somethin' as we still need to talk about. Could we have a word or two? In the library, mayhap, where there ain't so much noise as one can't hear?"

He looked down his great beak of a nose at her. "I cannot imagine—" He broke off as several people turned to stare at them. "The devil," he muttered. "Must you choose to make a spectacle of me?" He grabbed her arm and bustled her out.

Once in the corridor, she forced herself to overcome her distaste for entering the library and led the way in.

Sir William strode in after her and shut the door firmly behind them. "Now, what do you mean by accosting me like that?" he demanded.

"I'm that sorry, sir, but it ain't easy for me to get

out to call on you at your home. And when I seen you here tonight, it seemed too good a chance to miss. About my sister, sir."

"Oh, yes. That sister of yours. Your mistake, my girl, was allowing me time to think. Your story is preposterous."

"But—" Annie stared at him, too startled to fully take in what he said.

He folded his arms across his chest. "I utterly deny any responsibility for your sister and that child she has borne. Its father could be anyone. I doubt if she knows for certain, herself."

"How dare you—"

He raised his hand and took a menacing step toward her. "How dare *you?*" he countered. "This is an attempt to extort money from me, pure and simple. Well, I'll not let you get away with it. If you have the temerity to come anywhere near me again, I'll have the Runner arrest you on that charge. And mind, girl, I mean what I say."

With that, he swept out of the room, leaving Annie to stare after him, too shocked to move.

Frake reached the top of the servants stair, barely avoided falling over a bucket of soapy water, and turned down the service corridor toward the library. They needed a few oil lamps along here, he reflected. He didn't see how Annie got around without stumbling in the near dark. It was no wonder at all she'd taken that spill down the stairs last night.

Of course, that might have been no accident, as she claimed. The meager light practically begged some villain to lay his snares for unwary feet.

That reflection continued to plague him as he approached the library door. As he neared it, it swung open with a force that banged it against the wall. Annie herself stormed out and slammed it closed, then stood trembling, her hands scrunched into fists. Tears glistened in her eyes, but her expression denoted repressed fury, not sorrow.

"Annie?" Frake strode up to her.

She started, then dashed a hand across her eyes. "Don't you go talkin' to me," she said through clenched teeth. "I'm that angry, I—I could almost kill someone."

"Anyone in particular?" He inserted a touch of gentle humor into his words.

"Him." She jerked her head toward the door through which she had just come. "The weasel! It wouldn't hurt him none. He's got so much, and Violet and little Rose has nothin'."

"Sir William Templeton, I take it." Frake rocked back on his heels. "How much did you ask for?"

"I didn't! He didn't give me no chance. He said if I ever come near him again, he'd have you arrest me for tryin' to extort money from him."

Frake raised his eyebrows. "I take it he denies his uncle fathered your Rose?"

She nodded. "He said the cruelest things about Violet, and they ain't true! She ain't like that at all."

He liked the way her chin thrust out in defiance.

She had pride, as well as her loyalty. Curious, he asked, "What are you going to do now?"

She hesitated, and for a moment real fear shone in her eyes. It vanished the next second as she straightened her shoulders. "I'll take care of them myself. If he won't do what's proper—well, then, we don't need him."

Brave words. He could see the effort with which she held back despair. What hope did she have, unless her brother—

That thought arrested his attention. Her brother would shortly inherit five hundred pounds. How much of it, he wondered, would Annie see?

Of course, if Samuel murdered Sir Joshua, he wouldn't get any of it.

On the whole, it would be better not to raise her hopes. He'd wait and see what happened. But the moment Samuel laid hands on the money, he'd see to it that Annie knew about it—and got what she needed.

"I can do it," she said, though more as if she tried to convince herself rather than him.

"You will," he said, and realized he meant it. "No one can keep you down. Now," he went on, "why don't you just go along to the kitchen for a few minutes, give yourself a chance to calm down."

She shook her head. "I got my work. I shouldn't never of taken the time to talk to Mr. Templeton—*Sir* William, I should say." She corrected herself with a sniff of disdain. "I'd best get back to my rounds." She squeezed past him in the narrow corridor.

And that, it occurred to him, was possibly the best conversation he'd ever had with her. She'd been angry, true. But not, for once, with him. She confided in him, accepted his words without antagonism. Almost, she seemed to take comfort from him.

Suddenly, his whole night seemed brighter.

Except when he thought about Sir William Templeton. At the moment, nothing would please him more than to prove that gentleman guilty of murdering his uncle. Buoyed by that prospect, he opened the door to the library.

Sir William, though, had departed. With a muttered oath, Frake set off after him. He wouldn't remain in this house for long, not with him being in mourning and all. He'd best find him quick if he didn't fancy a trip to Duke Street.

He made a rapid tour of the rooms, but found no trace of the gentleman anywhere. Mr. Henry Wickham, when approached, could not say for certain when he had glimpsed him last. Some time ago, he rather thought. Frake returned to the entry hall, retrieved his hat, and started out the door.

The sound of a hushed voice brought him to a stop. An angry hushed voice. It was answered the next moment by a familiar tone slurred by drink that at once caught his interest. Samuel Gooden. Now, what did he do here this night?

"Your other pocket, man," Sir William said, his voice rising. "Don't put me off. I want to see what you have in there."

A loud sniff came from below. "Ain't nothin' a

fine gentleman like yourself would be wantin' to see," Samuel said. "Just my dirty wiper."

They must be in the tiny area outside the kitchen door, at the foot of the wrought-iron steps. Frake looked over the railing, but the porch light cast only the gentlest of glows, illuminating no more than the door and the three steps leading up to it. The area beneath him remained a region of dark shadows.

"Dirty from handling stolen goods, I'll wager. Will you have it out, or do I summon the Watch?"

"I didn't take nothin' from nobody." A whine crept into Samuel's voice.

"We'll see about that."

The sounds of a brief scuffle reached Frake. He tensed, ready to break it up, but it ended almost as soon as it began. For a moment silence followed.

"I knew it!" Sir William drew in a ragged breath. "A snuff box."

"I didn't steal it." Now, Samuel merely sounded sullen. "Found it, I did. This mornin' while I was exercisin' the prads in the park. Just lyin' there in the tanbark, it was, so I picked it up. There ain't no harm in that, is there?"

"Then what were you doing in the dicing room tonight?" Sir William demanded.

"Just lookin' around. A fine sight it is, sir, a real treat." His words positively dripped innocence and sincerity. "Even better'n Bartholomew's Fair, it is."

"And I suppose you never went near Lord Errington?"

"Lord who, sir?"

"Don't try to gammon me. With my own eyes I saw you dip your hand into his pocket."

"I didn't never!" Now Samuel betrayed pure indignation. "I just bumped into a gent, is all."

"We'll see if Lord Errington recognizes this, shall we?"

"Now," Samuel wheedled, "there's no call to go botherin' anyone. If it's his, I reckon he went and lost it at the park. I'll be right glad to see him get it back, I will. Right glad. Now," he suggested, as if the notion had just struck him, "why don't I just leave it with you to give t'him?"

"You may be very sure I will keep this. Good God, man, don't snivel. You're drunk as a wheelbarrow, I'll wager." Sir William's voice held a wealth of disgust.

"I ain't on duty," came the smug response.

"No, nor will you be again, with me. I don't see why my uncle bore with you, even if you did bring my cousin home from the Continent. I'm not so easily duped as he, though. I've tumbled to your thieving ways. Collect your things and clear out. I want you gone from my stables before morning."

A long moment of silence passed. Then Samuel said: "I'll be right glad to. And do you know why?"

"I couldn't care less." Sir William's voice took on a touch of ice.

Frake peered through the darkness, wishing he could see what went on between the two.

" 'Cause I knows a beetle-witted, nip-cheese twiddle-poop when I sees one," Samuel finished on a note of pure satisfaction.

"Insolent!" Footsteps started up the area stairs.

Frake ducked back into the entry hall. Was Sir William really as angry as he sounded? If so, it might be a good time to ask him a few questions. People, he'd discovered, tended to blurt out the truth, without calculated tailoring, when in the throes of a strong emotion.

"Mr. Frake?" Captain Palfrey crossed the hall to join him. "Is something the matter?"

Frake waved him back. The footsteps had mounted the shallow stairs to the front door, but now paused just outside. "Just waiting for someone. I'll do best on my own."

The captain looked him over and his lips quirked upward. "I believe you will. The front salon—" he nodded toward the small room next to them, "—is never used in the evenings, if you have need of it." He strolled back into the dicing room.

The handle on the door clicked, and Frake retreated a pace. The next moment it opened, and Sir William strode inside with all the air of a man who had just stepped outside for a breath of fresh air. Only the slightest line marring his high brow betrayed the anger he had displayed only minutes before.

Sir William's gaze fell on Frake, where he hovered only a few paces away, and he raised his eyebrow. "Are you now serving as major domo here?"

Frake awarded this sally a benign smile. "Now, what a fortunate coincidence to go running into you like this. Just like to ask you a couple of questions,

I would. In here?" He swung wide the door into the front salon.

No lights. He took a candle from one of the wall sconces and carried it inside. Sir William trailed after him, waiting while Frake lit the three tapers in the candelabrum on the side table.

"Now, that's better." Frake returned the candle to the sconce in the hall. "Just a couple more questions about the other night," he added as he returned to the room.

Sir William looked up from where he had seated himself in one of the comfortable wing-back chairs. "Anything I can do to help, of course. I want my uncle's murderer found, and as quickly as possible."

"So do we all, sir." Well, all except the murderer himself, of course. Or herself. "Now, would you be so kind as to try and recall who you went and had supper with last night?"

Sir William rubbed his chin with his forefinger. "I'm afraid I don't remember much. Rather the worse for drink, you know. I believe—" He broke off, frowning. "Yes. I went down alone, I'm sure of that. Then Mrs. Leeds joined me."

"Mrs. Cornelia Leeds," Frake murmured, and drew out his Occurrence Book. He jotted down a quick note. "Did she come in alone?"

Sir William raised a supercilious eyebrow. "Now, how the devil should *I* know that? I never pay much attention to the woman. I was eating by myself, in a corner, when she came up and sat without so much as asking my leave. Devilish bad *ton.*"

"And what was it she wanted?"

He snorted. "Not *my* company."

Did he sound a touch resentful? Frake added a note that the man just might have been jealous of his uncle.

"Information," Sir William went on after a moment's silence. "The damned female tried to interrogate me." His brow clouded as if with irritated memory. "She kept after me, asking questions about my uncle." He snorted. "I didn't tell her anything, though. I knew she had to be up to no good."

"What sort of questions?" Frake waited, pencil poised.

The furrows in Templeton's brow deepened. "About Templeton Grange, I think. I don't really remember. None of it seemed important to me at the time. I thought she already knew all about the estate. Couldn't understand why she badgered me about it, unless—" He broke off, and his eyes gleamed.

"Unless?" Frake prompted.

"She knew I had my pistol with me. She'd been part of the group I'd shown it to, earlier. She might very well have joined me," he went on, growing more indignant with every word, "for the sole purpose of trying to obtain it from me without my knowledge."

"And could she have done it—if she had actually tried?"

"If you mean, my good man," he said, looking down his high-bridged nose at Frake, "had I had enough to drink so I might not have noticed her reaching into my pocket, I should think the answer must be obvious. *Someone* did just that."

"During the supper? Could anyone else besides Mrs. Leeds have taken it then?"

"How the devil should I know? Unlike you, I do not keep lists of everyone I speak to—or who speaks to me."

"Could the pistol have been taken before the supper?" Frake pursued.

Sir William rose. "I have no idea whatsoever. It seems to me, though, that Mrs. Leeds had both the best opportunity and the best reason for taking the dashed thing. Why do you not go and plague her with your questions and let me get about my business?" With a curt nod of dismissal, he stalked out the door.

Frake leaned back in his chair, considering. Interesting, how out of temper the gentleman became when questioned about the taking of that pistol. Could that be because no one did take it? A man would have to be very foolish—or drunk—to use the weapon he was known to be carrying to murder someone. Unless he counted on the authorities to make just that assumption. Frake sighed. Perhaps he should have asked him about his firing of Samuel Gooden.

Or maybe it would be more enlightening to speak to the groom. He just might try that. Frake let himself out into the entry hall, then headed for the kitchens.

Samuel Gooden, though, was nowhere to be seen.

He'd left nigh on half an hour ago, Ruby said, with a toss of her dark hair as if to say it was nothing to her what the groom did. Apparently, he hadn't come back in after his confrontation with Sir William.

Thoughtfully, Frake started up the stairs. Perhaps he could think up some reason to interview Annie again. That would certainly be more pleasant than speaking to Mrs. Cornelia Leeds, which he supposed ought to be his next step.

He continued up the second flight, and once more had to skirt the bucket at the top. Now, why would Annie leave it lying around like that? Normally, she seemed to have everything back in its place almost before someone took it out.

A bucket of soapy water. He knelt, running his fingers along the carpet. Only a few drops had spilled here. He tested the steps and found the third one still damp. A quick clean-up, apparently. But of what? He couldn't quite dismiss it as a normal household spill, not with the memory of Annie, pale and trembling after falling on these stairs, so fresh in his mind.

And Annie had headed down the main staircase a little while ago. Had someone set another trap for her back here? Then why hadn't she told him? Because he hadn't taken sufficient note of her first "accident"? He'd let her down. He should have followed his instincts from the start to trust her.

Still brooding, he set off once more in search of Mrs. Cornelia Leeds. He traversed the servants corridors until he reached the large card chambers, but found no sign of the woman there. Frowning, he made his way through the doorway into the piquet room.

"Frake." Mrs. Wickham's nephew Henry strode up to him. He cast a glance over his shoulder as if to see if they were overheard, then caught him by the elbow. "A word with you." He led the way to the library.

Frake entered, glanced around to assure himself the room stood empty, then waited. Henry Wickham pulled the door closed behind him. "I just remembered something and thought I ought to tell you." He didn't look happy.

Frake drew out his Occurrence Book. "Right glad I'll be to hear something of use, sir."

"As to that, I'm not sure." Henry Wickham clasped his hands behind his back and paced to the fire. He stared into it for a long moment before turning to face Frake once more. "It might be nothing. But last night—early in the evening—I overheard Sir Joshua's groom, Gooden, bragging to Ruby—she's the kitchen maid. He was saying something about coming into a good deal of money in the near future." He drew a deep breath. "I can't really see where that might be involved in Sir Joshua's death, but he struck me at the time as being up to no good."

Frake tapped his pencil on the edge of his book. What might Samuel have been referring to? Picking pockets, blackmail—or murder for his inheritance? With his abilities at dipping his fingers into others' pockets, he could easily have gotten the pistol from

Sir William—once that gentleman was drunk enough. But that was nothing more than guesswork.

"What we need to know," Frake said slowly, "is who came near enough to Sir William last night to get his pistol from him. Did Gooden?"

"I didn't see him. But that doesn't mean anything."

"Can you think of anyone else?"

Henry Wickham shook his head. "I suppose almost anyone who was here. Let's see." He frowned. "No. The only one I can actually remember is Captain Bevis. That was late in the evening. They played piquet. I only noticed them because of the way Templeton swayed in his chair. Badly foxed. By that point, I imagine someone could have asked him for the pistol and he would have handed it over without ever remembering."

Which didn't help Frake in the least. Nor could he ignore the fact Templeton might have kept the pistol himself.

With a sigh, he went in search of Captain Bevis. He found that gentleman at last in the dicing room, idly tossing a pair of ivories from hand to hand while he watched the play. Frake touched him on the sleeve. "A word with you in the salon, if I may?"

Bevis's eyebrows rose, and a touch of amusement lit his eyes. "Am I to entertain you, or you, me? What interesting possibilities." He followed Frake across the hall, then asked, "What may I do for you?"

Frake rocked back on his heels. "I understand as how you played with Templeton late last evening. How did it go?"

Bevis's lips twitched into a smile. *"Sir* William, do you mean?" He stressed the title ever so slightly. "He lost. Heavily. He was three parts disguised, by then. Not a sensible way to play, if one is in as bad straights as he seemed to be."

Frake looked up from his notes. "Was he? In bad straights, I mean. How did you know?"

"He kept muttering about it." Bevis drew out his snuff box, but didn't open it. "He said—" His expression became abstracted, as if with an effort of memory. "He said he'd be rolled up if his uncle didn't come through with a loan. Yes, that was it." Suddenly, Bevis's eyes widened. "Good God, you don't think he went to his uncle, begged, and was turned down, do you? Templeton was so drunk he might have struck his uncle, then been afraid he'd killed him and staged the suicide."

"That's as may be." Frake tucked away his Occurrence Book and drew out his pipe. Absently, he tapped the gnarled bowl in the palm of his hand. By that time of the night, Sir Joshua had already—and quite publicly—refused Templeton a loan. Had the man tried again? Or had he taken more stringent steps to assure his getting his hands on his uncle's money?

Ten

Annie, head held high in nervous determination, defiantly carried the load of bottles up the main staircase to the floor devoted to cards. A good crowd, she noted. If anything, news of Sir Joshua's murder had only increased the appeal of the gaming establishment among the members of the *ton.* The members of the *ton,* Annie decided, were a right gruesome lot.

She emerged into the hall from the loo rooms just as Captain Bevis mounted the steps. He paused before a heavy gilt-trimmed mirror beside the door to the main gaming salon, straightened his cravat, then drew a watch from his pocket and checked it. He smiled, gave the watch a jaunty swing on its chain, then instead of going inside, he headed down the back hall toward the servants stairs.

Annie ducked among the milling people, her curiosity roused. There wasn't any reason for a gentleman to go back there. So what was he up to? Could he be her villain bound now to lay another trap for her on the steps? Whatever he was about, he bore all the air of one prepared to enjoy himself very much indeed.

She reached the narrow staircase in time to hear footsteps somewhere above her. He went up? But no visitors to the house ever did that. The next floor held nothing but the private quarters of Mrs. Wickham, Mr. Henry, and Captain Palfrey. What would take Captain Bevis up there?

It wasn't any of Annie's business what he did— unless he *were* bent on doing her harm. At any rate, he shouldn't be going into the private areas of the house. She hesitated for several moments, torn, half afraid, then gave in to her puzzlement. Setting her tray on the floor, she started after him.

Shadows closed about her as she climbed. Only a low-burning oil lamp in the hall above cast any illumination down these steps. It would be the same in the main corridor, too. Mrs. Wickham wasted no oil or candles when they were all busy in the gaming rooms. Annie clung to the banister, dreading at any moment to feel her feet skidding out from under her.

At the head of the stairs she paused, peering through the darkness. No one. The doors she could see stood closed: Captain Palfrey's on the right; Mr. Henry Wickham's just beyond that; an empty chamber on the left; Mrs. Wickham's at the front of the house. Opposite that. . . . She crept along the hall, as noiselessly as she could. Which was just plain silly, she chided herself. The low roar of noise that assaulted her from below would cover any slight sound she made.

She caught herself holding her breath, and forced herself to let it out and draw in another. It wasn't right, her being so nervous here, where she worked.

This should be as familiar and comfortable to her as her own home. But Captain Bevis, vanishing the way he did, had set her on edge.

As she reached Mrs. Wickham's door, a man's deep chuckle sounded from the chamber across the hall, which was used as a family sitting room. Annie started, then eased closer. Probably only Mrs. Wickham having a private chat with Captain Bevis about some business matter. That would make everything all right. Still, she'd better make sure.

The door stood slightly ajar, as if the last person to enter hadn't closed it properly. She'd just have a quick peep inside, Annie decided, just to be certain Mrs. Wickham was there. She put a hand on it and eased it open another inch.

A couple stood within, locked in an embrace, silhouetted against the light from a single three-branched candelabrum. For one startled moment Annie stared in disbelief, then the woman moved and she realized it wasn't Mrs. Wickham in Captain Bevis's arms. These blond ringlets appeared a more natural shade. Slowly, Mrs. Cornelia Leeds disentangled herself and patted her curls back into position.

"Must you always be late?" She pouted, then drooped her long lashes over her eyes and glanced sideways up at Bevis.

He laughed softly. "I could hardly walk out in the middle of a game, could I?" He caught her gently by the shoulders and kissed the base of her throat.

"I don't know why I put up with you." Mrs. Leeds tapped his hand playfully with her fan, which fastened about her wrist with a satin riband that matched her rose silk gown.

"I'll be happy to remind you." He slid one arm about her waist.

She pulled away. "Not here." She opened her reticule and drew something out, which she handed to him. "This," she said with a sneer, "is the great and wonderful present my adoring viscount had promised me."

Bevis gave a snort of laughter. "My poor Cornelia. Isn't he spending that vast wealth he supposedly won from Sir Joshua last night?"

Cornelia folded her arms. "I don't think he did win anything. He was loud in his claims last night, but he hasn't approached Templeton about it. And can you see Daylesford not demanding payment at once?"

Bevis poured whatever he held from one hand to the other. "Hasn't he so much as a single vowel with Sir Joshua's signature?"

"All he got were his own." She hugged herself. "I—I don't think they played at all."

Bevis ran his fingers along the back of her bare neck. "Are you having second thoughts about dragging your little viscount to the altar, my sweet?"

She moved away from his touch. "I don't think I care to be leg-shackled to a murderer, thank you."

Bevis closed the space between them and kissed the nape of her neck. "Marry him quickly, then see him convicted. You'll be a widow again in no time, and a wealthy dowager viscountess in the bargain."

"And if he's innocent?" She looked up at him over her shoulder.

"Then you'll be a wealthy viscountess, and I shall still worship at your dainty feet." He opened his hand and turned what he held in the light of the candles.

Annie held her breath and craned to see, but she couldn't quite make it out.

"Pretty baubles," he said after a moment.

"I shouldn't be surprised if they're paste," Mrs. Leeds snapped back. "That shrew of a sister of his holds the purse strings, you mark my words."

"But not when he gambles," Bevis reminded her. "Go back down and captivate him again. Lure him from the tables as soon as he's winning, and drop hints about those sapphires. Those should be easy enough to sell."

Mrs. Leeds turned, and her arms slid about him. "At least Sir Joshua didn't get to tell him about us."

Bevis kissed her forehead. "We lead a charmed life, my sweet. But it would be far more charming with those sapphires in my pocket. Go and see what you can do."

Annie hurried away before either could emerge. She shouldn't have eavesdropped. That fact alone troubled her. But not as much as what she had just overheard.

She descended the stairs, retrieved her tray from where she had left it near the landing, then tried to gather her flying thoughts. This wasn't any of her business, rightly speaking. Her job was to clean the gaming establishment and bring the customers their wine, not to listen to their private conversations.

Even if they did have bearing on a murder inquiry. Investigating murders was the job of the Runners.

And this particular murder investigation was the job of a very particular and very disturbing Runner.

She had only taken a few steps away from the foot of the stairs when she realized Mr. Frake stood calmly in her path. He didn't move; he simply waited, his steady gaze resting on her countenance. She flushed. She'd been so lost in thought—about him—she hadn't even seen him.

He continued to gaze at her for a thoughtful moment, then he nodded to himself. "This way, my girl." He took her elbow and escorted her into the library.

Annie, perforce, went with him. The flesh of her arm tingled with the contact, and nerves fluttered through her stomach. Embarrassment? Or just fear? Runners always unsettled her. And this Runner, with his piercing blue eyes that missed nothing, she found profoundly disconcerting.

He removed the tray of bottles from her hands and set it on a table. "Sit down."

She hesitated, shifting uneasily from foot to foot. She'd never met anyone before whose mere presence could so totally disrupt her thinking. She'd be glad when he solved this murder and she never had to see him again.

Unless he arrested Samuel, or her.

She ought to tell him what she'd heard. Yet—

"What happened?" He voiced the question gently. "What's occurred to upset you?" His gaze narrowed. "You learned something, didn't you? And you don't like to carry tales to me?"

She stared at him, surprised that he understood her predicament.

He clasped his hands behind his back and paced toward the door. "I won't go and insult you by telling you how much I need your help," he said over his shoulder, "or by trying false flattery about how important your information probably is." He turned back to face her. "I do need all the help I can get, make no mistake about that. And there's no way of knowing whether or not what you have to say might be just what I need to hear."

"No, sir." Annie searched his face. Runners weren't reasonable. So why did this one sound like he was? Could it all be part of an act to trick her into helping him?

"Now," he said, and his voice took on a compelling note. "You know what's right and wrong. Even if you had reason to hate Sir Joshua, I think you'll do what's right in helping me find his killer. Especially," he added with emphasis, "if what you've learned might go a long way toward clearing others."

She jerked her head up and glared at him. Oh, he was clever, this Runner. What she'd heard might remove suspicion from Samuel, and he knew she'd do that at any cost. But would he believe her—or would he think she made up stories about others on purpose to clear her brother? You never knew, with a Runner.

He was right on the other count, too. She did think the person responsible should be caught. She'd never gotten her chance to make her appeal to Sir Joshua. He might have listened—or at least been willing to buy her silence. Whoever killed him might, by that single evil act, also cause Violet's death.

Annie straightened. "I heard someone talkin'," she said, and briefly related the scene she had just witnessed upstairs.

Mr. Frake listened in frowning silence. As she finished her tale, a slow smile lit his eyes, then spread to his generous mouth. "So, Sir Joshua *had* found out about Mrs. Leeds and Captain Bevis. Well and well and well. Glad I am to get that little point all cleared up."

Annie watched him, guarded. "You think since she went and lost her chance of marryin' Sir Joshua's fortune, she up and killed him to keep him from tellin' Viscount Daylesford and queerin' that suit for her, as well?"

"She or Captain Bevis. It's a very good chance." He drew out his pipe, looked at it, then replaced it in his pocket. "Good girl," he said absently, his mind obviously still sorting what he'd learned.

Annie sniffed. She didn't feel good. She felt like a tale-bearer. But at least she'd given him someone other than Samuel to think about. She picked up her tray. "I'd best be gettin' on with my rounds," she murmured, and realized she used that excuse frequently to escape from him. She hurried out the door.

Samuel, she reminded herself. If it hadn't been for

the suspicion hanging over him, she'd never have said a word about Mrs. Leeds and Captain Bevis. She drew a shuddering breath. She wanted to see Samuel. Something had happened between him and Mr. William Templeton this evening. She'd heard their voices just outside the kitchen door, but not what they'd said. And she intended to find out what it was. She'd go as soon as she left here tonight.

She ought to get home, though. Mrs. Appleby would have departed long ago, leaving Violet alone with little Rose. What if they needed something? What if Violet's fever took a turn for the worse? Yet she had to know what happened with Samuel. She'd have a look-in at Violet, she decided, then see to her brother. She could get by with an hour or two less sleep again.

The remainder of the night seemed to crawl past for her. Not that they lacked customers to keep her busy, but her thoughts kept drifting far away, to Violet, to Samuel, to all the things she wanted and needed to do, but couldn't. At last, the final patrons laid down their cards, and she breathed a sigh of relief as she saw them into their greatcoats and hats, and out the door.

Now, she had only to do a cursory straightening of the rooms—more a check to make sure no gentlemen remained slumbering in an armchair or passed out from drink beneath a table. She hurried through this, driven by her desire to make sure her sister was all right and to confront her brother. Happily, tonight everyone seemed to have gone home.

She went to the library last, held back by her reluctance to enter the chamber. Ridiculous, she scolded herself. She had had no real qualms entering while others were around. Before she could turn tail, she threw the door wide.

Inside, a number of candles blazed. Annie stopped short, then saw Mrs. Wickham seated alone at the far end of the room. Relieved, she went in, only to come to an abrupt halt as she saw the object in the proprietress's hands. A pistol.

Mrs. Wickham looked up, an abstracted frown creasing her brow. "What is it, girl?"

Annie opened her mouth, but no sound came out.

Mrs. Wickham regarded her in surprise, then followed the direction of Annie's gaze. Her eyebrows rose. "This?" She held up the pistol she was cleaning. "Now, there's no reason to make a fuss. I am perfectly capable of handling a gun. Sir Joshua himself taught me when I started this house." Her frown deepened as she mentioned the man. "I know," she added with emphasis, "how not to injure anyone."

"Yes, mum." Annie bobbed a curtsy and turned to her work. If Mrs. Wickham knew how *not* to injure someone, that must mean she also knew *how* to injure someone. Should she tell Mr. Frake? But that seemed horribly disloyal. Mrs. Wickham would never shoot anyone—would she?

Annie filled her tray with dirtied glasses, all the while railing at Mr. Frake under her breath. She hated being in this position, of learning things that might incriminate people, of knowing the Runner would probably want to know. And she resented Mr. Frake for making her feel this way.

She hurried out the door, only to collide with the very solid figure of a man. With a startled gasp she staggered backwards, balancing her wobbling burden, and found herself facing Mr. Frake himself. "What are you still doin' here?" she demanded. And had he seen Mrs. Wickham's pistol and heard their brief exchange? She couldn't decide if she hoped so or not.

"Waiting for you." He bestowed an amiable smile on her that mirrored the innocence of his eyes. "Just thought as how I'd see you home."

She eyed him in uncertainty. "That's very kind of you, I'm sure, sir." The prospect of walking home alone through the dark streets didn't appeal to her, not after the fright she'd had early this morning. But she didn't want him around when she talked to Samuel.

The door opened behind her, and Mrs. Wickham looked out. "Annie, I—Mr. Frake. Excellent. I'd like a word with you."

A slight frown creased his brow. "Annie—"

"There ain't no need your seein' me safe, sir," she said quickly. "You've got ever so much more important things to do." She pushed past, checked at the dark steps, and instead made for the well-lit main staircase.

In the kitchen she deposited her burden, dragged off her soiled apron, then faced the door. A full minute passed before she could force herself to go outside. To her immense relief, no one lurked in the shadows—yet.

She ran through darkened streets which were never quite silent. Other figures passed by her, and she clutched her shawl about her shoulders and forged ahead. Only tonight, she wasn't assailed by that eerie sensation of being watched. Only the bold sallies of drunken gentlemen and the piteous cries of the occasional beggar besieged her. The advances of the former she ducked with the adroitness of long practice, the pleas of the latter with an aching sadness that she had nothing to give. With considerable relief, she reached the crooked alleyway in which she lived.

She mounted the several flights of steps, and found herself gasping as she at last stopped before her room. A creaking sounded from within: the old chair. Annie opened the door to find the ever-dependable Mary Appleby, her strawberry blond hair wisping out from beneath her mobcap, doing her best to rock little Rose in a chair meant to stay in one position. A single candle cast a soft glow over the woman as she crooned softly to the infant she cradled in her arms. Annie drew a deep breath, and the welcoming scent of lavender and peppermint enveloped her.

Mary Appleby offered her a tired smile, which displayed one broken front tooth. "The poor mite, she wasn't givin' her mama no rest."

Annie hugged her shawl about her and shivered. The night chill crept through the room, as if in flagrant denial of the heat of the day. "I thought you'd of gone and left hours ago."

"I come back. Right poorly your sister was doin'. So I left my own little Danny with me 'usband and come back to check on 'er." Mrs. Appleby shook her head. "That worried I am and make no mistake."

"The weather ain't helpin' her fever none." Annie crossed to the bedside and touched her sister's hot forehead. If only she knew more of herbs, or could afford the services of someone who did. "Can you stay a little longer? I'm goin' to see my brother. If he got even a shillin' from some gent—"

She broke off with a sigh. It was far too rare an occasion when one of the gentlemen who frequented Mrs. Wickham's give *her* a shilling. But wishful thinking didn't pay for anything, not even the essentials, let alone the extras like medicine.

Mrs. Appleby broke off her gentle crooning. "You hurry along, dearie. I'll gets me sleep when you comes back."

Annie cast one last helpless look at her sister. Violet's deep, even breathing offered some reassurance, and Annie grasped at it.

And maybe Samuel might have something he could let her have. Buoyed by that hope, she dared to venture forth again into the dark, forbidding streets. It would be a long walk. Tonight, despite her jumpiness, she didn't dare spend the extra money for a hackney—even if she *could* find one. If only Sir William had given her something—anything!—to help Violet. But "if only's" paid no more toll than wishful thoughts.

She might as well go on foot anyway, she told herself. Samuel wouldn't be up yet for another hour or more. By the time she got there, it would be late enough so he wouldn't be too angry when she slipped up the stairs to the loft where he and the other grooms slept above the stable. And by the time she finished with him, the others should be waking. Maybe Loomis would offer her a share of whatever breakfast the grooms would have before taking the horses out for morning exercise and training.

She walked quickly, listening with all her might. Every doorway seemed to her lacerated nerves to hold a lurking figure. Every sound she interpreted as footsteps following her.

She spun about, her straining gaze searching through the pre-dawn blackness. Did someone draw back into the deeper shadows of an alley? She backed away, her heart pounding, but no one came after her.

At last she reached the mews where Sir Joshua had stabled his cattle. All lay in darkness and silence here, with a shrouded stillness that did nothing to ease her growing tension. She ran the last hundred yards to the door that led into the stable. She dragged it open, darted inside the barn-like interior, and pulled it closed behind her. Safe.

A single lamp glowed, and the scent of fresh straw reached her, mingled with that of oiled leather and other stable smells. She started toward the rickety stairs, only to stop at sight of a slightly built man sprawled in the bedding straw at the foot of the steps. She bent over him, peering through the near darkness to make out the features. The bedraggled coat, though, told its own tale.

"Samuel?" She shook his shoulder. "What're you about, sleepin' down here? Samuel?"

A rattling snore escaped him. He stirred, groaned, then hunched his arm away from her and tried to bury his face beneath the other. Annie grabbed with both hands and tugged.

"Go 'way," he muttered.

"Samuel, you wake up this instant." She bent low, modulating her voice to penetrate his drink-fogged brain, but not to penetrate to the sleeping loft above.

He gave a low groan and opened one bleary eye. "What're you doin' here?" he muttered.

"I needed to have a talk with you. What was you doin' at the gamin' house tonight? And don't you try tellin' me you wasn't there. I saw you, and heard you, too, talkin' to Sir William. Did you go askin' him about Violet?"

Samuel struggled to a sitting position and rubbed both hands over his face. "What're you goin' on about, Annie? Can't you leave a feller to sleep?"

"What was you talkin' to Sir William about?"

He yawned cavernously. "Nothin' as is of any interest to you, Annie-girl. Never mentioned Violet."

That, at least, relieved her of one worry. She hesitated only a moment before plunging on. "Samuel, have you got a few shillin's I can have? For Violet? We need more herbs, for her fever. She's not gettin' any better."

"Shillin's." He snorted, then gave her an exaggerated wink. "We're goin' to get ourselves some real money, Annie-girl." He leaned toward her to confide drunkenly: "I knows me a thing or two, I does. About ol' Rumguts's murder, sure as I'm standin'—sittin'—here. That sort of knowin'll bring us pounds, not shillin's. Lots an' lots of pounds. Buy Violet anythin' she needs. Jus' got to wait a few days, we does."

Annie tensed. "What do you know, Samuel?"

He lay back in the straw, his arms folded behind his head, and regarded her with a drunken grin. "Enough, Annie-girl. I knows enough."

"That don't sound safe, Samuel." She drew her shawl closer about her. "If you knows somethin', you'd best tell that Runner."

"There ain't no sense in doin' that, Annie-girl. No money, neither. And what we needs is, we needs money. A whole lot of money."

"What we need—" She broke off, her nose twitching to an acrid smell. "What's that? Sammy, is that smoke?"

"Couldn't be." He waved a dismissive hand, then shoved it behind his head once more. "Now, you stop worryin' and—"

"It is smoke." Annie backed away, looking around, trying to find the source. "Samuel, if there's smoke, there must be a fire somewheres near."

He raised himself up on one elbow and peered about. "What—"

Flames erupted near the front wall on the far side of the stable. They licked up the wood, flared across a pile of straw, and raced along the floor toward the first of the stalls.

"Let them loose!" Annie shouted, and dove through

the billowing smoke for the door to provide the horses with a means of escape. She grasped the handle, but it wouldn't budge. Startled, she tugged at it, but it remained jammed. They were trapped.

Eleven

The smoke caught Frake's attention first. It filled the air, biting in his lungs. He looked about, alert, unable to discover in the darkness from where it came. Then flames crackled into life, licking the boards of the building a scant hundred feet ahead of him. The stable, where Annie had entered only a few minutes before.

He broke into a run, all desire for caution and silence abandoned. He grabbed the handle and tugged, but the door didn't budge. Locked? Or jammed?

From within, Annie's shaky voice rose on a note of fear. "Sammy, come on. We've got to get the horses out. The horses, Sammy. Pull yourself together and help me. Is there anyone upstairs? Sammy!"

The fool must be drunk, probably set fire to the hay. Frake backed off, set his shoulder, and rammed the door. It quavered but held. He repositioned himself and ran at it again. This time it broke free and swung wide, and he staggered to a stop several paces inside.

Smoke billowed everywhere, burning his eyes, scouring his throat. In their stalls, the horses paced and threw their heads, whickering their fear. From above came the shouts of the grooms as the racket roused them from sleep. And on the ground—

Annie, on her knees coughing, tugged at the prone figure of her brother.

In three steps, Frake reached her. He swung her up into his arms and carried her outside, where the night breeze dissipated the smoke. Men came running, jostling past him, some bearing buckets of water. The alarm, it seemed, had spread already. Tenderly, he set Annie on the cobble stones, her back against a wall. She turned her head aside, her slender shoulders still shaking with spasms of uncontrollable coughs.

Nothing more he could do for her now. He touched her hair, then turned back to where smoke still billowed forth from the open stable doors. More men had arrived, most sketchily clad in breeches dragged on over nightshirts. Buckets of water sloshed past, spilling half their contents before reaching the front line of workers who threw them over the flames.

Frake elbowed his way through the growing crowd and back inside. The other two grooms had joined the fray, and grasped halters and ropes as they tried to throw blankets over the horses' eyes to lead them out. Samuel teetered toward the door, a foolish grin on his face as he watched the turmoil, as if he enjoyed the show.

Frake grabbed him by the collar and dragged him outside, shoving his way once more through the crowd. Annie remained where he'd left her, limp and still coughing. She didn't appear to notice their approach, Frake saw in dismay. "Here." He thrust Samuel toward the ground. "You watch over your sister. Mind you don't leave her."

Samuel straightened his coat. "I always takes care of her, I does," he informed Frake with careful hauteur.

"You'd better," Frake muttered, and returned to the stable.

The two grooms brought out the first of their charges. The horses trembled, their coats gleaming with sweat, and the men fighting the blaze stepped hastily aside to give the blindfolded animals a wide berth. Frake grabbed two waiting buckets, waited until the grooms had passed, then forged once more into the smoke-filled interior.

He could only thank God he'd followed Annie. What had prompted his action, he couldn't tell. Curiosity about her, perhaps. He heaved the contents of his buckets at the base of the flames, then headed out for more.

As he returned with his fourth load of water, he became aware that men now stood about in small groups rather than racing back and forth. A low buzz of conversations replaced the yells and cries that had filled the night for what seemed an age. He raised his tired head and saw only the glow of embers and wisps of smoke.

He poured his buckets over anything that still smoldered, then set about inspecting the structure. Far less damage had occurred than he had expected. The straw had gone up, a portion of the front wall would have to be replaced, and the partitions between stalls needed work, but the building itself had suffered little real damage.

He tested the stairs to the loft above and found them sound. Still, he mounted them with caution, noting that one near the top squeaked ominously. The door stood ajar, and smoke, which had invaded the area through the cracks and crevices in the floor boards, hovered thick and acrid in the air. The place would need a good airing before it would be habitable again. Better than burning to the ground, though.

He returned to the stable below to find Loomis, the head groom, gloomily kicking through the ashes of the first stall. "Everyone safe?" Frake asked as he joined the man.

Loomis raised his eyebrows. "Now, whatever is the likes of you doin' 'ere?"

"Just keeping an eye on things." Frake rocked back on his heels. "Any idea what started this?"

"Lantern, I supposes." Loomis led the way outside. "Got the 'orses settled." He nodded his head along the mews toward the road. "Bad up there?" He jerked his thumb toward the sleeping quarters.

"Smoke," Frake told him.

"Aye." Loomis stared at his filthy boots, lost in morose thoughts. "Well, best get the lads off to other quarters for a couple days. But now, we've got ourselves a right lot of work to do, I reckon."

Frake left him to it. Outside, the early dawn light filtered through the buildings, throwing shapes into a soft blur. The crowd had begun to disperse, ambling away, still talking about the early morning excitement. The toils of the day would soon replace it in their minds.

Annie still sat where he'd left her, eyes closed as she hugged her shawl about her shoulders. Her brother, far from standing guard over her, lay in a heap, his snores leading the symphony of awakening sounds of London. Frake prodded him with a toe and derived immense satisfaction from the groan the groom emitted.

"Loomis will be wanting you, lad," Frake announced. He dragged him to his feet and shoved him in the direction of the stable. Samuel shambled off.

Annie coughed and looked up at him, wide-eyed, her face smudged with smoke and dirt. He held out his hand to help her to her feet, and to his surprise she gripped it as if finding comfort in his touch. Well, he could dream.

"Come," he said gently. "Let's get you home."

For once, Annie didn't protest. She accepted his help, and made no demur when he took her elbow to steady her uneven step. That, he reflected ruefully, should let him know how badly the fire had shaken her—and possibly how much she suffered from the effects of the smoke.

They emerged onto a street just coming to life. Already, vendors trundled their barrows over the cobble stones, crying their wares. Even a few hackneys plodded by, carrying the gentry home from their parties of the night before. Frake hailed one that looked empty and bundled Annie inside.

She sat silently next to him, as if too drained to

speak. He fought the urge to draw her against him, to gain comfort from the feel of her head resting on his shoulder, of having his arm tight about her. She smelled of smoke instead of the usual light lavender scent that always clung to her.

They got out at the corner where he'd seen her set off for the mews such a short time ago. He accompanied her along the crooked alley and up the dilapidated stairs to an ancient building. Inside, the odor of mildew and dirt assaulted him. He drew a deep breath and followed Annie up the dingy steps, past landings and passageways along which stretched a series of doors. From behind them shouts and snatches of conversation emitted. Squalor was the word that came to mind, and it revolted him that Annie should live in such oppressive conditions.

She turned down one of the corridors and opened the third door on the right, at the back of the house. Frake entered after her, and the mingled odors of sickroom and herbs brought him up short. In a crudely constructed cradle near the wall, a tiny baby wailed its unhappiness. A frail, dark-haired young woman lay in the room's single bed, struggling to rise. Frake crossed the uneven floor boards and picked up the blanket-swathed Rose.

"Well, hello there." He settled the infant on his shoulder and had the satisfaction of seeing it settle down almost at once.

"Annie?" The young woman leaned back against the pillows and ran a trembling hand through curls lank and lusterless from fever.

"This here is Mr. Frake." Annie cast him an uncertain glance. "He's a Runner. Where's Mrs. Appleby?"

The young woman—Violet, she must be—stiffened. "What's a Runner want with us? What've you been about, Annie?" Her fingers tightened in the bedclothes, and she cast an apprehensive glance at Frake, then back to Annie. "You're filthy, you are. The both of you."

"A fire in the mews where Sir Joshua Templeton stabled his horses." Frake bounced the baby gently on his shoulder. "Your brother is all right," he added.

"Everythin's all right, Violet." Annie sat down on the edge of the bed as if her legs would no longer support her. "But where's Mrs. Appleby?"

"Had to go, she did. No, don't you go blamin' her, I told her as how it would be all right and you'd be back right soon."

Annie sniffed. "And you not able to get up for little Rose."

"She's all right now." Frake brought the baby over and handed her to Violet.

Violet eyed him with suspicion and clutched her daughter to her. "What're you doin' here?"

"Seeing Annie all right and safe. She was overcome by the smoke."

"Annie?" Violet's eyes widened in worry.

"Mr. Frake here got me out, me and Sammy." The glance she cast him held a measure of shyness. "We ain't neither of us taken no harm."

"No," Frake said. "Nor will you, not if you have something warm to drink and get a good rest."

He looked about the small room, searching for the means of boiling water. A damp chill clung in the air, not healthy for either mother or baby—or Annie. Someone—Annie, no doubt—had tried to make the apartment habitable with bright curtains at the window, but nothing could alter the pervasive odor of mildew, not even the scattering of herbs probably used for that purpose.

"It was right good of you to go bringin' her home," Violet said. She smiled weakly, a pale phantom of what it must have been before she took so ill.

The chamber smelled of smoke, now, too. Annie must be saturated with it; he knew he himself was. Smoke, from a fire that might or might not have been an accident—and well might have proved fatal. Like her fall on the stairs. Was she safe even here, in her own home?

She coughed again, and somehow, that decided him. He took one last look about the place and said: "What will you need for a couple of days? All of you?"

Annie's eyes widened. "You're takin' me into custody? But I didn't kill Sir Joshua."

"And no one's saying as how you did. Now," he faced her, hands on hips. "This here room is cold and damp, and if you two stay in it, you're only going to get a lot sicker. You, too," he added as Annie started to protest. "From the smoke. Now, where will your taking ill leave this poor little mite?" He nodded toward Rose.

Annie's chin rose, though her worried gaze strayed toward Violet. "Don't you go thinkin' as we don't know all that, 'cause we do. There just ain't nowhere else for us to go."

"I know of one place. Just until you're better. No, I'll have no arguments from either of you. You're coming with me, and that's final."

Annie rose, the picture of uncertainty. "Where?"

He avoided that. "You'll be safe and warm and I know a very good woman who understands her herbs. Nanny Gossett, she's called, and she's been a midwife more times than anyone can count. She'll know what'll be best for your sister."

As soon as he said those words, he knew he'd found the way to reach Annie. She still hesitated, but her gaze rested on Violet, who lay back against the pillows, cradling little Rose. For her sister, Annie would do anything. Perhaps even trust him.

"We can't." She sounded a touch wistful.

"What's more important? Your sister's health or your pride? Your health, too," he added as she tried unsuccessfully to smother another cough.

"Where?" she asked after a long minute.

"Just off Covent Garden, it is. Now, you show me what you need."

There was pathetically little. The few pieces of clothing and other articles easily fit into the cradle. This Frake carried down the steep stairs while Annie helped Violet to dress. In a very short time, Frake hailed a hackney and bundled them all into it.

The expression on Annie's face when he helped them into his rooms some twenty minutes later assured him he had done the right thing. She advanced

two steps into his sitting room, looking around with
wide-eyed pleasure. Violet sank onto a chair in exhaustion from the short outing, but Annie, still holding Rose, explored. She ran her fingers along his
shelf of books, circled through the area he used for
preparing and eating his meals, then peeked through
the doorway into his bedroom.

She turned back, her expression clouded. "This
here's your rooms," she accused.

"Aye." He carried the cradle into the bedroom.
"You and your sister, you make yourselves at home
in here. I'll make up a bed for myself on the couch."

Annie clung to the baby. "We can't go puttin' you
out of your own room. We got a place of our own."

"True." He waited until she looked up, meeting
his gaze. "One where your sister will only get sicker.
No, there's no backing out, now. Here you are and
here you'll stay. Your sister's in no fit shape to go
traipsing across town again in a drafty carriage. You
put her to bed while I make us all something nice
and hot to drink."

Tears misted her eyes. "Why are you doin' this for us?"

For you, he thought, but didn't say it aloud. " 'Cause
Sir Joshua can't, and Sir William won't. Now, you get
going, she's like to fall asleep where she's sitting."

It seemed odd having other people moving about
his rooms. Odd, but very comforting. Annie, with
ease and efficiency, set about readying his room
while Violet lay on the sofa, a warm blanket thrown
over her. Frake lit a fire in the hearth, and with a
murmur Violet turned toward it. A deep, quavering

sigh shook her shoulders, then she closed her eyes once more in contentment.

He set water on to boil, then slipped down the hall to knock on the door at the back of the house. After nearly a minute, it swung wide and he found himself face to face with Nanny Gossett. She peered at him through thick-lensed spectacles, her country gown covered by a voluminous apron and a tatted shawl drooping from her elbows. Her white hair, straight as a pin, protruded at odd angles from beneath her starched muslin mobcap.

Her gray eyes lit with pleasure. "Benjamin. Come in for tea. Now where did I put the kettle? Dear me, it was here just a moment ago. Or was that yesterday? Dear, dear." She scooped up a gray tabby from the tabletop and deposited her on the floor beside three others who rubbed against her ankles.

Frake caught a black tom that peered into the hall between his feet. "Come and have tea with me, instead. Got a patient for you, I have. Fever after childbirth. And another one who was caught in a fire this morning and breathed in too much smoke."

She tilted her spectacles and examined him. "You, too, or so it would seem. Well, you'll be wanting herbs, won't you? Let me see." She wandered about her sitting room, scanning the shelves which were lined with herb-filled bottles and boxes. She selected several, depositing them in a large wicker basket. "No, Octavius, not you," she murmured, absently shooing out a gray cat who sniffed at her collection.

Frake herded another back into the room and held

the door for Nanny Gossett. She bustled along before him, murmuring to herself. Frake prevented a black tabby from following them by the simple expedient of closing the door in its face.

"Mugwort," Nanny Gossett muttered. "No, best not in this case. Borage, yes, that's what we need, borage. And fennel. Benjamin?" She turned back to him. "Fetch the fennel seeds and my strainer, would you? Oh, and the anise. Heavens above, where is my mind? Anise, of course we need anise. Why ever didn't I put it in my basket?"

"You did." Frake strolled up to her and drew out a small bottle. "And here's the borage, if it's the leaves you're wanting."

"And the fennel." She shook her head. "Heavens above. Now, you just show me this poor lamb of yours."

As they entered the apartment, Annie came out of the bedroom. She stopped, clutching a pillow to her, and stared at Nanny Gossett. His blankets lay in a neat pile beside the sofa, he noted. Over Annie's shoulder he glimpsed Violet already in the freshly made up bed.

"There, now." Nanny Gossett eyed Annie in an appraising manner. "You must be the one with the cough. Never you fret, dearie, I've brought just the thing for you—or at least I think I brought it. Never you mind. A nice tisane we'll make you, and you'll be as right as rain in no time. Now, where is the other poor dear?" Without waiting, she bustled past Annie and into the bedroom.

Annie started after her, but Frake caught her arm. "Let them be," he said softly, and closed the door.

"But—" Annie cast a worried glance at the room. "Does she know what she's doin'?"

"That she does. She's more to be trusted than any doctor as ever I've met."

Annie looked down at the pillow she still clutched. "I don't know how I'm ever to go payin' her, sir. I ain't got no money. I'd been hopin' Samuel—" She broke off.

The devil take her brother. Frake rocked back on his heels, gauging the worry on her expressive countenance. She wouldn't be easy to appease. "Let's just say," he tried at last, "as how you're helping me with this here case. Now, that's a job and more, you may be sure of that. You'll be my assistant. No, now's not the time for argle-bargle. You just stay here and mind you heed what Nanny Gossett tells you. I'll be back shortly."

He collected a jug and a basket from a shelf in his eating area, gave Annie a cheery nod, and set forth to see what he could find by way of breakfast provisions. Already, the streets teemed with life; if he'd waited much longer, he'd have been too late. He strode forth, inspecting the contents of the various barrows as the vendors cried their wares.

He loved the early morning. But he preferred waking up to it, not coming to it at the end of a long, trying night. When he retired, he reflected, mayhap he just might buy himself a small farm in some quiet village. Feeding chickens, growing his own garden, breathing fresh air. He couldn't help but wonder if Annie would like that kind of life.

But then it wasn't likely Annie ever would want anything more to do with a Runner than she had to.

The aroma of fresh bread laced with sage reached him, and he waylaid a man carrying two huge baskets heaped with loaves and rolls. After some good natured haggling, he stowed a loaf and some sticky buns in his basket. Next he bought some apples, then recklessly added cabbages, potatoes, and onions, as well. After all, he had a family—albeit a borrowed one—to feed.

He bought milk from a girl carrying huge cans suspended from a yoke about her shoulders, then a small round of a creamy white cheese. Laden with his finds, he returned to his rooms to find Nanny Gossett measuring the contents of various bottles into paper packets. Annie stood at her side, washed clean of the soot and with her hair tidied.

His heart tightened at sight of her there in his home, looking almost as if she belonged. She embodied everything missing from his life—a fiery warmth, impulsiveness, fierce loyalty. He wanted to protect her, to clear the worry from her huge eyes. He needed her.

And while she would accept from him a measure of help for her sister now, that was probably as much as he ever could hope for.

"Ah, Benjamin." Nanny Gossett handed the packet she had just finished to Annie, who dipped a quill in Frake's ink pot and wrote a note on the paper. "Such a sorry state as she's in, the poor dear, though at least she's able to nurse the baby some. Time, of course, that always helps, but how long?" She shook her head and added a measure of seeds to the dried leaves on the paper before her. "What she needs is rest and good food, tinctures, and tisanes. Now, I've given Annie here some instructions. She knows which packet to brew and when. She'll do just fine. And I'll bring the salve with me when I come back later. So I'll just be going, shall I?" She started for the door.

"Stay for breakfast." Frake set his basket on the table. "I've brought plenty."

Nanny Gossett beamed at him. "Now, if that isn't ever so nice of you, Benjamin. I'll just pop on home for some herbs to brew us some tea, shall I?" She bustled out the door, carrying her basket with her.

"She even left some packets for little Rose," Annie said as she brought dishes down from the cupboard. "She rambles so when she talks, but she knows ever so much."

So, Nanny and her herbs fascinated Annie, Frake noted. He smiled with indulgent pleasure. Mayhap she'd like a garden of her own some day. He'd bear that in mind. He went to fetch cups.

"No, you just sit, sir. Let me." Annie laid out breakfast for the three of them, then set a special tray for Violet.

Nanny Gossett returned with her tea, and Annie, to Frake's added pleasure, removed the kettle from the hearth and poured the boiling water into the pot. Quite at home she looked, already. Mayhap she wouldn't take too much convincing to stay for a few days.

She carried the tray to Violet, then returned to join the others for their lavish repast. She eyed every little treat with awe, Frake noted, then she ate them with relish. He'd remember to get more delicacies next time. Certainly more of that sage bread.

Nanny Gossett finished her repast and rose. "Now, I've got some tinctures that need minding, and a syrup to make to see to it that cough of yours doesn't come back. I'll bring it along in a bit. Now, dearie, you just come right down the hall any time you like and learn all about herbs." She patted Annie on the shoulder and took her leave.

From the other room a gurgling cry began, quickly rising in volume. Annie jumped to her feet, found one of the neatly labeled packets, and poured the contents of dried leaves and seeds into a cup. She poured boiling water over it, then left it to steep while she hurried into the other room. A moment later the wails subsided.

Frake read the instructions on the packet. Honey. He'd have to buy more for the little mite. At least he had enough to make up this batch of syrup. With a pleasant feeling of satisfaction, he brought his crock of strained honey from the cupboard.

On the whole, the contentment he felt in this simple domestic arrangement worried him. He'd always wanted a family. Moira, he realized, was still a part of him, despite the many long years since her death. Annie was like her in some ways, he reflected as he strained the tisane. And she was very different in others. He was different now, too, than he'd been when he married Moira. The death of his wife had changed him, as had the numerous years as a Runner that had followed.

He dragged his mind from this melancholy reflection and returned his thoughts to the problem that brought Annie and her sister under his care. He had his suspicions about the cause of the fire—especially in light of Annie's fall on the stairs. Did someone want to kill her—or Samuel—or both? Or was Samuel himself, out of sheer carelessness, responsible? He chewed on his pipe, pondering possibilities.

Behind him he heard the window open. Turning, he saw Annie standing beside it, the huge marmalade Sylvester in her arms. The cat purred his pleasure.

Annie glanced at him in uncertainty. "He insisted he should come in," she apologized.

Frake nodded. "He also insists he lives here. Is there anything left for his breakfast?"

Annie set the tom on the floor and checked the leftovers. The cat happily stropped himself against her ankles, then deigned to accept her offerings. Annie watched the cat, Frake noted, with the air of one determined not to look anywhere else.

"What is it?" He kept his voice friendly, gentle.

"I—I just want to thank you for all you're doin' for us. You're bein' ever so kind."

Frake waved it aside. "Sylvester and I need the company. Keep us civilized."

She still studied the cat. "A good sleep in a room

that's warm and dry will do her a world of good, sir, and I—I can't thank you enough. I'll take them home just as soon as Violet wakes up."

"No!" Frake surprised himself at the strength of his objection.

Annie blinked, and the wary look crept back into her eyes.

"She'll be more comfortable here," he assured her, recovering. "She's too ill to keep moving, and here we have Nanny Gossett just down the hall. Best arrangement possible, in the circumstances."

"But we've taken your room," she protested.

"I'll be fine here on the sofa."

She regarded him with a touch of suspicion. "Are you doin' this to keep a watch on me?"

"Now, I don't see as how there's any need for that. But there is another need, there is. With little Rose here, I need someone to look after her. I've never had children."

The intensity of his regret surprised him. He turned away, accepting the heavy-footed arrival of Sylvester in his lap as his excuse to break off the conversation. He settled all sixteen pounds of fur and claws more comfortably. "Get some sleep," he suggested to Annie over his shoulder.

Annie hesitated. "I'll have to be goin' to Mrs. Wickham's in a few hours, sir."

He frowned. "Are you sure you're up to it?"

"Oh, yes, sir. The place has to be tidied and readied for the night."

He turned to look at her, curious. "What on earth do they do when you're ill?"

"I'm not, sir, not often. And I haven't been since I started there."

"Why did you?" he asked. "Start there, I mean."

Annie began straightening the table, clearing away the few dishes they'd used. "I went and left Sir Joshua's estate three years ago, when I was sixteen. I come to town to try and earn a bit of money. Bein' in service, that isn't what I want. There's no chance for a real life of my own."

She poured some water to start washing up. "When Violet come to me and said as how she was in the family way, well, I knew there was no one but me to confront Sir Joshua with what he'd done. Samuel, he was too afraid of losin' his position. Said as how Sir Joshua would come around and acknowledge the baby as his, if we'd only wait a bit."

"But Sir Joshua didn't try to see your sister?"

Annie laid down her scrub brush, then picked it up again. "I tried to call on him at his house, here in town, but Mr. Daniels, as his butler, he up and turned me away. As if we'd never sat down at table in the servants hall together!" She sniffed and scrubbed industriously at a plate. "I tried to speak with Sir Joshua several times on the street, but he brushed past me as if I had some disease and wouldn't give me a chance to open my mouth. Probably didn't recognize me, or thought I was beggin'," she added with a touch of charity.

She must have been getting desperate, Frake reflected, watching the agitation with which she applied herself to the drying. Anger surged in him, at the deceased Sir Joshua, at the servants who protected their master instead of helping one of their own. Of course they'd feared for their jobs.

"Then Samuel," Annie went on, "started complainin' as how his Ruby, who is kitchen maid at Mrs. Wickham's, was always workin' extra, and how he never got a chance to talk to her no more, and all on account of the maid quittin' to get married, and I seen my chance to get to speak to Sir Joshua with no one to stop me." She put the last dish away and turned to straighten the bowl of fruit on the table.

"Only you could never find him alone?" Frake suggested.

Annie nodded. "He didn't always come, and when he did, he would sit at the same table for hours on end, all intent on his cards. And there was poor Violet, needin' just a tiny portion of all that money he up and throw'd away or won each night—" She broke off, biting her lip, a guarded expression in her large eyes.

Frake studied his pipe, giving her a few moments to recover her composure. "You could have gotten his attention by creating a scene," he said, his tone mild.

Her eyes widened further. "No, sir. He'd've hated that, he would. He'd never of given poor Violet a farthing if I'd up and done anythin' of the sort."

Frake refrained from pointing out that he hadn't

given Violet anything, anyway. Except a baby. He looked up to find Annie watching him.

"What now, sir?"

Benjamin, he thought. My name is Ben. And he would give a great deal to hear it on her lips. Aloud, he said: "Time for some thinking. Why don't you go and take a nap while you can?"

She hesitated, then with a quick, shy nod, she slipped from the room into what had been, until a few hours before, his bedchamber.

He stroked Sylvester's fur, earning a resounding purr for his efforts, and refused to think of Annie moving about among his things, lying down on his bed . . .

His hand clenched on his pipe stem. Some things were just best not thought about.

At least he'd made progress in one area. Unless he was much mistaken, she no longer regarded him as a dreaded enemy. He'd seen real gratitude in her eyes, and something else, possibly a touch of warmth. If they spent a little more time together, here in the informality of his home, she might even come to think of him as a person.

Twelve

Sylvester batted at Frake's hand with an imperious paw, fixed him with an indignant glare, and presented his chin for rubbing. Frake obliged with a finger and resolutely turned his thoughts from Annie to the fire that had brought her here. There had to be a simple answer to what caused it.

An accident, perhaps? Samuel had been drunk enough to be careless. Or one of the other stable lads might be responsible. But a groom should be too aware of the hazards to take any risks.

What if it hadn't been an accident? Sir William had fired Samuel earlier that evening. What if Samuel had lit that fire in revenge, only been too drunk to save himself and his sister?

Frake's stomach clenched. The sight of Annie, fallen to her knees and choking, had affected him more than he liked. Even now, he kept wanting to check on her to assure himself she was all right.

If someone had wanted to kill her—or Samuel— they'd picked a safe way to go about silencing them. An accident would be the verdict. Only it had claimed no human victims—thanks to his own unexpected interference, he recognized.

Accident or design. Samuel or someone else. Annie the target or an accidental victim. That just about exhausted the possibilities represented by the fire. And at the moment, he found himself nowhere nearer to whittling them down. He'd go back and examine the scene once more and see if he could find any clues that had eluded him this morning.

Which left him, at the moment, to deal with the nagging question of the murder.

With a sigh, he returned to Samuel. If Frake had a sister who'd been treated the way Sir Joshua had treated Violet, he just might be roused to murder, himself. Yet Samuel Gooden did not look like the kind of young man to stir himself on another's behalf without considerable prompting. Still, put a few tankards of ale—or a measure or two of blue ruin—inside him, and he might well turn violent if provoked. He whined and wheedled most of the time, but a snarl existed just beneath the surface.

Of course, Samuel might know about that bequest in the will. Or Sir Joshua might have caught him picking someone's pocket—which seemed quite possible. Annie certainly thought her brother had been up to those tricks at the gaming house.

Did Annie suspect Samuel of more? Of the murder itself, perhaps? That seemed the most likely explanation as to why she had gone to the stable after leaving Mrs. Wickham's in the early hours of this morning. The prospect of Annie fretting over her brother's possible involvement in murder bothered him. She had enough worries. And knowing he was investigating her brother wasn't likely to make him very popular with her.

A light knock sounded on the door, and Nanny Gossett stuck in her head. "I just brought along that syrup for your cough, Benjamin. Now where—oh, yes, here it is. And that little Rose will be needing a wet-nurse, I make no doubt. I'll just have a talk with Violet. No, don't you trouble yourself none. I'll just pop on in there." Gesturing for him to remain where he sat, she bustled across the room and through the other door. A white kitten darted after her, dancing on its hind legs to bat at her swinging skirt.

Frake chewed on his pipe stem. Behind him, soft feminine voices rose in discussion. It had been too many years since he'd heard such a comfortable sound in his home. Far too many years. A man grew tired, living so long alone. With an effort, he dragged his thoughts away from pleasant domestic arrangements and back to the case.

The door opened once more, and Annie emerged. A soft flush touched her cheeks as her gaze came to rest on him. She looked away almost at once. "It's time and past I was goin' to Mrs. Wickham's." She kept her gaze lowered, studying her hands. "What will you be doin' this afternoon?"

Would she ever be able to look at him without showing signs of discomfort? Not likely, he reflected; not with her opinion of Runners. And not the way this case went. He cleared his throat. "I never got a chance to talk to your brother this morning. Intended to have a word or two with him, I did."

Annie tensed. "You suspect him, don't you? Don't you?" she repeated, louder, when he failed to answer at once.

"Why did you go along to the mews this morning?" he countered.

She hunched a shoulder. "Just wanted to know what brought him to Mrs. Wickham's last night, that's all." Her expression gave nothing away. Guarded.

"You suspect him yourself," he said simply.

She flushed. "O'course not! That's a—a right vile thing for you to say. It's you as thinks he's guilty." She sniffed. "I should of known never to go trustin' no Runner, not for—"

"I'm not just a Runner!" He surged to his feet, dislodging Sylvester. The wariness in her expression created an ache deep within him. He drew a deep breath. "I'm—I'm me." He paced across to her and placed his hands on her shoulders. "You can trust me to do what's right," he said softly. "Haven't you realized that yet?"

She met his gaze for a long moment, then lowered hers to about the level of his top waistcoat button. She nodded. "That you'll do. No matter the cost to— to anyone." She turned and left, going out into the corridor, heading down the hall, away from his rooms. Away from him.

He stared after her, torn. Did she think him so unfeeling? He did consider the cost of his search for truth. And the law could always be bent a little in the cause of true justice.

But where did that lie in this case? Sir Joshua's death hadn't righted any wrongs. He hadn't been the pleasantest of men, but he had done nothing deserving of death.

Frake's gaze strayed to the door of his bedchamber, he could hear the soft voices of the two women within. A wail started from little Rose, but it broke off as apparently one of her attendants met her need. Sir Joshua's callousness toward Violet's fate, his refusal to honor his obligations to her, did that constitute a reason—an excuse—for him to die? Did anything justify taking the life of another?

He strode to the window and stared blindly down the alley toward Covent Garden. Annie's slight figure, hurrying through the street, caught his attention. He watched her until she disappeared around a corner. Sylvester jumped on the sill and thrust his head under his hand, demanding more attention. Absently, Frake raked his fingers along the cat's spine, to the accompaniment of contented purrs.

He had sworn to uphold the law, and the law required the punishment of transgressors. Yet there were other factors involved.

Would arresting Annie's brother be a betrayal of her? He felt certain she would see it that way. Yet could he live with himself if he allowed a murderer to go free just because—

He drew a slow, steadying breath. Just because the thought of Annie's being unhappy tore at him? Because he wanted to spare her any worry or distress or pain? Because he wanted to protect her, share with her, hear her voice, and see her smile? Because, he realized with a tightening of his heart, he had fallen in love with her?

Love. He leaned his forehead against the cool glass pane. He hadn't thought himself capable of that emotion any longer. Love. And Annie.

But at the same moment he opened himself to its joys, he also recognized its pitfalls.

Did his love for Annie influence his judgment? Did it cause him to take too light a view of Samuel's criminal tendencies—or to focus too strongly on this wholly inadequate brother, while the real murderer escaped his attention? In a perfect world, Samuel would turn out to be innocent. Then he could prove it, and that trusting smile he'd glimpsed so briefly in Annie's eyes would return. Well, he could dream.

Never, he acknowledged, had he had a more difficult road to tread.

He rubbed his chin. He had to seek out the truth, of that he was certain. He would deal with the moral dilemmas once he knew where he stood.

He collected his hat and set forth, hailing a hackney only a short block from his rooms. The clamor of the busy, late-morning London surrounded him: the empty carts as they returned from bearing their goods to the markets; the vendors loudly singing their wares; people everywhere, all going about their daily routines.

A city alive—and yet he must deal with death.

That thatched cottage on a small farm in some peaceful village sounded better to him every day. One good bonus, added to what he'd saved over the years . . .

He climbed down at the entrance to the mews and paid the jarvey. A lingering odor of smoke, of burned lumber and straw, reached him as he approached. It was fortunate the alarm had been raised so quickly. There could have been considerable damage with so many structures crowded together, so much hay that would go up like a torch, so many animals frightened and stampeding from the flames.

He cut off that vision. They'd averted it. And on the whole, he decided, eyeing the fire-scarred stable before him, they'd gotten off very lightly. Very lightly indeed.

He nodded to the elderly head groom who was inspecting harness leather. The inevitable straw hung from the corner of the man's mouth; he chewed it with vigor. Loomis paused in his labors to squint at Frake.

After a moment, the groom's brow lowered, and he spat. "Gooden ain't 'ere," he called.

Frake straightened. "I'm investigating the cause of this here fire. His quarters are above, ain't they?"

The straw twitched. "Runners," he muttered, barely audible across the barn, and returned to his work.

Frake took that for permission—not that it would have mattered much except for taking longer if the man had protested.

The stairs to the grooms' quarters above stood to

the far right. These he tested again, found them not to have weakened any further, and mounted. The long bunkhouse met his gaze, lined with beds, each with a cupboard and trunk. Someone had opened the windows, but the smell of smoke lingered. No one here now, at least. Good.

He walked along the line, noting the names carefully printed on each trunk. Someone, it seemed, had an orderly mind. Gooden's he located third on the right.

He stood over it for a long moment, contemplating the lock, then with a shrug drew a selection of thin metal instruments from his pocket and set to work. He hadn't had recourse to them for some time, but he hadn't lost his touch. The mechanism sprang open after a scarce minute.

An odd selection of objects met his gaze: a torn halter of aged leather; a wine jug, probably long empty; boots; a variety of cheap trinkets apparently collected during his time spent following the drum with the late Captain Oliver Templeton; and three packages wrapped in newspaper. He selected one of these and carefully unrolled it, exposing a fine gold watch on a fob chain, from which hung a jeweled seal.

Frake gave a soundless whistle. The owner might be glad to discover what had become of it. Frowning, he returned it to its wrapping and examined the next. This proved to be a chased silver snuff box bearing a hunting scene on the lid. No initials to identify its proper owner.

The third package contained three silver spoons. Frake sat back on his heels, regarding them with a frown. Stolen, like the other two items, he supposed. And any one of them could have been disposed of for a tidy sum. Enough, definitely, to pay for a doctor for Violet.

His anger with Samuel grew. Only one understandable excuse existed for the lad's slide into dishonesty, and it obviously didn't here apply. He hadn't stolen things to help his sister. He helped no one but himself and probably never spared a thought for Violet's suffering or Annie's concerns and fears.

With an effort he brought his temper under control and returned to the questions at hand. *Had* Sir Joshua caught Samuel with some pilfered prize removed from a gamester's pocket? Frake could see the groom, worse for drink, striking his employer, then panicking.

But would he have had the coolness and presence of mind to stage the suicide?

Or might Annie have done that, to cover for him?

That thought left him sick at heart. She was so intensely loyal to her siblings, she might dare anything for their sakes.

He unwrapped the watch again and turned it over in his hand, then re-examined the snuff box as well. Could one of these things link the lad to Sir Joshua's murder? He shoved them in his pocket along with the spoons, relocked the trunk, and descended the steps, not at all pleased by the direction of the progress he made.

Once more on the street, he hailed another hackney and gave the direction on Duke Street of Sir William Templeton. It had to be done, he told himself, no matter his personal feelings. And mayhap he'd find himself proved wrong. That he'd be right glad of.

In all too short a while he arrived at the house where Sir William kept rooms. At the door he was met by a small, plump man, the retired valet who ran the establishment. Keen, clear eyes regarded Frake from beneath a shock of thinning white hair as the man listened to Frake's request to see one of his tenants.

"You're a day too late, sir." The former valet shook his head in regret. "He moved out yesterday. You will find him at Templeton House, the residence of his late uncle. On Albemarle Street."

Templeton certainly hadn't wasted any time, Frake reflected. He thanked the man, then set off with a swinging stride in pursuit of his quarry. It was a relatively short walk and the day fine; he covered the distance in record time.

A hatchment, he noted in cynical amusement as he reached the direction, hung over the door, and someone had tied up the knocker in black crepe. A house of mourning, at least on the exterior. He mounted the shallow steps and knocked.

He was admitted by a long-faced major domo with a morose expression. Sorrow or dyspepsia, Frake decided; he couldn't tell which for certain. His appearance went well with the funereal trappings, though.

The man regarded him with a noticeable lack of enthusiasm and said nothing.

"I've come to see Sir William," Frake offered, and gave his name.

The hooded eyes continued to stare at him for a

moment longer, then the man gave his head a short nod. "This way, if you please," he intoned in a deep, slow voice.

He escorted Frake into a front parlor. Elegant, Frake noted. Richly furnished. No expenses spared. Annie, Violet, and little Rose could live quite comfortably for a very long while off the proceeds of just one of these carpets.

The opening of the door behind him dragged him out of his contemplation. He turned, frowning, to see Sir William, resplendent in his mourning attire, stroll in. Here, again, no expense had been spared.

"There you are, my good man." Templeton struck a languid pose before the window. "It's about time. Have you word for me about this murder?"

A general air of ease and contentment hovered about Sir William, belying his somber garb. No love lost here, Frake reckoned. He doubted the man would mourn a moment longer than propriety dictated.

Frake joined him where the sunlight streamed over the sill. "I have a few things I'd like you to take a look at, if you will, sir." He took from his pocket the watch and fob chain.

Sir William raised his quizzing glass and examined it. "A very pretty piece," he drawled. "Are you by chance trying to sell it?"

Frake rocked back on his heels, studying the man's face. "Just wanting to know if you recognize it, like."

Sir William examined the seal. "I fear not, my good fellow." He handed it back.

Frake returned it to his pocket, and his fingers closed about the spoons, which he drew out.

Sir William took one, and his brow snapped down. "The devil!" he exclaimed. "Where did you get this?"

"You do recognize it?"

"I should," Sir William declared with considerable heat. "It's my uncle's. Mine, now."

"You are certain?" Frake pursued.

"A man should know his own things." Sir William ran a loving finger along the intricate pattern. "Several from the set here are missing. It put Uncle in the devil's own temper. I can't say I blame him," he added, brooding.

Frake nodded and held out a hand for the spoon.

Sir William stiffened. "It *is* mine," he pointed out, reproachful.

"That's as may be, sir. But it's also evidence."

Grudgingly, Sir William released his hold. Frake stowed it away with its fellows, then brought out the snuff box.

"Good God," Sir William exclaimed. "Have you been looting the place? That's mine! I lost it—" He broke off.

"When?" Frake asked, trying to keep any sense of urgency from the question.

"The night my uncle died. I was so shaken by that, I didn't realize it was missing at first. Thought I must have misplaced it. Where did you come by it?"

"I'll tell you when I can, sir." This, too, he reclaimed and put away.

He thanked Sir William, then took his leave, dismayed by the outcome of the inquiry. So Samuel had been within the house here, helping himself to the spoons. And on the night of the murder, he came close enough to Sir William to dip his fingers into his pockets.

Was the snuff box his only prize—or did he find another, deadlier item? The carriage pistol, with its carved ivory handle, might prove quite a temptation in its own right, even if he had no plans as yet to kill Sir Joshua. He might have taken it for its value, then later found it all too ready at hand. If Sir Joshua had seen Samuel stealing the snuff box, and taken him to task about it, anything might have happened. If the gun already rested in Gooden's pocket, action might have been quicker than thought.

In any case, Annie, when she learned of this, would not be happy. And that depressed him.

Thirteen

Frake let himself into his rooms with dragging steps. He had walked the considerable distance from Albemarle Street, but had found no peace from his troubled thoughts. Nor had he found any viable solutions to Sir Joshua's murder. At least, none that he liked.

An insistent meowing at his feet brought him out of his reverie. Not Sylvester, but a gangly concoction of black and white fur with half an ear missing. He scooped it up. "What're you doing here?" He rubbed its considerable stomach and was rewarded with a deep, vibrating purr. "Doesn't Nanny know you're missing?"

His bedroom door inched open on silent hinges, and the little woman slipped out, trailing her shawl behind her. In one arm she held a brindle kitten. "There, you're back now." She spoke in hushed tones. "Now, Mortimer, you were supposed to let me know the moment he came in." She took the heavy cat from Frake's arms. "I just came back to check on them. Sleeping, they are, the dears, and doing very well."

"That's good to hear." He scooped a long-haired tortoiseshell cat from off his table.

Nanny clicked her tongue. "Really, Dahlia, where are your manners? Oh, and Annie—" She broke off and looked up at him sideways. "Such a sweet little thing, isn't she? She promised to tell Mrs. Appleby, who is Rose's wet nurse, where they are. I expect the woman will be along shortly."

His rooms would be positively bustling in rapid order, he wagered. He thanked Nanny Gossett, saw her and her retinue of cats out, then stood in the middle of the room as exhaustion crept over him.

Sleep sounded like a very good idea. He hadn't had any for far too long. He dragged off his boots and stretched out on the sofa, drawing up the blanket Annie had arranged for him. Pity she had left for the gaming house. He wouldn't mind talking to someone about the case, just to help him get his ideas straight in his mind. Still thinking of this, and trying not to miss her presence, he drifted off.

He came awake to Rose's wail and the sound of a woman's unfamiliar voice soothing her. The wet nurse, he supposed. What was her name, Mrs. Appleby? He never heard her come in, that asleep he must have been. The baby quieted almost at once, but Frake was now fully awake.

He looked into the bedroom to see, standing by the cradle, a tall, plain-featured woman with tired eyes. A thick braid of strawberry blond hair, fastened with a torn fragment of cloth, hung over her shoulder. A stained apron covered her much-patched gown, but both showed signs of frequent and thorough scrubbings. She held Rose in her arms, and a small boy of perhaps eighteen months clung to her ankles.

She glanced at Violet, then carried—and dragged—her burdens toward the door. "I'm Mary Appleby," she whispered. "You must be Mr. Frake. It's ever so kind o' you, what you done for 'em. That room, it weren't no place for 'em, not with 'er so sick and all. But this—" she gestured about her, "—this is what a 'ome *should* be. Now, little Rose 'ere needs 'er feedin', she does." Firmly, she excluded him from the room.

Frake found himself facing a closed door, and smiled. Leave it to Annie to have found such a respectable wet nurse. He'd wager the task hadn't been easy. But he had no qualms leaving his charges in this young woman's care. Nor, it seemed, had Nanny Gossett.

He refolded the blanket and placed it on top of the pillow on the couch. He'd better get started on his day's work. Might as well get on with having another talk with Samuel, no matter how much he didn't look forward to the prospect.

But where to find him? Back in his old quarters with Sir Joshua's other two lads? Or would he have packed up and moved on by now? Not if Samuel could avoid it, Frake guessed. Which meant that unless William Templeton had told the other two grooms of Samuel's abrupt dismissal, Annie's brother would be right where he'd always been.

He returned to the mews, to be greeted by the sounds of hammering. A young lad, under the supervision of Loomis, repaired one of the stalls. Both looked up as Frake entered, and Loomis strolled over.

"You keeps right on a-workin'," the man called over his shoulder. "I gots me eye on you, I does. Now," he turned to Frake. "What would you be wantin' *this* time?"

"Samuel Gooden. Where's he off to?"

Loomis spat out the straw he chewed. " 'E's gone off to the park, 'e 'as."

The park? Frake drew out his watch and raised his eyebrows in surprise. Five-twenty. Already into the hour of the promenade. Had Samuel gone there in hopes of finding some gentleman in need of a groom? Or to dip his fingers into the pocket of some poor unwary?

Curious, he set forth for Hyde Park. For a long while he strolled along the walks near the tan bark, keeping a close eye on the passersby. Carriages made their way along Rotten Row, natty sporting curricles with tigers sitting up behind, phaetons, tilburies, all driven by fashionables out to show off their fancy equipages and horses, and exchange greetings with acquaintances. He maneuvered down the paths among the strolling throng, keeping alert for any stir, any glimpse of his quarry.

The drivers of many of the carriages he knew by sight. Some he'd helped over little matters of stolen property, others he'd investigated as suspects. Many he recognized simply because it helped him in his work to know who was who in this world where birth and fortune meant everything. Crazy world, he reflected, where the good-hearted went poor and ignored by their ill-mannered and self-centered "betters."

He had been searching the faces about him for close on half an hour when he spied Sir William Templeton, garbed in the severe black of his mourning, driving a matched pair of gleaming blacks before his spanking crane-necked phaeton. Samuel, looking smugly content, sat at his side.

Well and well and well, Frake reflected. Now, how did this come about? Last night, and in no uncertain terms, Sir William had dismissed Samuel. Frake stepped forward and flagged them down.

Sir William glowered at him as he drew to a stop at the side of the carriage drive. "What the devil brings you here, man?" he demanded.

"Well, now." Frake rocked back on his heels. "As I remember it, last night you up and fired Gooden, here."

A flush crept up Sir William's face. "I didn't mean it, and so he knew. It's the strain, my uncle being murdered." His gaze strayed toward Samuel, who winked at him. Templeton winced. "I—after all he did to save my uncle's—*my* cattle last night, you know."

Samuel assumed a virtuous expression. Too virtuous. A touch of blackmail here, perhaps? Except under the circumstances, Frake would have expected Samuel to be the subject of blackmail, not Sir William. Just what went on here? Did Samuel know something that implicated Sir William in the murder? Or was it something else?

Sir William directed a dismissive nod at Frake and

gave his horses the office. Frake remained on the tan bark, staring thoughtfully after them. Well and well and well, indeed.

And what, now? Temporarily, he found himself stymied on this line of enquiry. He might as well pursue another. Never ignore other possibilities, that was his motto. It had been a long time since he'd talked to young Viscount Daylesford.

He made his way out of the park and to the nearby town house on Mount Street. Here the door was opened to him by a very proper major domo, who regarded him with a supercilious air. The viscount, this individual informed him in lofty tones, was not at home.

Frake frowned. Had he missed him in the park? He could have sworn he wasn't there. But there were any number of other places a gentleman might be. He asked, and received a forbidding look.

"I am sure," the major domo intoned, "I couldn't say."

Frake nodded. "I'll just wait, then."

The man's lips twitched in obvious annoyance. "You will not want to sit here and do nothing for what might well be hours." The man began to close the door, only to stop with an exclamation of vexation.

A covered carriage pulled up at the side of the street, and a groom jumped down from his perch at the back. With practiced swiftness, he let down a step and opened the door of the vehicle. A hatchet-faced young woman, dressed in a severely cut gown of dull green, stepped to the paving. A moment later, Daylesford followed in her wake.

The woman mounted the first step, then stopped at the sight of Frake. She looked him up and down with an imperious hauteur. "Rogers," she demanded in a low, carrying voice, "who is this person and what does he want?"

Frake bowed and identified himself. "I've just come to have a word or two with Daylesford."

"I am Eugenia Mountbank," the woman declared, as if that said it all. She regarded Frake once more, then nodded. "You might as well come in and explain yourself." She swept through the hastily opened door into the front hall, then led the way into a salon.

Daylesford hesitated, cast Frake an unfathomable glance, then hurried after his sister.

Frake caught his arm before he'd gone two steps. "A word with you in private?" he suggested.

The viscount made a strangled noise and gave an uneasy nod in the direction of his sister, who had stopped just inside the elegant chamber.

She raised supercilious eyebrows. "In private? Nonsense, my good man. My brother has no secrets from me. Now, you will tell me what this is about." She settled herself on a blue brocade sofa with elegantly carved legs. She did not invite Frake to be seated.

Daylesford made a beeline for the window. From this position, strategically beyond his sister's line of sight, he made a beseeching face at Frake.

Frake rocked back on his heels. "I just want to

clear up a little matter concerning the death of Sir Joshua."

Miss Mountbank blinked. "Sir Joshua? What ever has that to do with Edwin?"

Edwin? She didn't call him by his title? Frake stored that little bit of information to be examined later.

"Knew him." Daylesford's voice came out on a cautious squeak.

"I cannot help but feel certain that any number of people knew him," Miss Mountbank said in condescending tones. "But I doubt very much if Bow Street is paying personal calls upon all of them. Are you?" She regarded him down the length of her patrician nose.

"No, ma'am," Frake admitted.

"And did he not die at *that woman's* gaming establishment?" Miss Mountbank persisted.

"He did, if you mean Mrs. Wickham." The questioning, Frake realized, had been taken out of his hands by this formidable young woman.

She nodded. "Then it has nothing to do with Edwin. He does not frequent establishments of that order. He spends his evenings at meetings of one or another of the societies to which he belongs. He would never be involved in anything so sordid as a murder." She spoke the word with distaste. "Edwin, do come away from that window and sit down."

He did so at once.

She returned her attention to Frake. "What can you possibly wish to see him about?"

"If I may have a moment in private with him, I—"

"Nonsense." She straightened. "If it is a matter that cannot be discussed in my presence, then I feel quite certain it can hold no interest for Edwin. We will not detain you any longer, my good man." She rose, clearly indicating the interview to be over.

Frake met Daylesford's uncomfortable gaze. "Perhaps we might meet tonight." He offered his blandest smile. "At the meeting of one of your societies?"

Daylesford went limp in relief, but managed a nod. "Tonight," he promised.

Frake bowed to Miss Montbank and left. Formidable female, he reflected. It didn't surprise him in the least she hadn't been able to bring any gentleman up to scratch. No wonder Daylesford appeared such a poor little mouse, if he lived under such a dominating thumb. He obviously went in terror of his sister. And equally obviously, she had no idea whatsoever he spent his evenings in a gaming hell.

What would she do, he wondered, if she learned of the vast sum her brother lost to Sir Joshua? And if he hadn't won it back, to what lengths might he go to keep her from learning? Murder, perhaps? Frake hadn't a doubt she held the purse strings in that household.

He looked forward to going to Mrs. Wickham's that night, he realized, to see what the viscount would have to say for himself. Or was it just that he looked forward to seeing Annie?

He had a quick look-in at his rooms and found Nanny Gossett happily arranging dinner for her patients. Sylvester, from the safe vantage point on the top of a bookcase, regarded with studied indifference the interloping cats who had arranged themselves on various pieces of furniture about the sitting room. Frake made sure no one needed anything, then took himself off for a quick bite to eat.

Fortified by a tankard of ale and a steak and kidney pie, he made his way to the gaming hell feeling better than he had all day. Annie would be there. A nice chat, he promised himself, without one mention of the word "murder." Just talk about her sister, and Nanny Gossett, and that nice young Mrs. Appleby, and if she really liked living in London.

Not many people had arrived yet, he noted as he strode into the entry hall. Captain Palfrey greeted him with a questioning look, to which Frake shook his head.

"Just looking around a bit," he assured him. Annie would probably be in the kitchen, or laying out wine in one of the rooms. He'd rather catch her when she wasn't under the eye of the ill-tempered cook. He headed up the stairs instead of down.

She came out of the piquet room as he reached the top of the steps. A broad smile spread across his face—probably besotted, he reflected, but he couldn't help himself. It warmed him just to see her gentle face, that soft fluff of dusky curls which he wanted to brush from her cheek. Those huge, brown eyes that held such a wary expression when they saw him.

"Good evenin', sir." She hesitated, clutching her

tray. "I hope as how Violet and little Rose didn't disturb you none."

"No. Not at all. And Mrs. Appleby arrived." Hardly witty and engaging small talk, but the disturbing evidence of Sir William's snuff box which he'd discovered that day in her brother's possession came to mind, and suddenly he felt guilty in her presence.

She looked down at the bottles she carried. "I—I'm right glad to hear it, sir." She hurried away as if only too glad to escape from him.

Depressed by his lack of address, by his inability to captivate her, he entered the card room. He wandered about the scantily populated tables, soliciting reminiscences about Sir Joshua, until he found an elderly gentleman who was quite willing to ramble on about the late baronet. Frake listened for a little more than an hour before escaping. During that time, the man had consumed two bottles of wine but provided not a single new insight.

At least more people had now arrived. Frake resumed his tour of the gaming salons, and had the satisfaction of spotting Viscount Daylesford sitting at a table in the dicing room. At his side, with one beringed hand just resting on his shoulder, stood Mrs. Cornelia Leeds.

"The most delightful of parties, I make no doubt," she said to the viscount as Frake approached. "But so very far from town." She gave an exquisite shiver. "Hampstead Heath, of all places. Are you going?"

The viscount's hands clenched. "No."

Mrs. Leeds fluttered her long lashes. "So very

frightening, the prospect of crossing the Heath. I do so hate to do it alone."

Captain Bevis, who stood at the table behind them, turned. "Is that the Armitage party? What a pleasant surprise. I am bound for there myself, later tonight. Would you care for an escort?"

She raised delicate eyebrows to Daylesford, who merely hunched a shoulder and looked away. Her lips pursed, then she turned her flirtatious gaze on Bevis. "Would you be so kind? I would love the company. I know it is silly, but I can never be comfortable crossing the Heath. I always fear a highwayman."

Bevis laughed. "They're a rare occurrence now, I assure you. But I should be honored if you will consider me your protection."

Frake watched the little interplay with interest. Was this an attempt on the part of Mrs. Leeds to make Daylesford jealous? The young man certainly glowered at Bevis. But if she'd hoped to induce the viscount to offer to go in the captain's stead, she'd failed. Instead, he took a curt leave of the two. Mrs. Leeds smiled, a very self-satisfied smile, as she watched his departing back.

The viscount paced to one of the other tables. He didn't join it, though; he stood behind the players and glared at the dice as they bounced across the cloth. Frake started forward to speak to him.

One of the gentlemen at the table looked up. "Have a seat, Daylesford. Take a turn?"

The viscount's mouth tightened. "No. Thank you." He stood, shoulders slumped, staring blindly before him. Then his eyes widened. He straightened and turned to stare at Mrs. Leeds, who now sat at a table across the room. An expression of grim determination settled over his vapid features.

Well, well, well. Frake eased himself back a few paces. What had the gentleman in mind?

Daylesford strode out the door, collected his hat and walking cane in the hall, and let himself out onto the street. Now where, Frake wondered as he followed, was the viscount going in such a hurry? It just might be very interesting to find out.

The pursuit led through a number of dark, twisting streets. At last, Daylesford turned down a mews, strode along the line of stables, then stopped at one and let himself in. Frake hurried forward and peered inside. A harness room. With growing fascination, he realized if he intended to follow this promising gambit any further, he was going to need a horse himself.

Daylesford walked along the line of stalls, then finally selected a nondescript chestnut. Instead of summoning a groom, he bridled the animal himself, then set about fumbling with a saddle. It was a safe bet, Frake reflected, that this task never before had fallen to the young nobleman. This was like to take him awhile.

Which gave Frake a chance to think. There would be no way he could ride through the cobbled streets without making a racket. The viscount would hear him, and there would go any chance he had of finding out what was afoot. If only he knew where the man might be going . . .

To Hampstead Heath, of course. He must be intending to follow—or spy upon—Mrs. Leeds and Captain Bevis. To determine the exact nature of their relationship, perhaps? Daylesford was, after all, one of the two candidates Cornelia Leeds had set out to entrap into marriage. And now Bevis and Mrs. Leeds had staged an excellent explanation of why they might be seen leaving London in one another's company. Perhaps Daylesford merely wanted to assure himself nothing more than a party lay behind it.

Or maybe some other reason existed for these journeys out of town, something more pertinent to his investigation. After all, any one of those three might have murdered Sir Joshua.

Frake strode rapidly back to the street, and was fortunate enough to discover a hackney within a few minutes. He gave the direction of the livery stable where he normally obtained mounts and swung into the vehicle. He was going to have to hurry.

Some twenty minutes later, he set his heels into a black mare's flanks and headed for Tottenham Court Road. He could only hope he hadn't guessed wrong. But somehow, he didn't think he had.

How far behind was he? Or could he be ahead? Daylesford probably wouldn't ride at once for the Heath, but wait to trail Bevis and Mrs. Leeds.

Frake slowed as the houses thinned, the grounds around each one stretching into more luxurious space. Several carriages had passed him going in the opposite direction, but none had overtaken him. It must be going on eleven o'clock by now. Rather late to be going to a party so far from town, and much too early to be coming back.

If, of course, Bevis and Mrs. Leeds actually went to a party.

And if they didn't, what business was it of his? He pulled his mare down to a walk. He'd acted on impulse, reacting to suspicious-looking behavior. Or had he just been that desperate to find evidence against someone—anyone—other than Annie's brother?

Now that he had the leisure to reflect, it seemed highly unlikely this little jaunt had any bearing on the murder. What interest did he have in Cornelia Leeds's love triangles? He could be back at the gaming hell right now, seated in a comfortable chair interviewing Annie once more. He liked that occupation. Instead, he perched on a saddle in the chill night air on the back of the most rackety-gaited nag it had ever been his misfortune to throw his leg over. He might as well head back and talk to those who were willing to remain in one place.

Two horsemen overtook him, one astride a dark mount, the other riding a gray. Neither interested Frake. A few minutes later a light chaise pulled by four horses rattled past, but the shrill laughter emitting from within showed it to be occupied by at least two rather frivolous young ladies.

Somehow, that decided the matter for him. He spun his mount back the way he'd come and urged the mare into her bone-racking trot. Another carriage jolted by, then a group of three young sprigs of fashion, followed by a lone rider on a chestnut. Frake reined in at once, suddenly alert, but the man, a stolid gentleman of advancing years, merely awarded him an acknowledging nod and continued on his sedate pace.

He'd been right; he'd wasted his time. He—

The pounding of hoofbeats reached him as someone rode hell-for-leather. Moments later a dark figure, bent low over his mount's neck, galloped past, coming from the direction of London. A nondescript chestnut. Daylesford, at last.

Since he'd come so far, he might as well see it through.

Frake spun his own horse about and raced along the verge, trying to keep the sound of his pursuit as silent as possible. But Daylesford wouldn't be expecting to be followed—except by a carriage carrying Cornelia Leeds and Captain Bevis.

Abruptly, after less than three hundred yards, Daylesford slowed, jumped the ditch, and disappeared into the trees. Frake did the same, keeping a good distance back. He sat tensed, listening, but no sound reached him. Interesting, Frake reflected. Very interesting. What game did Daylesford play?

The pounding of more hooves interrupted his reflections. The creaking of a harness and carriage grew louder and louder as a vehicle emerged onto the heath proper. Expectant, Frake looked back to where the horseman had disappeared. Would he emerge and follow?

To his surprise, the man urged his horse onto the road in front of the equipage. A loud shot rang out through the night.

Over the neighing of the startled horses and the creak of the harness as the carriage lurched, a gruff voice shouted, "Stand and deliver!"

Fourteen

Frake fought the urge to go to the passengers' aid. There'd be time enough for rescues—if the situation called for such measures.

The coachman struggled to maintain control of his horses. For several seconds the animals reared and sidled; then they settled, still trembling, under their master's none-to-steady hand.

The window of the carriage lowered, and a man's head emerged. "What the devil's toward?" a deep voice demanded in the darkness.

The highwayman brought his mount forward a few paces, but the animal threw its head in protest. Young Daylesford must have wrought the poor animal into a lathering sweat of nerves, Frake wagered. He watched, keeping in hiding, curious to see how this little act played out.

"Stand and deliver," Daylesford repeated, a tremor in his voice. "Hand over your money and your jewels."

The man—Captain Bevis, Frake now saw clearly in the moonlight—jerked his head back inside. A woman's voice—Cornelia Leeds—rose, but her words didn't carry. Bevis shot back a response, his voice inching upward.

"Hurry!" Daylesford balanced his pistol while his horse sidled.

This time a woman's head emerged. She held something out, but as Daylesford approached, a flame flashed from her hand, and the sound of her pistol rang through the dark. Daylesford's horse reared, and she yelled to the driver: "Get us out of here!"

The man hesitated only a fraction of a second, then drove his uneasy team forward with a crack of his whip. The horses sprang ahead, breaking into uneven gallops, leaving Daylesford struggling for control of his mount.

Frake waited, giving him time to recover, reflecting on what had just occurred. It seemed Mrs. Cornelia Leeds had taken command of the situation. That must have irritated Captain Bevis, to be rescued by her.

Frake returned his attention to the would-be highwayman. When at last Daylesford's animal stood trembling, Frake brought his own horse forward. The viscount, who now patted his greatcoat as if seeking a smoldering hole, swung his head around, setting the poor chestnut dancing again.

"Interesting performance," Frake said, keeping his tone conversational. "May I ask what it was about?"

Hastily, Daylesford dragged a stocking mask from his face and stuffed it away. "Performance?" The word barely escaped in a croak. "What—I don't know—what are *you* doing here?"

"Following you," Frake informed him. "No need

to try to concoct some farfetched story, now," he added on a note of apology. "I seen you hold up Bevis and Mrs. Leeds. I really ought to point out, though, as how this here's far too well traveled a stretch of road to pursue such activities in safety. Which makes me doubly curious as to why. What were you hoping to get from them?"

Daylesford stared at him for a long moment, then dropped his gaze to his hands. "You heard me. Money and jewels." His voice was muffled, barely audible. "Oh, God, what a mess."

"You didn't win your fortune back from Sir Joshua, did you?" Frake kept his voice sympathetic.

"If only I had!" Daylesford wailed. "At least I retrieved my vowels and burned them. But Eugenia—" He broke off.

"Your sister found out you'd been gaming?" This time, his tone was that of one man beset by women to another.

The viscount shuddered. "Cut up pretty stiff, I can tell you. Need to get my father's signet ring back from those damned cent-per-centers before she finds out I pledged it."

Frake turned his mount toward town, and Daylesford fell in beside him. "Taking to the High Toby—" Frake began.

"Lord, I wasn't *stealing,*" Daylesford protested. "I was just going to *borrow* their gewgaws. Put them up the spout till my luck changes, then return 'em. Good God, I'm not the kind of rum touch who *steals* from his friends. Certainly not from Mrs. Leeds."

For a moment Frake hovered on the brink of asking if the viscount had thought to ask for a loan in a more conventional manner instead of taking such drastic measures to assure it, then abandoned the idea as pointless. Instead, he stated: "Sir Joshua was already dead when you went into the library that night."

Daylesford slumped in his saddle. His mount, with a companion now to steady it, walked sedately. "Thought I was done for, when I saw him like that. No hope of winning anything back from him. Sat down opposite and just stared at him for a bit, wondering if I should follow his example." He gave a short laugh. "Couldn't think of any reason why he should have done it. Thought he'd killed himself, you know. Kept thinking if it had been the other way around, if *he* had lost the fortune and I'd won it, it would make sense. That gave me the idea to say just that—" He shook his head. "He was already dead. I didn't see where the money would make any difference to him, where it did to me."

"Was there mud on the floor?" Frake asked suddenly.

Daylesford stared at him. "How the devil should I know? Wasn't looking at the floor."

Frake rode on, wrapped in thought. Did Daylesford tell the truth—or did he commit murder for the sake of that fortune? Of one thing Frake could now be certain. When Daylesford left the library, Sir Joshua had no longer been among the living.

After escorting Daylesford back to his mews, Frake

returned home. Somehow, there just didn't seem to be anything else to do at the moment. It must be the lack of sleep, he told himself resignedly as he mounted the stairs to his rooms. It had been a long couple of days with nowhere near enough rest. If he went to bed now, perhaps he'd be able to think more clearly in the morning.

As soon as he opened the door, he knew Nanny Gossett was there. By the light of a low-burning oil lamp, he could see four cats—none of them Sylvester—stretched out on various pieces of furniture, all regarding him with idle disdain. He strode forward and tripped over a darting ball of orange fur that flipped over on its back and tackled him around his booted ankle, all claws and teeth.

Frake detached it with care. "Nanny?" he called softly.

The door to his bedroom opened and Sylvester strolled out, head high, tail twitching. Nanny Gossett followed. "There you are." She beamed at him. "That Mrs. Appleby went home. A nice woman, she is, too. Violet is looking better. She's sleeping peacefully, and so is little Rose." She clucked her tongue. "The little dear. It's a good deed you've done, and no mistaking."

He waved that aside. If he wanted to appear a hero to anyone, it would be to Annie—the one person who insisted on regarding him as untrustworthy. That wasn't why he'd done it, though. It was pure selfishness on his part, wanting a family about him, even if it were not his own.

Nanny Gossett collected her basket, and Frake

scooped the great black and white Mortimer from a
chair and handed him to her. She headed out the
door, followed by the other cats. Even the kitten
raced along, trying to catch an orange and white tail
that waved just ahead of him.

With a sigh, Frake settled on his sofa. But instead
of sleeping, he found himself reviewing the night's
gleanings, sorting them, and reorganizing. He had a
couple of calls to make in the morning, he decided.

He must have drifted off, for a gentle knocking
brought him fully awake with a start. He swung his
feet to the floor, rose, and looked out to find Annie
standing nervously in the hall, her hands clenched in
her unease.

"I—I thought I should come in case Rose—"

"Come in." It was everything he could do to keep
from drawing her inside, into his arms. "They're both
fast asleep."

"Rose hasn't disturbed you none?" She cast an
anxious glance toward the bedroom. "I come as soon
as I could, though there was ever so much to be done
afore I could leave—"

"Don't worry." He reached out, brushed a curl
from where it dangled free of her mobcap, then realized what he did. Silently, he cursed the impulse
he hadn't been able to prevent.

She held very still. Almost, she seemed to stop
breathing. He could think of nothing to say, nothing
to do to ease the awkwardness of the situation. The
one thing he wanted, to kiss away the worry in her
eyes, to hold her and never let her go, he knew to

be impossible. He allowed his hand to drop to his side.

She moved away as if released from a spell, looked about, then crossed to the table to pick up a forgotten dish. "Don't seem proper, it don't, me bein' here like this and all."

"It would be much more improper, not to mention unkind, to leave poor Violet and Rose in my villainous clutches."

That brought a tremulous smile to her lips, which vanished at once beneath a yawn.

"You must be exhausted," he said quickly. "Go to sleep. You'll be disturbed soon enough, I wager."

She gave a short nod and scuttled into the other room, as if glad to escape. She probably was, he reflected. Still, she'd come. He could be glad of that.

He was disturbed by the baby's crying a little while later, but it quieted fairly soon. He had just drifted off once more when a heavy weight landed on his chest, and something warm and damp rasped his chin. He settled Sylvester in the crook of his arm, rolled over as best he could, and once more sought slumber.

Daylight roused him at last, flooding his room with warm, golden light. A good morning, he thought drowsily, then remembered it was because Annie was there. He sat up and looked over the back of the sofa, but his bedroom door remained closed.

He straightened his makeshift bed, and Sylvester promptly sprawled across the newly folded blanket and began an industrious washing of a hind leg.

Frake left him to it. He rinsed his hands and face at the basin, then donned one of the fresh shirts and neckcloths from the neat pile on the side table. Still, no one stirred within the room beyond.

He wanted to see Annie, to sit across the table from her over breakfast. But she needed whatever sleep she could get; on no account would he disturb her. Little Rose did more than enough of that.

He stretched, then rummaged through the cupboards to see what provisions he needed. His thoughts, though, kept returning to Annie. Just once, he'd like to see her free of worry, free of that ever-lingering exhaustion, free of her burdens. His shoulders were broad enough to bear them, but that was one place she was reluctant to turn. He was still a long way from earning either her trust or her liking.

He had just drawn on his coat when a light rapping sounded without, and Mrs. Appleby and Nanny Gossett came in together, followed by only three cats this morning. All the company he could want, he reflected, and slipped out. Once more he made the tour of the barrows and shops, loaded himself with a variety of delicacies, and carried them back.

The bedroom door stood open, now. Through it, he glimpsed Violet sitting up in the bed, her hair freshly washed and a towel about her shoulders. She looked very different, more of a bloom in her cheeks, he decided. Mary Appleby sat with Rose, and Nanny Gossett perched on a chair beside the bed, spinning a fine thread of gray wool onto a drop spindle. An orange paw appeared from beneath her skirts as one of the cats batted at it. The women's voices didn't carry.

A bundle lay curled under the bedclothes at Violet's side. Annie, buried beneath the covers, catching up on some badly needed sleep. The comfortable and comforting picture caught at him, awakening yearnings. She would be so warm and soft to hold . . .

He dragged his thoughts from his longings. Business, he reminded himself sternly. He needed to have a little talk with Samuel.

By the time a hackney set him down near the mews, the streets had begun to fill with morning life. He passed other grooms heading out for early exercise and training sessions, but no one he recognized. He reached Sir Joshua's stabling area and looked through the newly repaired door.

Gooden stood just within, saddling a horse. As Frake watched, the lad finished, pulled on a bridle, and turned to lead the animal out. He stopped in his tracks as soon as he saw Frake.

"Well, lad, so you got your job back," Frake said by way of opening.

Gooden tilted his chin in a cocky manner. "Now, Sir William, he didn't have no call to go firin' me. Saw the error of his ways, he did."

The groom added the last with such virtuousness, that Frake asked point-blank: "Are you blackmailing him?"

A dull flush crept into Samuel's cheeks. "Now, if that just ain't like a Runner to be goin' 'round bullyin' folks as ain't never done nothin' wrong. Tryin' to make me say things as I wouldn't never mean."

"Cut line, Gooden," Frake said. "That won't fadge, and so you know. What do you have on Sir William?"

Samuel hunched a shoulder and turned to tighten the girth. He swung onto the saddle, gathered the reins, then said: "I'm a loyal servant, I am. I ain't got nothin' on no one, and if I did, it wouldn't be no place of mine to go sayin' it."

For a sufficient price, Frake wagered, he'd say it soon enough. He watched Samuel ride out into the alley, then turned to see the old head groom leaning on a stall door, a wisp of straw between his teeth.

"That's one as knows 'ow to take care of 'isself," Loomis said, and grinned.

"What did Gooden do?" Frake strolled over. "Threaten to tell the old man as how Sir William had helped himself to all the best silver? Excepting, of course, Gooden couldn't do no such thing, seeing as how Sir Joshua is dead."

Loomis snorted. "Not likely, then, is it?"

Frake rocked back on his heels. "Must have threatened to tell something," he pursued, musing. "But what? And to who?"

The old man's eyes gleamed. "Be worth a pretty penny to find out," he said.

Frake drew forth his pipe and fingered it. "You know Sir William well?"

"Well as I needs to," came the prompt response.

"Meaning better than you'd like?" Frake quirked a companionable eyebrow.

That brought a considering frown to furrow the man's brow. "Not a bad sort, is Mr. William—Sir William, I should say. Can't say as 'ow I know anythin' against 'im." He sounded a bit aggrieved by this fact.

"Nothing to blackmail him with?"

"Not as one would think." The groom chewed the straw for a thoughtful minute. "Cares about 'is cattle, 'e does, I'll say that for 'im."

"Enough to kill in order to keep them?" Frake kept his tone one of only mild curiosity. "You don't think so?" he added as the groom's frown deepened.

"Can't say as 'ow I do," Loomis said with regret.

"Then what might someone blackmail him over?"

The groom shook his head. "Likes everythin' to go 'is way, 'e does. Puts up quite a fuss when it don't. Cares a good bit about 'is 'orseflesh, 'is cards, and 'is name, too. Might be somethin' in all that."

His horseflesh, his cards, and his name. Frake mulled those three over in his mind as he returned to the street. Templeton might have killed his uncle for his inheritance, to save his beloved horses from a precipitous trip to Tattersall's auction hall, or to have more money to game away.

He slowed his step. What about saving his name? If Templeton had committed murder, then he certainly had something he would wish to keep quiet. But if he hadn't? His uncle's head groom didn't seem to know of any disreputable secret in Templeton's past. And if any existed, he'd wager the servants would have some idea about it.

So what did that leave? Something potentially scandalous concerning another of his name? As far as he knew that could only mean Sir Joshua—or the late Captain Oliver Templeton. Perhaps he'd best ask a few questions concerning Captain Templeton's army career.

The only thing of which he felt sure, at the moment, was that Samuel had applied blackmail, of some sort, to regain his position. For a moment he toyed with the idea of hinting as much to Annie, to see if she could get the whole story from her brother, but dismissed the notion at once. Annie had enough worries.

At a few minutes before ten, he presented himself in Clarges Street, at the home of Mrs. Cornelia Leeds. A modest house, he decided. He applied the knocker and waited.

Several minutes passed before a footman, red faced from rushing, dragged open the door. He peered at Frake, then seemed to recall his responsibilities. He straightened, focused on a point just above Frake's left shoulder, and intoned: "Madam is not at home to visitors."

Frake offered him an encouraging smile. "That's all right, lad. I'm not a visitor. The name's Frake, and I'm from Bow Street. Just you run along and let your mistress know as how I'm here."

Dubious, the young man ushered him into the front salon and disappeared. Frake glanced about, noting the modest furnishings and the inexpensive trinkets decorating the chamber. Townhouse hired for the season, he decided. He paced the room, twisting his pipe stem between his fingers, while a considerable amount of time passed.

At last the door opened. Mrs. Leeds, draped in trailing shawls and holding a vinaigrette in one hand, tottered in. She raised a lace handkerchief, which reeked of violets, to her nose.

Frake, who had seen her in a very different vein the night before, raised his eyebrows in surprise at this invalidish demeanor. "I hope I haven't found you indisposed, ma'am."

She sank onto a sofa and waved him toward a chair. "You must forgive me. I underwent a most harrowing experience last night. So very dreadful. I vow, I was never so terrified in all my life. I doubt I shall ever fully recover."

Frake covered his skepticism with a show of startlement. "Whatever happened?" he demanded in tones of deep concern.

A quavering sigh escaped her. "Dreadful," she murmured, and went on to relate a highly colored version of being stopped by a highwayman and nearly murdered. "And as I cowered on the seat, in fear for my very life, Captain Bevis drove the villain off. Such an amazing show of bravery. I am quite in awe of him."

At the moment, Frake felt much the same about her story. In his memory, the situation had been quite the reverse. Now, why did the lady go to so much effort to make him think her the coward and Bevis the brave hero?

She drew the violet scented lace over her eyes,

then lowered it to flutter her lashes. "You must think me the greatest wetgoose. And I know I am quite silly, but I have the greatest fear of pistols. I cannot bear the things. And to have one waved about like that—" She gave an exquisite shudder.

Yet it had been she who quite coolly fired upon the highwayman—missing, it was true, yet still she had shown no hesitation or uneasiness in handling the weapon. Of course, she didn't know Frake had witnessed the scene. For some reason she seemed to feel the need to convince Frake she could never have killed anyone, least of all Sir Joshua.

Which meant she must have reason to believe herself to be a prime suspect.

Fifteen

Annie devoured the pages of *Marmion,* reading slowly, mouthing over unfamiliar words until they began to make sense. An unaccustomed moment of leisure, while Mary Appleby tended Rose, and Violet, for the first time in a very long while, rested peacefully. Annie actually had a few minutes without a single responsibility demanding her attention.

Sylvester, a warm lap-load of purring fur, twitched his whiskers and pressed his cold nose against her hand. Cradling him in one arm, she snuggled into the comfortable armchair, relishing the luxury of it all. His favorite chair, too, it was. Mr. Frake's.

Almost, she could hear the deep, resonant tones of his pleasant voice. If she closed her eyes, she could see in her mind the half smile that played about his mouth. And his eyes. . . . How could they be so piercingly direct, yet so gentle? So safe. Yet he was a Runner.

As if her thoughts conjured him, the door opened and his capable presence filled the room. Annie started, guiltily aware of committing the one unpardonable sin—wasting time. She sprang to her feet, dislodging the indignant cat, who vociferated his protest.

Mr. Frake smiled, apparently oblivious to her discomfiture. "I was hoping to find you awake and not gone yet," he said.

She thrust the volume hastily onto the table. "I'm that sorry, I am, sir, for takin' the liberty of pickin' it up. I won't never go doin' it again, I promise."

He raised his eyebrows. "You're welcome to pick up anything you like. Do you enjoy reading?"

Warmth touched her cheeks. "I don't do it very well, though I'm tryin' to get better. There're whole worlds between them covers." The reverence she felt for books slipped over into her voice, and her cheeks burned with embarrassment.

"Well, we'll just have to make sure as how you get the chance to explore them." He waved her back to the chair, and settled himself opposite her on the sofa. "I need someone to talk to. If you have the time?"

Her eyes widened. "Me, sir? What about?"

"The case. I always think better when I can talk it through. I usually only have Sylvester here to listen to me ramble. Not as how he doesn't do it very well, of course, but it's mighty hard to get a straight opinion out of him, it is."

The cat, as if in response to the mention of its name, stropped its length against his ankles. Mr. Frake obliged with a thorough scratch along its spine.

He seemed so calm and at ease, not in the least put out by her presence here in his home. Why did she have to be such a bundle of nerves? Yet it wasn't an unpleasant sensation. More exhilarating.

She perched on the edge of her chair and tried to will the tension from her muscles. "What was it you was wantin' to ask me, sir?"

"No need to be so formal." He looked up from Sylvester, his expression gentle. "And I wasn't wanting to ask you anything in particular. I just want you to listen, to think, to see if you can help me make any sense of all this."

"You mean help you, s—Mr. Frake?"

"That's right. Frake. Benjamin Frake." He put a slight emphasis on his first name.

She looked down, suddenly all a-glow. To call him by his first name—that was unthinkable. And suddenly, she found it difficult to think of anything else. Benjamin. Nanny Gossett called him that. Benjamin. Ben. A nice, comfortable name.

But it wasn't for the likes of her. She swallowed, trying to hide her embarrassment at the direction her mind had taken. "By all rights, you should still be thinkin' of me as bein' under suspicion."

"I suppose I should," he agreed. He drew his gnarled pipe from his pocket and studied it. The briarwood gleamed from so much handling. " 'Cepting as how I just can't seem to go bringing myself to believe murder—or anything dark and unpleasant—is lurking anywheres in your nature." He gazed at her steadily for a long moment, then returned his attention to the importunate Sylvester, who now stood on his hind legs, batting at the pipe bowl.

Annie caught her lower lip between her teeth and looked down. This glow that spread through her was all too much like a guilty secret, a dream she'd been refusing to acknowledge. To be sitting here, right across from him in his own home, with him speaking kind things to her and treating her like a friend. It was too wonderful to be true.

Which meant, most like, it wasn't.

She drew a steadying breath. She knew better than to be taken in by sweet talk, to believe a man's words just because he said them to her. Better she should figure out just what he was about, if he were trying to trick her into saying something to incriminate either herself or her brother. He'd be disappointed if that was his purpose. And she'd be disappointed, too. He looked—he sounded—so sincere. And he'd been so kind. But whenever she hoped for the best from someone, she generally got the worst. Just once, she'd like someone to live up to her ideal. *This* once.

He looked so tired, as if he really did just need a friendly listener. She owed him that. She owed him much more than she could ever say or ever hope to repay. She hesitated, torn, then decided to risk it. "Where do we begin?" she asked. "With me? Seein' as how I'm the most likely suspect?"

He leveled the gaze of those disconcerting blue eyes on her. He didn't say a single word; he just studied her face, searching for she didn't know what.

Heat crept once more into her cheeks. She stared back, refusing to look away, and suddenly found she no longer wanted to. He had strong features, a generous mouth and a firm chin. A pleasant face; one, she realized, at which she liked to look. And those eyes. If she weren't careful, she might lose herself in their smiling warmth and innocence. Deceptive innocence.

But the warmth, she could swear, was real. It enveloped her, its spark igniting a response deep within her being. It could so easily be fanned to a flame . . .

Something batted at her knee, and with relief she welcomed Sylvester back into her lap. She caught his front paws before his claws could shred her dress, and he contented himself with washing her wrist with his rasping tongue. She hugged him close.

Mr. Frake still watched her. She shifted Sylvester so he lay on his back, front paws hooked over her forearm, then raised her chin in defiance of the desires she didn't fully understand. "Mrs. Wickham, she come in and found me holdin' the pistol," she reminded him. As if she had to convince him of her guilt, rather than the opposite.

Mr. Frake shook his head. "That won't fadge. Daylesford now says as how Sir Joshua was already dead when he went in the library. So either that's true, or his lordship killed him. Either way, it means as how you couldn't have done it."

Annie tilted her head to one side. "I might of gone in there earlier, followin' right on Sir Joshua's heels, I might of."

He smiled, acknowledging her the point. "We know Mrs. Wickham was in there when he entered, so if you went in soon after she left, he was either still alive, which clears her, or he was dead, which implicates her."

"But I didn't go in— Oh. I almost wish I had," she sighed. "Only I seen my brother, and I went after him, and when I got back, his lordship was just goin' in."

Frake straightened, a gleam of hope kindling in his eye. "You could see your brother from the time Sir Joshua entered the library until the time young Daylesford went in after him? Think carefully, Annie."

"N—" She broke off. To admit he'd only brought her a message, then stayed behind while she went to the kitchen, would help nothing. Samuel couldn't be guilty of murder. She squared her shoulders. "Yes," she stated in her most positive voice.

Frake's gaze remained on her, and his expression clouded. "You mean, 'no.' " A deep sigh escaped him. "I was hoping you could, in all truth, relieve my mind about him."

"But—" Annie began, then broke off, seeing his understanding of her deception. She lowered her gaze to Sylvester, and her hands moved restlessly over his soft fur.

"Let's talk of the others," he suggested.

She gave her head a vigorous shake. "I want to know what you're thinkin' of my brother."

Frake studied his pipe, twisting the stem between his fingers.

"You know as how he went into the library," she pursued.

"But we don't know when," came back his answer. He hesitated a moment, then went on. "I know he removed a snuffbox from Sir William's pocket. He might have taken the pistol as well."

Annie's hands stilled with her effort to hold her reactions under strict guard. She hadn't known about that snuffbox. Why couldn't Samuel keep his fingers out of other people's pockets? "What you mean, is," she said with deliberation, "Samuel had the chance to kill Sir Joshua, he might of had that pistol, and he had a reason to want him dead."

Frake had the grace to look uncomfortable. "The same can be said for others," he pointed out.

"Like me?"

"If you wish. I was thinking more of Lord Daylesford. Or Captain Bevis and Mrs. Leeds. She's out to marry Daylesford now, and Bevis seems to like that just fine. Seems as how the viscount don't see more than is right under his nose. Now, they might have gone and killed Sir Joshua to keep him from tellin' young Daylesford what he's too besotted to notice for himself. Or there's always Mrs. Wickham. Sir Joshua's dying like that kept her from being in a bad way for money."

Annie hunched in her seat. "I don't like thinkin' as how it might be her."

"Then let's think about Sir William," Frake suggested. "He's certainly gained the most from his uncle's death. And your brother—" he broke off.

She looked up quickly. "What about him? What's Samuel gone and done now?"

"He seems to be blackmailing Sir William," Frake admitted.

Annie sank back in the chair, closing her eyes. What devilry would he be up to next? "About what?" she asked, and knew her voice sounded hollow.

"I've no idea."

"He—he might of seen Sir William enter the library," she suggested quickly.

"That he might."

Hope surged in Annie. "Then you can arrest—"

Frake shook his head. "It might just be something as your brother knows that would discredit the family. Do you know of anything like that?"

Annie rubbed Sylvester's chin. "Nothin' as I've ever heard. Except . . . But that don't seem likely."

"Tell me anyway."

For a moment she met the smiling encouragement in his eyes, then looked away before she became lost in it. "I—I don't really know nothin'. Just somethin' as Samuel said about Captain Oliver. Happened while they was away on the Continent, but he never said what. Samuel, he just kept laughin' to himself about it. It might be somethin' worth a spot of blackmail to keep it quiet. Then again, it might not."

"Well, well, well." Frake chewed on the pipe stem. "I'll have to see what I can find out from him, won't I? And now, time to do me a bit of ruminating, it seems, and see what comes up." He stared off into space, and the bowl of his pipe swayed gently as he became lost in thought.

Annie remained where she sat, stroking the purring Sylvester. If only Mr. Frake weren't a Runner, a potential enemy, she could enjoy sitting here with him like this. He radiated a certain peace and contentment, a quiet enthusiasm for solving a difficult problem. She found him restful and stimulating and exciting, and—

She shied from the direction her longings took. For her peace of mind, she'd better move herself and her sister from his home as quickly as possible. Perhaps in another day or two Violet would be stronger. Yet a flicker of relief touched her, knowing they couldn't leave quite yet.

And why did he let them stay? He seemed to enjoy having company—but why theirs? He was a handsome man, intelligent, and he moved with ease everywhere he went. People trusted him. Well, people other than her. He must have any number of girls setting their caps for him, many who could bring him something of advantage as a dowry. Why should he interest himself in a maid—except to win her trust so he could learn something about the case on which he worked?

That was the only reason that made any sense. Not that he meant to trick her. He just wanted her where he could keep an eye on her. If she betrayed anything about Samuel—or herself—it would be her own fault. He would probably even feel genuine sorrow. He'd looked as if he honestly hoped she could clear Samuel, and had been disappointed when she couldn't.

She eased Sylvester to the floor and rose, excusing herself to make ready to go to the gaming house. Mr. Frake merely nodded as if he barely heard her, and remained where he sat. When the opportunist

Sylvester changed laps, he calmly accepted the cat. Annie slipped away.

She no longer needed to work at the gaming house, she reflected as she donned her working gown. She had nothing more to gain there. She might as well look about for another position. But what sort of job could she find?

She didn't really want to go back into service. That was why she'd left Templeton Grange to come to London, to find something better, something where she could have a life of her own. But she hadn't found much.

She checked the mirror and adjusted her gown. Perhaps it would be better, after all, to seek service with some important family. A really hard-working maid could advance, perhaps even become a lady's abigail or dresser. She'd earn good money, then, not just the salary of a scullion. And she'd be an important person in the servants hall. That wouldn't be the same as having a family of her own, though.

She pulled on her mobcap and tucked most of her ringlets beneath the starched muslin. A servants hall was sort of like a family. She'd never be really lonely, not like she felt on occasion now.

She knelt on the floor, took little Rose from Mary Appleby and bounced the gurgling infant gently. Babies weren't always fun, she reminded herself. Rose woke constantly during the night and sometimes cried until Annie felt like joining in out of sheer frustration and exhaustion. But they were someone to love and love and love.

"What's Samuel doin', Annie?" Violet asked from the depths of the comfortable bed.

Annie sat down on the edge, still holding Rose. "He's groom for Sir William, now. Don't you go frettin' for him, none. Sammy's like a cat, always landin' on his feet, he is."

Violet plucked at the coverlet. "Sir Joshua—"

"Now, don't you go thinkin' about him, none. Not yet, leastways." Annie turned a bright smile on her sister.

Violet managed a weak one in return.

"Now, aren't you lookin' better." Annie beamed at her. "You've done her wonders, Mrs. Appleby, you and Nanny Gossett."

"Bless you, dearie." Mrs. Appleby smiled shyly at her. " 'Tis a joy to have little Rose and her mama both. Now, you run along and let me tend them."

Violet, Annie noted, had turned her head on the pillows, her eyes closing once more. Only a little fever remained; she had started the slow process of healing. Annie stood, more grateful than she could express to Mr. Frake, whatever his true reason for taking them in.

The early evening preparations passed quickly in the gaming rooms. Once she had everything clean and orderly to her satisfaction, Annie descended the stairs to the kitchen to help Cook and Ruby. She was arranging little cream tarts on a large tray when Samuel stuck his head in the door from the area steps.

She looked up, and something in his expression caused an uneasy sensation in the pit of her stomach.

"What are you doin' here?" she demanded, taking the offensive.

Behind her, Ruby giggled.

Samuel ignored the kitchen maid. "I wants a word with you, Annie, my girl. Now." He took her arm and dragged her outside.

Annie pulled away. "I've got my work—" she began.

He glowered at her. "Where're you stayin'? Went to your rooms, I did, and the old bat what lives down the hall says as how you left with some gentleman. *Gentleman!* I'll not have you goin'—"

"You'll not have me what?" Annie glared at him. "If you think as how you can come here and try tellin' *me* what to do or not to do, you can just up and think again, Samuel Gooden!"

"Where're Violet and Rose?" he demanded.

Annie drew a steadying breath. "With me. So before you go accusin' me of slippin' off with some gentleman—"

"It's that Runner, ain't it? He's gotten his grip on you to see what information he can squeeze out of you about me, I'll wager. Damn it, Annie, I didn't think as how you was the mooncalf of the family."

"No, you take the prize for that," she shot back.

His color darkened. "How you can go puttin' yourself in the hands of that Runner—"

"It ain't like that. He *is* a gentleman, and more deservin' of the name than them as is regular called it. He's given his own room to Violet and Rose and me, and brought in a woman as knows everythin' there is to know about herbs, and he's been that kind and all, and—"

Samuel's eyes narrowed. "You're in love with the damned fellow!"

Annie stared at her brother in shocked horror. "I never! It ain't no such thing." Why did her voice have to sound a touch uncertain? "If you just come here to make trouble and go spoutin' nonsense, you can just take yourself off again." She spun on her heel and stormed back inside.

Her face burned, and she dropped the first thing she picked up. In love with Mr. Frake. The idea was plain crazy! She couldn't be in love with him. He was a Runner! And besides, he'd never want her around, not permanently at least.

Oh, she'd seen that contented look of his, but it didn't mean anything, not really. He liked having company, that was all. And he was naturally a good and generous man who took real pleasure in helping someone in trouble. He'd be glad enough to have her move on in another week, then he'd probably up and find himself another poor soul in trouble, and he'd forget all about her.

She thrust the last of the tarts on the tray and shoved it out of the way. She'd caught a gleam in his eye, today, a glow that took her breath away. As if he might not mind seducing her. He was too honorable a man for that, though. That he was the first man she actually wanted to be seduced by, she refused to acknowledge.

She still refused. What she felt—what she wanted—

made no difference. She couldn't afford to end up like Violet, cast aside with a baby and no way to care for it. One of them had to stay respectable.

Only if he ever got her in the family way, Mr. Frake wouldn't cast her aside. He'd insist on marrying her, doing what was proper, and then he'd be stuck with a wife who wasn't good enough for him and whom he didn't really want. He deserved better.

Tears stung her eyes, and she tried to swallow the lump that welled in her throat. Why couldn't Samuel have kept his mouth shut and never forced her to admit to herself what she felt for Mr. Frake? She'd be ever so much happier if she hadn't. How could she face him when she went back to his rooms in the early morning? For that matter, what if he came to the gaming house this night? Could she keep him from guessing? She couldn't bear it if he found out and she had to watch his friendliness turn to pity and embarrassment.

The next several hours did nothing to ease her mind. The noise, the air of tense excitement, the gentlemen growing steadily more drunk and rowdy, only set her already strained nerves on edge. She was tired, tired of the work, of seeing the vast sums wasted on play, of the careless pleasure-seeking of the rich.

And their sloppiness. She bit back an angry word as some young sprig fell forward over his cards, knocking his bottle onto its side. Burgundy spilled out, flowing across his hand, over the edge of the table, and onto the carpet. With an exclamation of vexation, she dove to retrieve it before it did further damage.

Trying to keep her frayed temper from exploding, she hurried down the two flights to the kitchen, fetched several towels to mop up the mess, and started back up. She rounded the first landing and collided with someone. She staggered, almost falling, and the man caught her arm in a sustaining clasp. Mr. Frake.

Her heart leapt as she recognized him. Her hand twisted to catch hold of his sleeve, and she fought the urge to bury her face against his shoulder and feel his arms circle about her and hold her close. The memory of his carrying her, the night of that fire, haunted her dreams, both day and night.

With an effort, she shook off the entangling web of emotion and sensation he created within her. Work. Best think of work. She pulled free, and suffered a pang of regret. "Thank you, sir, I'm ever so sorry," she murmured, and hurried past. She could feel his gaze burning into her back as she continued resolutely up the stairs.

Had she acted too self-conscious? She ran up the last flight, glad she had her chores to occupy her. No use dwelling on the impossible.

The young gentleman no longer sprawled across the table. She glanced about and saw him lying on a sofa. Just as well, he'd only have been in her way. She dropped to her knees and scrubbed at the mess, only to have to snatch her fingers away as a careless, drunken gentleman almost trod on them.

Gentleman. She risked a peep over her shoulder to see if she could spot the only man she knew deserving of that name, but he was nowhere to be seen. Her sigh was only half relief, the rest regret. Yet she couldn't let herself get caught up in dreams of "if only."

Luckily, the carpet here was dark—probably on purpose for absorbing excess wine. When it was as dry as she could get it, she hurried back to the kitchen to deposit her wet towels, then collected another armload of wine bottles to bring to Mr. Henry. From him she received three new decks of cards, which she carried along the servants corridor to stow in the library.

The door stood slightly ajar. She pushed it wider on silent hinges, but at sight of a lady, her back turned, bending low over a seated man, she halted, then did a double take. That was her own brother Samuel in that chair, his gaze feasting on the revealing décolletage presented to him by Mrs. Cornelia Leeds.

The woman boosted a silk-covered hip onto the table and leaned confidingly closer, refilling Samuel's wine glass from the bottle she held. "I just need to be sure, you see, and you're such a—talented—young man, I feel certain you must know a thing or two."

Annie, indignant, watched her brother preen. Drunk, she realized. That, and dazzled by the eyeful he was getting.

"Whom did you see come in here that night?" Mrs. Leeds positively cooed the words. "I know you were where you could see the servants door, you must know who all came in, and I couldn't bear it if Viscount Daylesford were the only one. Tell me you saw someone else."

Samuel licked his lips, his gaze never wavering. "Oh, I seen a thing or two," he said. "Not that I wouldn't mind seein' a bit more."

"That—could be arranged." The voice held a world of promise. "Who came in?"

"Now, that would be tellin', that would. Me, I likes to be gettin' my price for information." He reached forward.

Annie, fortunately, couldn't see what he did, though her cheeks burned at the obvious conclusion.

Mrs. Leeds laughed, a throaty sound. "So Sir William Templeton is finding out, I'll wager. Are you telling things to that Runner?"

"There wouldn't be no advantage to me in that, now would there? Not like this."

Annie clutched the cards. She should go, she didn't want to be a witness to this, but she had to know what they said, what they might reveal. That Samuel knew something, perhaps guessed the identity of the murderer, seemed very likely.

Annie must have made some sound. Mrs. Leeds jumped to her feet and spun about, facing her. The woman's eyes blazed.

Flushed and uncomfortable, Annie pushed the door fully open and came in. "Cards, mum," she said and laid them on the table. She retreated at once.

She hurried down the corridor, teeth clenched. What had the woman been trying to find out? If Samuel had seen a particular person? Mrs. Leeds herself, perhaps? Pretty great lengths she seemed willing to go to, to find out.

Annie sniffed. The Quality weren't any better than they should be. Certainly not decent, respectable folk. Not like some she could name.

The thought of Mr. Frake brought her to a standstill, and the blood drained from her cheeks. Should she tell him about that little interlude? Should she let the Runner know that Samuel knew more than he was telling, and that Mrs. Leeds was that desperate to find out what it was?

Or would that be betraying her own brother?

Sixteen

Annie wove her way through the crowded rooms delivering her bottles of wine. She didn't see Mr. Frake anywhere in the house. She didn't even know if she wanted to. Yet a desire she couldn't quite analyze drove her on, searching for him.

The one spot she hadn't tried was the front salon which stood opposite the dicing room. He'd used it when he'd talked to people that night Sir Joshua died; he might have gone there to think, now. She preferred that possibility to the more likely one that he'd left.

She ran lightly down the stairs, collected a tray at the foot and made a quick tour of the hazard tables to pick up dirtied glasses and empty bottles. This accomplished, she deposited her burden on the hall table, then turned toward the salon. A prickle of nerves raced along her spine. If he were there, what would she say?

As she reached the door, the sound of a raised voice reached her. Anticipation mingled with apprehension, then faded into disappointment. A woman's voice. Mrs. Wickham's. And she sounded very angry.

The man's voice that answered wasn't Mr. Frake's.

Annie hesitated. Was the proprietress in trouble? Should she fetch Captain Palfrey or Mr. Henry? More likely Mrs. Wickham could handle matters on her own, and Annie would only be intruding where she wasn't needed.

"You killed him, didn't you?" the man declared, his voice rising in accusation. "You'd do anything to keep from paying what you owed him."

"You're a fool, William Templeton, and you've always been one," came the woman's furious response. "And don't think your uncle didn't know it. That's what really tortured him after Oliver's death, the thought that you would one day step into his shoes."

"Like Cornelia Leeds stepped into yours as his favorite?" The words came out with a sneer. "That might have weighed even more with you than the money, mightn't it? Jealousy. The woman scorned."

"After five years and who knows how many ladies between?" A forced laugh sounded in Mrs. Wickham's voice. "I had no idea I could be so slow to react."

William Templeton's response came out so low, Annie could barely hear the rumble of his words. She turned away, back to the comforting familiarity of her work. Mrs. Wickham, killing Sir Joshua, and all on account of money? The thought sickened her. Yet she couldn't deny the gaming house's monetary woes; she'd heard the proprietress lamenting them often enough.

But the possibility of someone she knew, someone she worked with every day, being a murderess. . . .

No, it simply couldn't be possible. She'd much rather it proved to be someone she barely knew. Not Mrs. Wickham, who had become a part of her everyday life.

And as for Samuel. . . . No, she could never believe her own brother capable of murder. Yet Mr. Frake considered it very possible. How could she love a man who might cause her brother to dangle from the nubbing cheat?

The night passed in a blur for her, so wrapped up was she in the misery of her reflections. Somehow she delivered wine, cleared tables, brought fresh cards. Yet the voices and activity about her didn't penetrate her cocoon of unhappiness.

What she really wanted, she realized, was to go far away, escape from her troubles and worries, just for a little while.

The sound of her name, spoken in Mr. Frake's beloved voice, brought her around in a whirl. He stood just behind her, smiling with a warmth that spread right through her, wrapping her in a happiness she would not have believed possible the moment before. A slow light sprang to life in the depths of his eyes, as if an ember burned there. For the first time in hours, the hope touched her that just maybe everything might turn out all right after all.

"Can you take some time off work on Sunday?" he asked abruptly. He started to raise his hand, then lowered it again to his side. "I thought as how we might take little Rose on an outing to a park, after church."

"I—" She broke off as emotion welled within her.

What a wonderful father he'd make, positively doting on his children. Unless— The familiar unease seeped back into her. Unless this was his way of telling her he'd be having his own time free soon. And that would mean finishing with this case. "Have you—do you know who killed Sir Joshua?" she blurted out.

The gleam in his eyes dimmed. "Not yet."

She didn't know whether to believe him or not. If he decided it was Samuel who was guilty, how would he tell her? By taking her for an outing with little Rose to soften the blow?

She hadn't trusted anyone for so very long, she realized. Not since her parents died. And with the death of her father at the hands of a Runner, how could she start by trusting a Runner now? Yet the temptation to do so proved almost overwhelming.

She'd never been so aware of a man before, so conscious of his power and gentleness, of his every move. When she closed her eyes, she could recall the sensations he created in her just by brushing a stray lock of hair from her face. Such a little attention— yet so breathtaking.

Vaguely, she remembered there were things she ought to tell him. Important things. Things that might help. Yet with him here, before her, smiling in a way that set her heart pounding, she just couldn't think straight.

They hadn't spoken a word for almost a minute, she realized suddenly. They just stood there looking at each other. For the moment, that was enough.

Something subtle changed in his expression, and

her knees turned to water. How could blue eyes burn so hot, mesmerizing her with their blaze? She swayed toward him, drawn to his flame, oblivious to her fears of being scorched. In his expression, in every line of his dear face, she saw a place where she could rest, lose herself, perhaps even find a measure of peace.

"Annie," he breathed her name.

He touched her cheek, a caress that set her pulse racing.

"I—" He broke off and drew a deep breath. His mouth tightened and he drew his hand back.

Annie flinched. Had she done something wrong? Had she—

"Damn this case," he said with unaccustomed harshness. "Annie, when this is all over, I want to talk to you. Promise me you won't vanish with your sister until I've had my chance."

Talk. And a little more, perhaps? Was this what she wanted, or— No, it was all too soon to decide, to think. He was right, they had to wait and see, to find out if he would be forced to arrest Samuel. Annie looked at her slippers, nodded, and pushed past toward the table where her tray waited. Her hands trembled.

Heavy footsteps approached, and Captain Bevis appeared. "Frake, a word with you, please."

Annie pretended to busy herself restacking the glasses, keeping her face averted. Mr. Frake was amazing, how he could calmly go on with business, as if nothing bothered him personally. As if a whole world hadn't just unfolded between them, only to be whisked closed again.

Mr. Frake rocked back on his heels. "And what might I do for you, Captain?"

Bevis frowned, then gave a short, embarrassed laugh. "I don't really know, I suppose. A little matter bothered me, that's all. It's Mrs. Leeds. She's been behaving in a very odd manner this night, hobnobbing with that groom of Sir Joshua's. You know the one, Gooden. I don't like it one bit."

Mr. Frake raised his eyebrows but said nothing.

Annie's hand clenched on the crystal stem of a glass. Why did everyone have to go trying to make it look like Samuel was guilty?

"I wouldn't normally interfere," Bevis went on, "but I owe something to Sir Joshua's memory. He and his son were fine men, they were both good friends to me. I want to see Sir Joshua's murderer brought to justice."

Mr. Frake smiled in that winning way of his. "Seems we have a common goal, then, sir."

Bevis paced a few steps, then stopped once more before Mr. Frake. "I don't suppose it's any secret from you that I have been an ardent—admirer—of Mrs. Leeds?"

"Well, no," he admitted.

Bevis nodded. "I've never had a chance with her, myself. She's a woman who needs wealth and position." He shrugged his shoulders, which could be no easy feat in his exquisitely cut coat. "I have neither to offer her. I'd always thought—" He broke off, and his mouth tightened.

"There's something you think as I should know, but don't feel comfortable telling me?" Mr. Frake suggested.

"It's a damned business." Bevis resumed his pacing in the short hall. "So much uncertainty. Learning things you'd rather not know about people. Look," he said, and went on to relate the tale of the holdup. "I was stunned to find Mrs. Leeds at home with a pistol. She's always told me she hates the things. It's been weighing on my mind, so I decided to confront her with it tonight. And I came upon her in an embrace with that groom!"

Annie cringed. Did he have to speak of her brother with such loathing?

"What," Bevis went on, "if Sir Joshua had discovered she was no better than an alley cat? Indulging her fancy for a groom, all the while she was inveigling him into marrying her? She'd told me they'd had a falling out, but I hadn't realized it might have been serious."

"You think it likely he might have found her with Gooden?" Frake asked.

"Here? Yes. I caught them myself, just a little while ago. She'd also been casting out lures to young Daylesford, you know. I can't get it out of my mind she might have killed Sir Joshua in order to keep him from revealing her character to her other suitor. And you'll never know," he added, raising a haggard face, "how I hate myself for my suspicions. Kindly clear them for me, will you?"

Annie moved off, recognizing the part about her

brother had ended. This wasn't the first time someone had told Mr. Frake about Mrs. Leeds's not wanting her behavior revealed to Daylesford. Last night she had inveigled Captain Bevis into joining her in an attempt to make the viscount jealous. Was she attempting to spring her trap for him quickly, before he learned the truth about her, and his title and fortune escaped her clutches? If she'd committed murder for their sake, she must be desperate for the power and security they offered. She'd waste no time before securing them for herself.

Curious, Annie worked her way through the crowded rooms, trying to spot the woman. At last she caught sight of her, playing cards at a table in the large gaming room. And yes, her opponent was the viscount.

A flush covered the young man's face as he gazed at Mrs. Leeds. The woman leaned forward in the same provocative way she had used with Samuel, awarding the viscount the same seductive view of her décolletage. Playfully, she reached out with her fan and rapped his knuckles. He laughed, caught her hand and, dropping his cards, kissed first her fingertips, then her palm.

A fish, Annie reflected, snapping at the hook, begging to be reeled in. Mrs. Leeds wasted no time.

It was some while later before Annie realized she had not seen Mr. Frake since she'd left him with Captain Bevis. She resumed her rounds, this time watching out for him, but nowhere did she catch a glimpse of his familiar figure. Perhaps he'd gone home to sleep. She longed to go there, too, just to be in the sanctuary of his home. Just to see him.

Finally, after what seemed like hours more, the last of the patrons began to make their unsteady ways out the door. Annie did a hasty clean-up, preparing everything for the morrow, then went down to the kitchen. Ruby and Cook had left already, she noted with a touch of envy. With a sigh, she dragged off her sullied apron and picked up her cloak.

As she started out the door leading to the area steps, someone came down the kitchen stairs behind her. She turned as Mrs. Wickham entered the room.

"There you are, Annie." The proprietress, her face lined with strain and the lateness of the hour, advanced several more paces, then stopped. "What has that Runner learned?"

"Mum?" Annie regarded her with uncertainty.

"Don't be witless, girl." A note of irritation crept into her voice. "What is he thinking? Whom does he suspect?"

Annie drew back. "How should I be knowin' a thing like that, mum?"

The woman fixed her hands on her hips. "I have heard," she intoned, and her voice grew cold, "that you are staying with him." She made it sound as if she accused Annie of consorting with the enemy. "I am making no judgments, mind," she went on, "and if you want to behave in such a manner, I am sure it is of no concern to me. But I will have no disloyalty from someone in my employ. If you are acting as his spy among us, girl, I'll have you out of here this minute."

Annie stared at her, too astounded to speak. "It's no such thing," she finally managed. "I wouldn't—he wouldn't—" But how could she explain Mr. Frake's unselfish kindness?

Mrs. Wickham's lip curled. "I cut my eye teeth long ago, girl. I've seen the way you look at him. You'll do anything to ingratiate yourself, I suppose. Even carry tales. A pack of lies, most of them, I'll wager."

The blood drained from Annie's cheeks, leaving her chilled. "Of—of all the unkind, unjust, downright cruel things to say."

"Deceitful wretch! I don't know why I've borne with you. You're nothing but that Runner's spy."

Annie stiffened. "If—if you think as how I'm the kind of person who'd do that, who'd spy on you, then I'll be leavin' right now. And I want my wages, I do, them that are comin' to me."

A triumphant smile flickered across the woman's face. She reached into the reticule that dangled from her wrist and drew out several coins. "This should more than cover it." She turned on her heel and left.

Annie opened her hand and found herself staring at five shillings and several pennies. She had just lost her job—and probably any hope of getting a character reference so she could find other employment.

Five shillings and four pennies. All the money she had in the world.

And to one extent, she realized with an aching

heart, Mrs. Wickham's accusation was true. Mr. Frake said as how in exchange for his paying for Nanny Gossett's tending of Violet, Annie should help him with the case. And hadn't she considered telling him everything she'd overheard this night? If that didn't make her a spy, what did?

She sagged against the door jamb, disgusted with herself and angry with him for putting her in this position.

The chill of the pre-dawn air finally penetrated, sending a shiver through her. She straightened and looked about in the darkness. Pretty soon she might find herself living out in this.

That sobered her. How could she have done anything as senseless as quit her job? But it had been forced on her. Mrs. Wickham had been determined from the start of that conversation to get rid of her.

That realization shocked Annie. But looking back over the woman's stance, the gleam in her eye, she knew it to be true. But why? Because she thought Annie a spy? Or because she *feared* her to be a spy and had something to hide?

Annie mounted the steps to the street, her mind whirling. This all happened *after* she heard Sir William accusing Mrs. Wickham of killing his uncle. Had Mrs. Wickham realized they'd been overheard—and by whom? Had this been an attempt to get Annie away from where she might overhear something even more incriminating—or to make her feel so guilty she'd never mention to Mr. Frake what she'd already heard?

And what was she to tell Violet about losing her job? How was she to care for her and little Rose? Violet mustn't know yet, mustn't be allowed to worry. Not now, not when she'd just begun to get better.

Tears forced their way into her eyes, stinging; she fought them back, refusing to give in to her fear for the future. Somehow, she'd make everything work. She had to. No one else would do it for her.

She trudged through the streets. Not to the rooms off Covent Garden where her sister slept in blissful ignorance of this latest disaster, but toward the mews where she would find Samuel. She needed to talk to him, to reassure herself he had nothing to do with this dreadful business, to warn him of Mr. Frake's damning amount of evidence against him.

That, at least, she could do. She could try to save her brother.

By the time she at last reached the stable, the first gray of approaching dawn tinged the sky. She let herself in, to be greeted by two lanterns burning low within, as if they'd been left on for the entire night. Only then did she realize the oddness of the hour. Her brother would be neither slinking in late from some convivial gathering nor rousing for his morning's work. He'd be up in the loft, asleep. She couldn't disturb everyone; she'd have to wait.

One of the horses stuck its brown head over its stall door and nickered, a nervous sound. It threw its head, its eyes rolling, its ears laid flat back. Then it swerved away, paced the length of its confines, then returned, nickering once more.

The other inmates of the mews didn't display the same restlessness. Curious, Annie went to the stall while the bay circled once more. As the animal passed by, she saw its neck glistened beneath its black mane. So did the hair at the base of its ears. Nervous sweat. She glanced down its body, noting the other gleaming damp patches, and saw a bundle of clothes lying in the straw behind the animal.

An all too human-shaped bundle.

On the horse's next pass, she caught its halter. The animal jerked its head, but when she opened the door, it bolted past her, dragging her from her feet. She caught her balance and made it with her charge to the far wall, where the bay stood trembling. Murmuring soothing words, she found a rope and tied it securely.

The man in the stall hadn't moved. As she approached, the reek of gin almost overpowered her. Jagged tears, spotted with blood, showed in his clothing where the animal's iron-shod hooves had clipped him. She knelt at his side, but even before she reached out to move the upflung arm that covered his face, she recognized him. Samuel.

For one awful moment, panic filled her. He lay too still. Something, surely, should move. She caught his wrist and checked for a pulse. Nothing.

The cold lump in her chest that was her heart skipped a beat, then thudded painfully. With a hand that trembled, she loosened his knotted neckerchief and collar. For frantic seconds she felt at his throat for a faint flutter of life, but it eluded her.

She sat back, hugging herself. He'd been knocked

unconscious. That had happened once before when he'd been trampled by a frightened horse. He'd recover in just a few moments.

Or maybe it was the gin. He was drunk, as well. That's why he didn't stir. He'd sleep it off, then wake up with a splitting headache and no memory of how he got here.

He'd wake up.

She grabbed his shoulder and started shaking, but instead of rousing, he merely slumped sideways. His head lolled on the straw at an unnatural angle.

Seventeen

Annie swallowed as her surroundings swayed. She knelt in the straw, her brother's body in her arms, her mind silently crying for Mr. Frake. She needed him, she couldn't think straight, this had to be a nightmare. Why couldn't she wake up? Sammy—

Shock, she realized hazily, must be numbing her. This couldn't be real, yet how much more proof did she need?

Samuel— He could be so unreliable, he stole things, she worried constantly about him, he drank too much, but he was her brother! She couldn't accept this, that he was dead. And all because he'd gotten too drunk to handle a horse safely!

She drew in a quavering breath. She had to do something, she couldn't just sit here, dazed. She had to think.

She needed Mr. Frake. Not just for his comforting presence, either. He'd know what to do.

And he'd need to know, too. His prime suspect for the murder of Sir Joshua was now dead, and he'd probably consider the case to be closed. He'd look no further, and the real murderer would get away free. She had to convince Mr. Frake of Samuel's innocence. And Samuel—

Samuel . . .

She should go and get someone, but she couldn't leave him. Why hadn't anyone come down stairs from the grooms quarters? Didn't anyone hear the horse pacing about? Hadn't they noticed Samuel wasn't in his bed?

"Is anyone up there?" she called, then realized her voice, shaky and weak, couldn't have carried. She tried again, but no answer came in return.

Where was everyone? Out? But it was almost morning, and they had to be up and about their duties tending the animals soon. Surely they wouldn't all leave the mews.

She caught her lower lip between her teeth. There wasn't anything she could do for Samuel by sitting here. She had to get up, move, find someone. Tenderly she laid his head back on its straw pillow and dragged herself to her feet. She'd check upstairs, then if she had to, she'd go to the next stable or the next, until she found someone to ride for Mr. Frake.

As she neared the top of the rickety, creaking steps, a shaky snore reached her. That single sound heartened her. She wasn't alone here, after all. But why didn't the man wake up?

She opened the door at the top of the landing and entered the long sleeping quarters. No light at all penetrated here. She groped through the darkness to the first bed, found a recumbent form, and gave the shoulder a vigorous shake. A broken off snore was the only response. She tried again with the same results.

Don't panic, she told herself. Not now. Not yet.

She searched for the next bed, found its occupant, and shook harder than before. This time, she received a low groan for her efforts. Why weren't they waking up?

Here, too, she realized, everything reeked of cheap gin. Drunk, she deduced with disgust. There was poor Samuel, lying dead downstairs—and he'd probably been as drunk as his comrades.

Tears filled her eyes, and she stumbled back down the steps and went to stand in front of the stall. Why couldn't he move, jump up and laugh at her, say he'd really gone and made a May game of her this time? Why had he deserted her like this, leaving her the sole support of Violet and little Rose, and on the very night she had lost her job, at that?

She straightened and turned away. Shock was taking her in strange ways, she realized through her daze. But she didn't have time to indulge in grief yet, not until she'd found someone to do the decent thing for Samuel. She'd be the one to lay him out, of course, see all things done proper as they should be. But now—now she needed Mr. Frake.

That thought drove her, giving her new purpose. She let herself outside into the chill pre-dawn light, then hesitated, not sure which way to turn, what to do next. Then in the distance she heard hoofbeats on the cobbled stones, and at the end of the mews a carriage creaked as it pulled to a halt.

A carriage! Someone who could be sent for Mr. Frake.

She ran toward it through the darkness, shouting she didn't know what. She couldn't see more than the dim outline, but the carriage didn't move on. It stayed, waiting.

A shadowy shape moved before her, and she slowed. Someone—

"Annie?" Relief mingled with concern sounded in a deep, beloved voice.

With a half sob, Annie found herself wrapped in Mr. Frake's arms, her face buried against his solid chest.

He crushed her against his greatcoat. "Annie, love," he murmured in her ear. "It's all right, all right, love. I'm here, I've got you safe. You're trembling." It didn't seem possible, but somehow, he pulled her closer and his lips brushed her temple. "Easy, love, easy. What's happened?"

She drew a shuddering breath. "You're here," she gasped.

"Yes, I'm here." He proceeded to prove it by kissing her hair again.

"How—?"

"When you didn't come back to my rooms, I went to the gaming house to find you. Mrs. Wickham told me as how you'd quit and stormed out. I tried your old room, but someone else had moved in. The only other place I could think you might have gone was here, to your brother. So I came."

"I—" She gulped back the sob that welled in her throat. "He's dead."

"He—your brother?" A sharpness edged his voice. He gripped her upper arms and set her a pace from him, peering through the dark at her face. "Steady, Annie. Tell me what happened."

"Come—" She turned, and his arm went about her shoulders, drawing her close to his side, supporting her as they walked. He didn't say another word, but his presence, so stolid and dependable, eased the cold hollow within her. She allowed the top of her head to rest against his shoulder, a position to which she could become accustomed all too quickly.

They arrived at the door of the stable. She reached out to open it, but he was before her.

Gently, he set her aside and went in. "Where is he?"

Annie hugged herself, shivering. "In that stall." She nodded toward it.

Mr. Frake dragged off his greatcoat and draped it over her shoulders. She huddled into the warmth he'd generated, welcoming it, welcoming his nearness. Part of her wanted to cling to him, but she remained by the door while he crossed to the stall and went inside.

Minutes passed, then he called: "You found him like this? You didn't move nothing?"

Annie frowned, trying to remember. It all seemed a blank now, except— "A horse. This horse here was in there, all nervous and pacin' about. I led it out. And when I couldn't find no heartbeat, I—I moved his head—" She broke off, suddenly nauseous at the memory of the way his head had lolled.

"Horse was there?" Frake backed out and stood looking down at Samuel. "He's been—" He broke off. "Damn it, I'm sorry, Annie." He came to her and held her once more. "My poor love, what you've gone through. Did you look at him closely?"

"No, I—I just knew as how I had to find you, to tell you." To know the comfort of being with him, of feeling his arms about her, like they were now.

"What do you think happened?" he asked, his tone gentle.

She hesitated. "He'd been drinkin' gin. You can smell it. He must of fallen under the horse and been—been trampled."

He nodded, and his chin rubbed against her forehead. "Did he get drunk on duty much?"

"He know'd the danger. Somethin' must of come up, or he wouldn't never go near a horse in such a state."

"So something came up. Where're the other grooms?"

"Up there." She indicated the direction by raising her chin. "Snorin' in their beds. I couldn't wake them."

"You couldn't?" His frown deepened. "I'll just go see what I can do. No, you stay here."

Annie remained where she stood, but her gaze followed him as he mounted the stairs. As he trod on the one near the top that creaked, he caught the railing, then eased himself over it. A minute later, she heard his footsteps moving about above her.

He wasn't gone long. He returned, the creases in his brow more pronounced. "Do you think as how you could go to where I left my hackney? I told him to wait, and gave him something, but it's been so long he may have up and left. I need him to fetch a doctor."

"For them upstairs?"

He nodded. "I think they've been drugged."

"Drugged?" she repeated, startled. "But why? Then Sammy—"

"We won't know nothing until those two up there come 'round. Now, be a good girl and go find that hackney, will you? There's a few things I've got to do here."

Annie went, glad to have some purpose, something to occupy her. The dark outside held no terrors for her, now. Those all lay back in the stable.

As she reached the end of the alley, the welcome creak of leather reached her and she made out the dim shape of the carriage. He'd waited. She hurried up to the vehicle, and the jarvey peered down at her. In the pale, creeping light of dawn, she saw him shake his head.

"Busy," he told her. "Waitin' for a gentleman, I am."

That pleased her, that he referred to Mr. Frake in that way. "I've got a message from him," she gasped, breathless from her run. "He wants you to fetch a doctor. Do you know as where there's one nearby?"

The jarvey thought a minute, then announced that

mayhap he did, though not what one might rightly call *near*. Satisfied that this would do, he set off, leaving Annie standing at the mouth of the alley.

About her, shapes took on more definition as the morning dawned. This was one morning she didn't want to face. Samuel—

She shied from thinking about him. She didn't even have her job to keep her busy. At least she had Violet and Rose—though how she was to care for them now, without even Samuel's sporadic help, she didn't know. They couldn't continue to impose on Mr. Frake. He should have his own rooms to himself again.

She walked slowly back to the stable. Nowhere inside could she see Mr. Frake, but he had thrown a blanket over Samuel's body. Then creaks and scrapes sounded from above, accompanied by a heartfelt groan. He must be up in the loft, rousing the other two grooms at last.

The extent of her relief surprised her. Had she feared those two might die, as well? Then they might never know what happened to Samuel.

She sat on an old tack trunk and clutched the greatcoat about her. Thought was too difficult. A fog enveloped her as she stared, unseeing, straight ahead.

Burning heat against her hand made her start. She blinked and saw Mr. Frake standing before her, holding out a chipped cup. The pungent aroma of coffee enveloped her, blotting out even the stable smells. She took it, grateful, and swallowed a scalding mouthful.

She didn't even ask how he came by it. He seemed to her a man quietly capable of anything.

"The doctor's come," he said. "Those two upstairs will be fine, once they have a few cups of this inside them."

She didn't look up. "Samuel—that wasn't no accident, was it?"

"No. He was hit on the head afore the horse trampled him. There ain't enough—" He broke off. "I think it happened out here," he went on, "then he was put in the stall and someone scared the horse so it would run over him. Looks like an accident on the surface, but no horse shoe got his head like that. I'd be willing to wager there's more gin sprinkled over him than there is inside of him. The older fellow says as how your brother brought a bottle here, which he shared out between them. They'd drained their glasses before they realized he hadn't been drinking his, just pretending. Then they don't remember anything else."

Annie forced her mind to function. "Then Samuel up and drugged them himself," she said slowly. "Why? And where would he be gettin' the drug?"

"Offhand," Frake said, "I'd guess he was planning something to take place here that he didn't want no one else to know about. Or mayhap he had someone coming for to visit with him."

"But who—you mean the person who murdered Sir Joshua?" She swallowed more of the strong, sweet brew.

"He was blackmailing Sir William into keeping

him on here." Frake took his briarwood pipe from his pocket and fingered the stem, frowning. "There's only one sure way to stop someone as is blackmailing you."

Annie shuddered. "You think as how Sir William set it up to meet him here, then killed him?"

He rocked back on his heels. "Seems like a real good chance, it does. Blackmail. Now, I wonder—"

She looked up quickly. "What?"

"If it wasn't over the blackmail—"

Annie's eyes widened in dawning horror. "You mean you might of given my brother a fright? You've been checkin' up on him, and a lot of what you found out seemed like to make him out to be the killer. What if he thought you was about to nab him for murder? That might make him do somethin' desperate-like, it might."

Mr. Frake frowned. "If he'd helped someone else kill Sir Joshua, then went to that person to save him when I started closing in on him—"

"Samuel didn't never take no part in no murder!" She spoke with more conviction than she felt. "But you might of scared him enough to confront the real murderer," she declared. "Or mayhap you scared the murderer into silencin' Samuel."

Mr. Frake didn't move. "That's very possible, Annie."

She fought back the lump welling in her throat. "I've learned a lot about my brother of late, and none of it makes me feel no better about him. But that don't alter the situation none. If you hadn't been after him so determined-like—"

"He knew something," Frake pointed out. "If he would've told me, instead of trying to turn it to his advantage—"

"How could he tell you? You was so busy thinking as he was the killer, you'd never of listened to him." She sniffed and dashed the back of her hand across eyes suddenly brimming.

"Annie—" He reached for her hands.

She pulled away, rising as she did so, putting more distance between them. She trembled inside, and the tide of rising hysteria threatened to carry her away. It would be so easy to let go, drown in it, to scream and scream until it brought oblivion.

She fought against it. She couldn't break down, not yet. She sought a focus for her rampaging emotions and found it in the man who stood before her. "You! If it hadn't of been for you and all your investigatin' and scarin' folk, our Samuel would be right as rain this minute, not lyin' there like—like—" She shook her head, struggling to hold back the tears that threatened to overflow. "You—you as good as killed him."

He remained very still. "He chose his own path, Annie. If a man takes to blackmail—"

"We don't know as how that's what got him killed! You're just guessin'! All I know is that if you hadn't been so cocksure as how he was guilty of a murder he didn't never commit, he'd still be alive!"

"You're upset—"

"Am I? *Am I?* Why should I be any such a thing? Just on account of I've gone and lost my job and my brother's been murdered and my sister—" Her voice broke on a quavering sob.

He took a step toward her. "Annie, love—"

"Don't you go callin' me that." She spun away, breathing hard, trying to regain control.

The stairs creaked as someone began to descend, and Annie fled outside, into the early morning light. Drained, empty, too raw with pain to think— She stumbled over the uneven cobble stones and slowed her wild pace.

Where did she go now? She had no home, no job, and her sister—

She swallowed, struggling to hold back the emotions that tore her apart. She couldn't leave Violet and Rose with Mr. Frake. Yet her sister was starting to get better. How could she take her away from Nanny Gossett's healing care?

And even if she did, where could she take her? What could she possibly do now?

Eighteen

Frake, kneeling in the gloomy, smoke-reeking loft, glowered at the trunk before him. He wanted Annie, and instead he had this.

Under the direction of the two other grooms, he had packed up Samuel's things. His search of them so far had revealed nothing, but he hadn't really expected it to. He'd already found the stolen treasures.

But Annie would want everything. And maybe she could find something he'd missed, something that only someone who knew Samuel well might recognize as being important or out of place.

If Annie would even talk to him.

He should have gone after her— No, he'd been through all that. She needed time to accept what had happened. As long as she blamed him, his presence would only upset her more. And he'd had his job to do here and couldn't leave. Later, perhaps she'd accept comfort from him, and let him find a measure of comfort himself in her forgiveness.

The younger groom helped him carry the trunk down the stairs, then along the alley to the street. There he hailed a hackney and returned to his own rooms. As he lugged Samuel's belongings up the two flights, he wished he could turn back the clock to the previous day at this time. He'd give anything to spare Annie what she'd suffered.

And as for Violet— One more task lay ahead of him, one he'd give a great deal to avoid. Unless Annie had already faced it herself.

Annie. Perhaps she'd gone straight to her sister. She might be there even now, safe in his home . . .

As soon as he opened the door, he knew his hope to be in vain. She wasn't there. He felt it in his heart. There might be any number of people in his rooms, but without her, they loomed empty for him, like a barren wasteland.

As he laid the trunk on his sitting room floor, Violet called to him from the bedroom. He tensed, and a dull ache started in his stomach. He'd have to tell her something; how much would depend on her condition. Bracing himself, he opened the door and managed a smile of greeting.

Violet sat up in bed, a shawl about her shoulders, her dark hair soft and curling with new vitality. She'd improved a great deal in just the last couple of days, he realized. Her expression, though, showed her worry.

Her fingers creased the coverlet. "Where's Annie?"

Frake's mouth tightened. He wanted to know, too.

Violet's gaze narrowed. "What's happened? Somethin' has, and you can't tell me different. Is she all right? She never come back after workin' last night."

All at once, Frake felt old. Why couldn't Annie be here? Her sister would need her. Damn it, *he* needed her.

"Somethin's wrong," Violet said. "Don't you worry, none. I'm strong enough now to take it, whatever it is. Is it Annie?" Her voice rose in growing fear. "Is she—"

"No," Frake broke in quickly. "I saw her just above two hours ago."

Violet leaned back against the pillows, the worst of her fears relieved. Her gaze, though, remained fixed on his face. "Samuel?" she hazarded. "It's him, ain't it? No, don't you go tryin' to deny it, I can see it in your face. Have you nabbed him?"

Frake sank into the chair. "I wish I had."

She swallowed. "Tell me. What's he gone and done now? Something dreadful, ain't it?"

"No, not exactly. It ain't him that's gone and done it. He—" He broke off, unable to bring himself to say the words that would cause her so much pain.

Violet studied his face. "Meanin' as how it's been gone and done *to* him?" She managed an encouraging smile. "He ain't never dead is he?" The half-joking light faded from her eyes as she must have seen the confirmation in his expression. "Dear God, he is. He—" She shook her head as if trying to deny the fact.

Frake nodded. "I—I'm sorry."

Violet closed her eyes and reached for Rose, asleep in the cradle at her side. Disturbed, the baby cried and fussed for a couple of minutes, then subsided against her mother. Violet held her gently close, burying her face in the blanket wrapping.

Haltingly, Frake related the events of the early

hours of the morning. Violet listened, the whole while rocking back and forth and murmuring to Rose. When he finally trailed off, silence fell over them.

At last, Violet looked up. "Annie's blamin' you, ain't she?"

A bleak half-smile of acknowledgment tugged at the corner of his mouth. "She could be right."

"No." A shuddering sigh escaped Violet. "He is— was—always such a one for tryin' to snatch his opportunities and leapin' into trouble. It's—" Tears filled her eyes and she broke off.

"I shouldn't have told you," he said quickly.

She shook her head vigorously, then wiped her eyes on the muslin sleeve of her night dress and averted her face again. "Better I hear it at once. I always knew as how he was headed for a bad end. But it's still a shock when it up and happens. Annie, though—she always hoped as how he'd change. I knew he wouldn't, that it was just a matter of time afore someone come to bring me the news. Where's Annie, now?"

"I don't know. She ran away. It seemed best to let her go at the time, but now—" He grimaced. "I don't know where she could have gone or how to find her, and the worry of it will drive me right into Bedlam."

Violet blinked back the moisture that brimmed in her eyes. "She—she'll have gone to Mrs. Appleby. There ain't no one else she could turn to."

Mrs. Appleby. Relief flooded through him, and he let out a long, shaky breath. He should have thought of the wetnurse. Annie would be safe and comforted, and he'd have word of her when the woman came to tend Rose.

"She can't blame me any more than I blame myself," he said.

Violet turned her head into the pillow. She'd cry as soon as he left her, he guessed, but she'd accepted his story and her brother's ill fate. She would mourn for someone who had been so close a part of her life, but she didn't make it into any great tragedy. As she'd said, with a brother like Samuel, this was going to happen sooner or later. One just always hoped for the later, though.

When she spoke at last, her voice sounded calmer, more controlled. "You was only doin' your duty. Them as runs afoul of the law takes their chances. Don't you never go thinkin' as how it's your fault."

"I doubt Annie'll agree with you. Do you need anything? You're sure?" He stood. "I've brought your brother's things here. I thought as how Annie might go through them to see if she can discover some clue as to what he might have known that I missed."

"I'll help, but—"

"You rest," Frake stuck in quickly. "I don't want Annie blaming me for you collapsing again."

Violet managed a weak smile. "I won't do that. I'm not the stubborn member of my family."

Meaning Annie was, he supposed. He made Violet a pot of tea from one of the packets left by Nanny Gossett, placed everything she might need by her bedside, then left her to grieve after her own fashion. Sylvester ran past him into her room as he went out.

Somehow, that cat always seemed to know where he'd be of the most use.

He stopped beside the sofa, frowning. He had a great deal to do that morning. Specifically, he wanted to lay his hands on the villain who murdered the brother of Annie and Violet. But since that didn't seem possible at the moment, he'd settle for making any real progress on the case for a change.

His first call was on Samuel's employer in Albemarle Street. He found Sir William at home and awake, lounging back in his chair in a sunny salon overlooking the street. On the table before him rested a tankard of ale and the remains of a rare beefsteak.

"I've already heard about young Gooden," Sir William announced as his major domo ushered Frake into the room. He didn't sound in the least bit upset. "My grooms have been before you with the news. I have been expecting you." He made no move to offer Frake either a seat or a share in the meal.

Frake eyed him, his expression bland. "I thought as maybe you might tell me where you were last night."

"Where I—" Sir William's eyebrows rose. "Really, my good man, I utterly fail to see what that has to say to anything."

"Do you? Then let's just say as how I'm naturally curious, like."

A flush inched up the man's neck and spread across his face. "If you really must know," he said, and a touch of petulance crept into his voice, "I was here. All evening. Where else should I be? I'm in mourning for my uncle, must I remind you? I should think that rather than running around, asking me ridiculous questions, it would be your primary business to be discovering who murdered him."

"It is." Frake kept his steady gaze on Templeton, and had the satisfaction of seeing the flush deepen. "You're quite sure as how you didn't go out nowheres?"

Templeton opened his mouth, then closed it again, casting Frake a resentful glance. "Now that you mention it, I believe I might have gone out briefly to Mrs. Wickham's. Needed to see someone—not that it's any of your concern. You haven't come even a bit closer to settling this affair, have you?" he demanded, going on the offensive.

Frake shook his head, his expression mournful. "There's someone out there who knows something, and whoever it is ain't talking. At least," he added, "not yet."

A cunning expression settled over Templeton's features. "You need help." His tone held a note of smugness. "I'll tell you what I'll do, my good man. I will offer a reward of one—no, two—of two thousand pounds, to anyone who helps find the real murderer of my uncle. Will that be of assistance to you?"

Frake rocked back on his heels, trying to hide his surprise. "A very big inducement to talk, is two thousand pounds," he said after a moment. "I'll be mighty surprised, mighty surprised indeed, if that don't bring forth some result."

It had, already, he reflected as he took his leave.

So Templeton wished to play the role of the outraged and grieving nephew. But for whose benefit? Frake's?

That seemed most likely. The sum he named was staggering. And somehow, he doubted Templeton had any intention—or even expectation—of parting with that much money. No, the offer had been to convince the law that he had an earnest desire to discover the identity of the murderer. Why? Because he *didn't* want it uncovered? Or because he knew it *couldn't* be?

Frake slowed his step. Who else should he see this morning, and what could he gain? Cornelia Leeds? There was a real possibility. She'd been flirting with Samuel Gooden last night, trying to pry information out of him. Could Samuel, in hopes of luring her into a romantic tryst, have implied he knew a dangerous amount about her involvement in Sir Joshua's murder?

Or what of Captain Bevis? Could the captain have followed Mrs. Leeds to the mews, then killed Samuel—either in a jealous rage or to protect himself or his mistress from what Samuel knew?

Then there was Viscount Daylesford. That young nobleman would do just about anything to keep his sister ignorant of the extent of his gaming—and perhaps worse sins, as well? If Samuel tried blackmail on him, killing the groom would probably have seemed to the desperate viscount like his only choice.

As for Mrs. Wickham, a comfortable little coze with that woman just might prove interesting. Samuel had haunted her gaming establishment, visiting the kitchen maid Ruby, for months before Annie appeared on the scene. Mrs. Wickham might have become familiar with his presence, perhaps even employed him to undertake a few little tasks for her. He doubted Samuel would be too particular about the nature of any odd jobs he did, as long as the pay was good.

His first thought had been that Samuel's murderer had been a man. But that didn't necessarily have to be true; it would have been very possible for a woman to have killed him. The groom was slightly built. A woman could have hit him over the head as easily as a man—more easily, perhaps, since Samuel probably wouldn't have expected it.

Neither Mrs. Wickham nor Mrs. Leeds could have carried his body into the stall, though; either one would have had to drag him. And if Samuel had been dragged, there might have been traces left, such as marks of boot heels in the dirt, or even disarranged straw. If no such traces existed, that would make it more probable his suspect was a man. Why hadn't he checked?

Because his mind had been on Annie, not where it should have been, on the task at hand. Annie. . . . Mrs. Appleby, he told himself sharply. Remember Mrs. Appleby. Annie had to be there, and safe.

With an effort, he brought his reflections back to the stable. By now, so much time had passed, the normal activities of the grooms and horses must have disguised any lingering traces of dragging. He was probably wasting his time. Still, for Annie's sake, he'd try anything to discover who was responsible for her brother's death.

On that determined note, he set forth to pay one more visit to the mews. As he let himself in, he found to his surprise that a number of stalls stood empty. More horses were missing than usually went out at the same time, considering only one lad could be with them. Only the head groom remained, the inevitable straw hanging out of his mouth, combing out the mane on a black gelding.

Loomis looked up, saw Frake where he stood in the doorway, and strolled over. "Now, what might you be doin' back 'ere? More questions? Already told you, we did. Don't remember a thing once we'd started on that blue ruin."

"The place looks almost empty. Where're the horses this morning?"

The straw twitched in Loomis's mouth. "Sellin' 'em, is Sir William. All 'is uncle's cattle. Sendin' 'em off to Tattersall's."

Frake drew out his pipe and twisted the stem between his fingers. "How long has he been planning this?"

Loomis turned his head and spat. " 'Appened all a-sudden-like, this mornin'. Could've knocked me over with a feather, you could've."

"Did he give any reason?"

"Says as 'ow 'e can't afford to keep two stables 'ere in town. This one, it's got more room and is closer to Templeton 'Ouse, so's 'e's movin' 'is own animals over and gettin' rid o' these."

Getting rid of them, was he? And on the morning after one of them had been used to trample a dead man to make it appear an accident. Frake cast a rapid glance down the line of stalls. Five horses missing. Including the one found with Gooden. Coincidence? He could think of no advantage to the murderer in thus quickly disposing of the animal.

He turned his attention to the ground of the stable, but it was as he'd feared. The passage of people and animals had obliterated any signs of a struggle or the dragging of a body. If any had ever existed. Now he'd never know.

He had run himself out of ideas, he reflected as he turned his frustrated steps toward home. Yet the solution must be out there somewhere, some scrap of information on which he had yet to lay his hands that would make everything else fall into place. He just had to find it.

Several people had reason to hate or fear Sir Joshua, possibly enough to murder him. But only one of them did it. That meant one of them had a very great deal to gain by his death—or a great deal to lose by his continuing to live.

Samuel, somehow, must hold the key.

Frake's brow puckered in thought. Samuel. What he did, to whom he talked, where he went. That's what he had to concentrate on. His step picked up as one more avenue of enquiry occurred to him. The kitchen maid Ruby.

Ruby herself opened the door of Mrs. Wickham's for him. Not Annie. That only served as a painful reminder that on top of everything else Annie'd had to suffer, she had lost her job last night. If only she'd let him comfort her, take care of her . . .

Ruby eyed him with a speculative gleam in her wide-set gray eyes. "Well, now, if it ain't the Runner. Ain't none of 'em up yet." She fluttered her lashes and leaned on the edge of the door, making no move to close it.

"That's all right, then." He pulled himself together and gave her his best smile. "It's you as I've come to talk to, anyways."

"Me? And 'ere was me thinkin' as 'ow it were Annie you liked." She stepped back into the hall, drawing the door open, inviting him within. "Now, what would you be wantin' from me?"

"Just to know a little about Samuel Gooden. In here?" He crossed the hall to the front salon and opened the door into it, holding it for her.

"Oh, 'im." She gave her head a flirtatious toss and strolled past, slowing to brush against him as she did so. Inside, she seated herself on the sofa and looked invitingly up at him.

He took the chair opposite, then leaned forward in a confidential manner. Immediately, she copied his pose. "What time did Gooden leave here last night?" he asked.

Her brows rose. "Last night? Whatever 'as last night got to do with old Sir Joshua?"

"Possibly quite a bit. When did he leave?"

She frowned, her gaze unfocusing as she thought. "Earlier than usual," she said at last. "About one, I'd say. Afore we carried up the supper. That I remember, on account of 'ow 'e weren't 'ere to 'elp set things out, as 'e does sometimes."

"Did he tell you why he was leaving—or where he was going?"

She sniffed. "Said as 'ow there was someone 'e 'ad to see. Some business deal. 'E said as 'ow we're goin' to be rich, and 'ow 'e's goin' to buy us an inn somewheres far from London." She shook her head. " 'E's always talkin' big like that, but I never listen. Big boast, small roast, I says."

"Where do you think he went?" Frake pursued.

Her expression set in a hard line, though she gave a casual shrug. "Maybe to see some other girl. I don't care."

He couldn't help but wonder how much she really did care, what she actually felt for Samuel Gooden. Whatever it was, it didn't rule out throwing blatant lures at other men.

"Now," she rested her chin in her hands. "Why're you askin' so many questions? You ain't goin' to nab 'im, are you? 'Is sister, she wouldn't like that none."

He met and held her gaze. "I'm afraid it's too late for that." Gently, he told her of the staged accident.

For a very long minute she said nothing, just stared into space. Then, in slow motion, she lowered her hands, folding them together, clenching them until her knuckles showed as white as her face. "We was goin' to 'ave an inn," she breathed, her voice barely audible. It quavered as she added: "We was goin' to— Oh, damn 'im!" She shook with the violence of her oath. "Damn 'im! The fool! 'E know'd somethin', 'e did, and now it's gone and gotten 'im killed! I didn't need no inn. I was 'appy just as we was."

Frake leaned closer and caught her trembling hands. "What did he know?"

" 'E wouldn't tell me. Maybe it weren't nothin'. 'E likes—liked to talk, to make everyone think as 'ow 'e's—was someone important, which 'e weren't." She sniffed, but no tears showed in her eyes.

Too early, Frake realized. "You have no idea who he was going to meet last night?"

"If'n I knew 'e meant it, that 'e was plannin' on doin' somethin' dangerous—" She broke off.

"You'd have stopped him?" he suggested.

She nodded, then tilted her head sideways to look at him. "Never could believe a word 'e told me. I know'd I wasn't the only girl 'e was seein', but—" She buried her face in her hands and bent forward, then rocked gently back and forth.

Frake waited, watching, but no sobs broke from her. They would soon, he wagered.

The door opened and Captain Palfrey paused on the threshold, eyeing them in surprise. Frake drew him back into the hall, closing the door behind him, and once more made his explanations about Gooden.

Captain Palfrey listened, frowning. "Poor Ruby. You needn't worry on her behalf, though. There's a line of young men, any one of them more reliable than that Gooden, just waiting for a chance to see her."

"Popular, is she?" Frake felt a wave of relief.

"If you ask me," the captain confided, "this is the

best thing that could have happened to her. That damned little wretch was too good looking by half. He turned Ruby's head. She'll get over him soon enough."

But for now, Frake reflected, he was glad Samuel had someone besides his two sisters to grieve for him. It didn't seem proper for a man to leave this world without people regretting his absence.

Somewhere, though, someone quite possibly celebrated that leave-taking.

A strident knocking on the door interrupted his reflection. Palfrey himself opened it, and Captain Bevis strolled in. The new arrival cast a dismissive glance at Palfrey, then spotted Frake.

"Thought I'd find you here." Bevis eyed him with a mixture of satisfaction and distaste. "You seem to be making quite a mull out of this case. All this time, barging about, disrupting people's lives, asking endless questions, and what do you have to show for it? A second murder!"

Frake rocked back on his heels, cutting off his flash of anger. He didn't need to be reminded of how abominably he'd failed Annie. He schooled his features into an expression of only mild interest. "Now, how did you come to hear about that, sir?"

"Templeton told me, of course."

"Sir William?" Frake's eyebrows rose in polite enquiry. "I only just left him a short while ago myself."

"Are you implying undue haste on his part to bring me the news?" Bevis's lip curled. "He merely did me the courtesy of paying me a call to inform me of the sad event."

"Why would he think you'd be interested in the death of one of his uncle's grooms?"

Bevis straightened and his eyes took on a glint of steel. "My good man, you seem to be forgetting that I was somewhat acquainted with the fellow."

"That's right, so you was. Knew a lot about you, did he?"

"I fail to see why—" Bevis broke off, and a look of exasperation tinged with amusement settled over his countenance. "Good lord, man. You still consider me a suspect in Sir Joshua's death! In my own defense, I must point out that there are several people who benefited considerably more than I ever could have by that murder. I might find Mrs. Leeds to be a delightful companion, and we have certainly shared a measure of pleasure in one another's company, but I fail to see why I should kill the gentleman whose suit she most favored. She had made it quite clear to me from the beginning that she would not accept mine."

"Well, now, what you say is certainly true. Especially considering as how Sir Joshua already knew about you and Mrs. Leeds, and had up and abandoned any—er—pretensions to the lady's hand."

Bevis gave a brisk nod. "Glad to have that settled. Now, would you be willing to tell me *why* someone felt it necessary to murder young Gooden?"

"Easy enough. Seems as how he was blackmailing someone."

"Blackmail! The very devil of a business. What have you found out?"

When Frake finished the tale, Bevis drew out his snuffbox and helped himself to a pinch. "Blackmail. Good lord. I—" He broke off, his expression arrested. "I think I may know what it was about."

"What?" Frake reached for his Occurrence Book.

"I told you I was acquainted with Gooden." Bevis replaced the snuffbox in his pocket. "I got to know him a little when he served Oliver Templeton in the army. At the time, I didn't think he had an ounce of loyalty in him that couldn't be bought with a drink. It surprised me, what care he took of his master in bringing him home. It—it formed a bond between us."

"Yes, sir?" Frake prompted as Bevis fell silent.

Bevis frowned. "The lad started drinking heavily after Oliver died. Took it to heart. That's when he took to stealing things, too, I think. Trying to get up some money to have a better life while he could." He glanced sideways at Frake. "I believe he was blackmailing William Templeton, and not just to get his job back after being fired. He told me he'd served too many Templetons to be treated like dirt."

Frake stopped his rapid writing. "Told you that, did he? When?"

"Early last evening. We talk—talked—about Oliver sometimes. And other things, too, when he was foxed." Bevis paced several restless steps. "I don't like bearing tales," he said, "but I owe it to Oliver and Sir Joshua. You know that Gooden had gotten a bequest from Sir Joshua. What you don't know is that he wanted it doubled. I heard him arguing with Templeton, saying he'd tell the world what he knew if Templeton didn't come through."

"And just what did he know?"

Bevis's mouth tightened. "That, I'm afraid, I didn't hear. But by God, I wish I had."

Frake left the gaming house a few minutes later, bound for home to see if Mary Appleby had arrived with any word of Annie. If not— He considered the propriety of calling out his patrol to help him search London for her. She would never forgive him, of that he felt certain, but he needed to know she was safe.

He strode through the streets, his thoughts flitting from Annie to his suspects and back again. Daylesford and his massive gaming debts. Sir William and the title and fortune. Annie . . .

Captain Bevis and his determination to see Mrs. Leeds marry a fortune. Mrs. Cornelia Leeds herself, for the same reason. Mrs. Wickham to save her gaming house.

Annie . . .

Frake increased his restless pace. He needed to know why Samuel died. That he was blackmailing his murderer seemed most likely, after what Ruby had divulged. But over what? He'd heard guesses, but they weren't necessarily right. Was it over the murder of Sir Joshua? Or over something else?

Whatever it was, it had to be sufficient to warrant a murder. Unsubstantiated accusations could be laughed off. Therefore it seemed most likely that

Samuel possessed some sort of physical, damning proof of whatever iniquity the person was guilty.

And that meant searching Samuel's belongings once more.

Nineteen

Frake strode through the streets, determined this time not to miss a single clue that might be contained in Samuel's trunk. Gooden died for a reason. That fact kept repeating over and over in Frake's mind. Gooden died for a reason. It might be the same one why Sir Joshua died, since Samuel, as his groom, might have overheard something said to or by his master. Or he might have died to protect the murderer. Either way, solving Samuel's death should lead him to much needed answers in Sir Joshua's. And it might induce Annie to regard him more favorably.

Annie . . .

As he let himself into the sitting room, the sound of two female voices greeted him. For one fleeting moment his hopes rose, then he recognized the carrying tones of Nanny Gossett and the softer speech of Mary Appleby. He knocked on the bedroom door, and the scraping of a chair sounded within. Nanny and the black and white Mortimer looked out at him. "Has Annie—" he began.

Nanny gestured for silence and slipped out to join him. The orange kitten darted out between her feet and latched onto his ankle. Mortimer watched with interest, sniffing Frake's boot to see if it offered anything promising.

"Where's Annie?" Frake asked, his gaze intent on Nanny's face.

"At Mrs. Appleby's. Now, don't you worry, Benjamin. You just give her time. Violet's asleep, which is the best thing for her, and I've made up a special tisane. I'll just be going, now. Octavius? Ah, there you are." She collected the gray cat from the sofa and headed out into the hall. Mortimer followed, with the kitten batting at his swaying tail.

At least Annie was safe. But she wasn't here where he wanted her. Where he needed her. Relief gave way to despondency, and he sank into his chair. No use dwelling on her absence, he told himself sharply. For her sake, he had to get on with the business at hand.

Bending over the trunk, he unlatched the lid and swung it back. He had thrown everything in in a haphazard manner, just wanting to collect it all in one place so he could move it. Now he took out the boots, which had landed on top, and began a painstaking inch-by-inch search. He found nothing stuffed inside, nothing slid into any cut seams, nothing inserted into the heels.

He set them aside and drew out a much stained and mended shirt. This he folded and placed on the floor. Next he brought forth a pair of breeches, but as he started to lay these on top of the shirt, Sylvester joined him, settling on the garment, adjusting it with his kneading paws to better fit his feline contours.

Frake scooped him up, positioned him on his lap where the cat couldn't hook anything with his claws, and resumed his labors.

He'd been at this for perhaps twenty minutes when a hesitant knock sounded without. Frake froze, not daring to hope, yet every part of his being crying out for it to be Annie. With slow, deliberate movements, he ousted the indignant cat and opened the door.

Annie, her cheeks unnaturally pale, her eyes red-rimmed, stood stiffly erect in the hall, her hands folded before her. She didn't look at him, but rather studied the toes of her shoes that peeped out from beneath her dress. She was all right, unharmed—and she was here. Without conscious thought he reached out to take her into his arms, only to stop as she flinched away.

"I've come for my sister." She kept her gaze lowered, as if afraid to meet his.

He fought back the pain of her rejection. Time, he reminded himself. She needed time. She suffered from the shock of her brother's murder. She was trying to shoulder all her burdens by herself. She still needed help, whether she realized it or not. Somehow, he would see that she got it.

He retreated a pace, allowing her room to enter without having to brush against him. She remained where she stood, as if loathe to cross the threshold into his apartments. She regarded him as little better than a murderer himself, he reflected, and the dull ache within him throbbed with a new rawness.

"If you want Violet and Rose," he said more

brusquely than he'd intended, "you'll have to come in sometime." He struggled to regain control while she advanced three reluctant steps onto his carpet. He closed the door. Still, she didn't look up.

Stay calm, he reminded himself. She'd gone through too much. Her responsibilities must terrify her, believing she had no one to help her. Well, she did—if he could only convince her to let him. At the moment, he didn't see how.

"I—we'd best be goin' straight away." She cast an uncertain look toward the closed bedroom door.

"Where're you planning to take her?" He studied her pale face, willing her to acknowledge him.

A film of tears misted her eyes. "We'll manage."

"Annie." Concern—love—overpowered caution. He reached for her, placing his hands on her shoulders, rocking her gently, wanting to draw her close but knowing the wisdom of refraining. "Annie, love. You have no home, no job, no one to turn to. Please, let me help." With one finger he brought her chin up so he could study her face. Her eyes remained swollen from prolonged crying, but she'd washed away the other traces.

He wiped away the tear that trembled anew on her lashes. "Now, let's be practical. You can't move Violet yet. Even if you won't listen to me, I doubt Nanny Gossett will allow it."

"But—"

"Annie—" His hold on her tightened. He could feel the warmth of her skin through the thinness of her gown. It proved highly distracting, making him want to trace the line of her throat. "Annie, if there was anything as I could do to bring him back, if there was anything as I could have done different to prevent this—" He broke off as a spasm of pain crossed her face.

"It's over and done with, and too late to change." Her words came out with repressed violence. She pulled away from him. "I just want to take my sister and Rose and go as far from here as we can get."

"And what about Samuel? Are you just going to forget about him? Or is blaming me for his death enough? I thought you was a fighter, Annie. I thought you'd want to help me find the person who murdered him."

"I do!" She spun back to face him. "But I ain't no Runner." She made the appellation sound contemptible. "I don't like spyin', and I don't like tellin' no tales."

"No, none of us does. But remember, we're trying to establish who is innocent as well as who is guilty. There's some as would consider that helping folk. And I have something I need for you to do that won't be a betrayal of anyone."

Her only response was a sniff.

He fought down his hurt and frustration. "If you won't do it to help me, then do it for your brother's sake."

For a long minute she said nothing. Then grudgingly, her voice rife with suspicion, she asked: "What?"

"Go through your brother's things, search everywhere. I've learned from Ruby that he was meeting with someone last night, and he expected to get a great deal of money."

Her eyes clouded with renewed pain. "Blackmail."

He nodded. "For that to work, he must have had some proof, something that would make me—or anyone else—believe whatever he said."

She regarded him with a steady glare. "Meanin' as how no one would rightly take the word of a groom over that of a lady or gentleman?"

Frake's mouth twisted wryly. "It's the way of the world, Annie. Your brother knew it. So see if he had any proof."

She studied the trunk as if reluctant to touch it. "Is this all he had?"

"All we could find. The other two grooms helped me gather it. I was checking the seams in his clothes to see if any slips of paper could have been hidden anywheres inside."

Annie nodded and set to work. Frake watched for a moment while she bent over the trunk. At least she was here, safe, where he could see her and hear her voice. He reached across her, took out a coat, and began his careful search.

Annie took inordinate care in folding the shirt she'd just checked. Her fingers traced the fine lines of a mended tear, then moved on to another. "I patched all these myself, I did," she said. "I don't hardly recall a time when he'd come callin' to see me without bringin' his latest tears and stains for me to tend." She laid the clothing aside, and her fingers lingered on the much-worn fabric.

Frake paused in his work. "Perhaps you could sell some of his things. Buy something for little Rose in memory of her uncle."

"Like food." Annie pulled out a waistcoat, and once again her fingers found each of the neatly mended tears and patches.

They continued for some time in silence, until the trunk stood empty, its former contents in neat piles on the carpet. Annie sat back in her chair, cradling Sylvester in her lap, as Frake checked the interior for a false bottom. Frustrated, he closed the lid, then placed the boots along the side.

"Nothin'," Annie declared.

Frake sat in silence across from her, glaring at the offending trunk as if it deliberately concealed secrets. "I was so sure as how there'd be something as we could lay a-hold of."

Annie caught Sylvester's front paws in one hand, disentangling his claws from her muslin skirts. "And now we've gone and searched in the most obvious place."

Frake looked up, his attention arrested. "Good lord, you're right."

She didn't look at him. "If it was me, and I had somethin' as I didn't want no one to find, I'd hide it where no one wasn't likely to go lookin' for it."

"Now, where—the mews?"

"Don't see as where he could of put it nowheres else." She rose.

"You check on Violet, I'll find us a hackney." He strode out the door.

Several minutes later, as a jarvey pulled his equipage up before him, Annie hurried along the alley. "Violet's still asleep," she told him as he helped her in. "And Mrs. Appleby's taken Rose to visit Nanny Gossett."

Frake gave the direction of Sir Joshua's stable and swung up beside her. As he settled into the seat, he asked, "Any idea where? Upstairs or down?"

"Up," she said after a moment. "Down, there's no tellin' as who might stumble across it."

"In his mattress, I suppose," Frake muttered. "No, that would be obvious, too. Well, we'll just have to look. Unless— Could he have given it to Ruby?"

Annie's brow puckered. "No," she said after a long moment. "He never trusted nothin' to nobody. He'd want it where he could check on it, he would. If he really had somethin'."

The hackney set them down at the end of the mews. They walked quickly through the bustle of carriages and horses departing for the park, and at last reached their destination. Frake let them in.

Neither of the other two grooms were anywhere to be seen. Probably at the park—or just avoiding this place where their comrade was so recently murdered. Just as well. He'd rather have this time alone with Annie. He might now have very little left with her.

Annie hung back in the doorway, her expressive countenance for once an unreadable mask. She drew a deep breath, then strode forward, staring straight before her, never once permitting her glance to stray toward the line of stalls.

Silently Frake cursed himself. He shouldn't have brought her here, to the scene where she had discovered her brother's body a scant twelve hours ago. Had dedication to duty blinded him to the feelings of others?

He reached out to her, but she pulled away, tension radiating from her in a tangible wave. She ran up the stairs to the loft, starting as she stepped on the stair near the top that squeaked. Frake eased himself over it.

Annie pushed open the door to the sleeping quarters, then stopped dead. A soft gasp escaped her. Frake took one look at her rigid stance, then set her aside and stepped within.

Clothes, boots, bedding—everything in the long chamber had been thrown about, ransacked, as if someone had made a desperate search. Frake's hands clenched. Annie took an unsteady step inside, then bent to start straightening up.

"It seems," Frake said, grim, "as how someone had the same idea we had."

Annie shook her head, her shocked gaze moving slowly about the chamber. In her hands she clutched a pillow from which feathers drifted through a long gash. "I—I'm ever that glad you had Samuel's belongings away from here. I don't think I could've borne it if they'd been invaded. Violated." She shuddered as she advanced farther, walking the length of the low-pitched chamber.

Frake kicked the broken bed frame nearest him. If

anything had been hidden in there, it would have been found. Offhand, he didn't think anything could have been secreted anywhere in the loft and escaped discovery. The beds, the trunks, the wall, the floorboards—

Annie turned back to face him. "Someone wants somethin' right badly."

"Which means something solid does—or did—exist." Yet somehow, he didn't despair. The hairs along the back of his neck prickled, as if he were on the verge of discovering something momentous that lay just beyond his grasp. "Now," he said slowly, his gaze scanning the torn-apart loft, "if only our villain didn't go finding what he wanted."

"Samuel must of known as how there'd be a search, once he tried blackmail." Annie looked about. "So he wouldn't go leavin' it where it could be found."

She circled the chamber, touching the walls, the long, narrow windows, the broken pieces of furniture. "Nothin' here seems likely. Too easy to search. The whole room is too obvious. That's not like Sammy." She paced out the door.

Frake followed, watching her, trusting her instincts when it came to her brother. She paused on the landing, gazing down the stairs, then descended first one, then another. The third creaked as her foot settled on it, and she grasped the railing.

"The stair." She descended two more, then turned and knelt. Her fingers searched along the edges. "Nothin'."

Frake found he held his breath. "Try the next one up."

She did, then the landing. "All I'm findin' are splinters." She looked up from where she sat. "That and dirt. I—" She broke off, staring over his shoulder. "The sconce." Her voice rose with excitement as she came to her feet and reached for the metal bracket on the wall. "Something . . ."

Frake brought out his pocket knife. She took it and pried up the backing plate. It came away easily, and a folded sheet of paper slid down several inches from where it had been trapped against the rough boards. She caught the corner of the page, drew it out, and handed it to Frake.

"If you don't mind," a man's voice drawled from below, "I think I'll take that."

Frake tensed, and his fingers closed about the paper. Captain Bevis stood just beneath them, looking up. And he held a horse pistol in his hand.

Twenty

Frake cast a wary glance at Annie. She remained on the third step, one hand still extended toward him as she'd handed him the page. Her steady gaze fastened on Bevis, her expression unreadable. Frake could see no way of getting her to safety, out of range of that pistol.

He'd have to stall, until an opportunity presented itself.

He caught her hand and drew her up the steps to his side. "Now, what would you be wanting this for?" he called down to Bevis. Slowly, as unobtrusively as possible, he inched her behind him.

"Let us say it is something that interests me." Bevis raised the pistol. "You will drop it down to me. Now."

"Really?" Frake twitched it open. He could think of no means to escape the mews from up here, un-less— "Crawl out the broken window and over the roof tops," he murmured, giving Annie a shove. "Hurry." She might be able to do it while he diverted Bevis. If only she'd just move! "Now," he said louder, "what's this all about, then?" He gave her another push, which she ignored.

Bevis's arm trembled. "Throw it down or I'll shoot. I mean it."

Annie plucked the sheet from Frake's hand, but instead of complying with Bevis's orders, she scanned the contents. "This here is signed by Captain Oliver Templeton and Captain Thomas Bevis," she announced.

Frake tensed as Bevis strode toward the base of the staircase. "Now, you won't go shooting in here." He kept his voice calm and reasonable. "Too many people would notice, out there in the mews. You don't want to go getting caught, now, do you?"

"I—I'll do what I have to." Bevis spoke through gritted teeth.

Frake eased Annie further behind him. "Get back in the room," he murmured.

"He killed my brother," she breathed back. "I want to know why—and I'm goin' to see him caught."

"Then get that paper—and you—to safety." With a frustrated mutter at her refusal to budge, he positioned himself squarely in front of her. "Now, why," he called to Bevis, his tone purely conversational, "is this here document so all-important to you?"

"I told you to throw it down here." Bevis put his foot on the bottom step.

Frake shook his head. "Two murders already, and all for this?"

Bevis gave a short laugh. "Who said anything about murder? I merely want that paper. It should never have been made." The pistol shook in his hands. "That damned groom . . ."

Annie, from behind him, said: "This here says as how Captain Bevis agrees to sell out of the army if Mr. Oliver doesn't expose his cow—" She stumbled over the word.

"Cowardice," Frake finished for her. He reached behind him and squeezed her hand.

Annie peered over his shoulder. "Why did you ever go writin' this in the first place?" she asked. "Once Mr. Oliver knew as you'd sold out—"

Bevis gave a short, mirthless laugh. "To keep me from rejoining. He took from me my one hope of earning a living."

"But not one you liked, I'll wager," Frake stuck in.

Bevis's lip curled. "At the moment, that is of no importance. You will give me that paper, and I will destroy it. Then we can all forget it ever existed."

"Except I have no intention of forgetting the murders of Sir Joshua and Samuel Gooden," Frake reminded him.

Bevis froze. "They have nothing to do with me. You couldn't possibly prove—" He stopped, and a slow smile spread across his face. "No. I'm no murderer."

"You are!" Annie clutched Frake's upper arm.

Frake's jaw clenched. Their "proof" might well *not* be enough. The paper might provide a motive, but it didn't actually prove anything except the charge of cowardice. Bevis would probably get away with both killings.

As if reading Frake's mind, Bevis grinned at them; the tension eased from his stance. "Even if I were," he said with deliberation, "it could never be proved. No clues were left. No one saw . . . the murderer."

Annie drew a ragged breath. "Oh, yes, someone did. My brother saw you."

"Gooden?" Bevis's lip curled in a sneer. "Even if that happened to be true, he can hardly testify to that effect now, can he?"

Annie straightened. "He already has."

Would Bevis believe Annie's bluff? Frake wondered. He cast a rapid glance about, measuring distances. He wanted to capture Bevis, bring him to justice, but not at the expense of any harm coming to Annie.

"Samuel, he went and wrote it all out," Annie continued. "How he seen you enterin' the library and heard the shot that killed Sir Joshua."

"Impossible." Bevis's sneer became more pronounced, yet the hand with which he held the pistol shook with more violence.

Frake clenched his teeth. They didn't have any proof; if Bevis continued his denials, the man would win. Unless—

Unless. Annie wasn't the only one who could bluff.

Frake reached into his pocket and drew forth a folded piece of paper. A request from Nanny Gossett for more mugwort and chamomile, but Bevis didn't need to know that. He squared his shoulders—covering as much of Annie as he could. "We already have all the proof we need as to your murderin' Sir

Joshua," he said steadily. "We only come here to discover the motive."

Bevis stilled. He opened his mouth, but no sound came out. Very slowly, he began to shake his head.

"Sir Joshua learned of your cowardice in battle from young Gooden, a cowardice that killed his son," Frake declared, at last understanding. "He intended to ruin you with that knowledge, didn't he? And not just socially, neither, seeing as how you live off patrons—or rather *patronesses* like Mrs. Leeds. And you needn't think as how killing us and taking the papers will help you none," he added as a spasm crossed Bevis's face. "This here is only a copy of Gooden's statement. The original is already safe in Bow Street."

"I—I might kill you just for the satisfaction of seeing you die." Bevis's voice rose toward hysteria as he braced the pistol with his other hand.

Frake spun and grasped Annie, throwing her backward toward the loft room. In the same motion he continued in a circle, dropping to the floor and drawing his own pistol from the waistband of his breeches. He took aim below, steadying his arm against the railing. Behind him, Annie crouched against the door frame.

Bevis quaked all over, and his mouth worked as he stared up at them. Then, with a sound somewhere between a laugh and a sob, he drew his pistol back, weighed it in his hand a moment, then raised it to his temple. In spite of himself, Frake flinched at the deafening explosion.

As Bevis started to crumple, a wordless cry escaped Annie. Frake turned to her, gathering her into his arms, burying her face against his chest. He held her close, allowing the rapid pounding of her heart to replace in his mind the sound of the pistol fire.

But as much as he needed her—as he hoped she needed him—this wasn't finished yet. He set her gently aside and ran down the rickety stairs. In the stalls beyond, the horses stamped and whickered their fright. And above, Annie sat shaken and drained.

He swore softly and bent over Bevis's body. No breath remained, not even the trace of a pulse. At least the man had made a clean job of it. There was nothing he could do for him—and nothing the world could now do to him.

He turned back to what was for him the more pressing need, and mounted the steps two at a time. "Annie, love?" He knelt beside her, gathering her once more into his arms.

"It's over."

She rested her head against his shoulder, her eyes wide and staring. "We—we couldn't of proved it," she managed.

"No. If it weren't for your quick thinking, he'd have gotten away with two murders. Possibly four, if you want to go counting us."

She shuddered and snuggled closer, clutching folds of his coat.

Below them, the door to the stable area burst open and a strange groom ran in two steps, then stopped dead. "Crickey!" he breathed.

With a muttered oath, Frake released Annie. She

pulled back, covering her face with her hands, breathing deeply. Frake rose, and the groom jumped back, staring at him with horror. "I'm from Bow Street," Frake announced as he began descending the stairs once more.

The young man hesitated, though his gaze shifted toward the door through which he'd just come. "What's goin' on 'ere?"

"A murderer has just killed himself," Frake announced in his most authoritative voice. "I need someone to carry a message for me."

"Murderer, is 'e?" The groom regarded Bevis's body with wide-eyed fascination, as if he were a raree in a freak show. "Cor," he breathed, apparently gaining enthusiasm now that he knew he was in no danger.

Frake drew out his pencil and Occurrence Book, scribbled a quick note, and ripped the page free. This he folded and handed to the groom, along with several coins. "For a hackney," he explained. "To Bow Street. Be quick about it."

"Aye." The groom stared at the largesse with wide, appreciative eyes.

"There'll be more when you get back with my men," Frake added.

The groom nodded with enthusiasm, then darted out the door.

"He'll probably run all the way there to save the coins," Frake said reflectively. He looked up to where Annie remained huddled on the landing. "Annie, love, I'm sorry. I'll have to stay here and wait. I'd rather escort you home, but you see how it is. I feel like I'm failing you again."

"That—" She broke off and shook her head. "About Sammy— There weren't nothin' as you could of done different." Her voice sounded hollow. She met his gaze, then looked down at her hands. "I don't blame you none for it, and—and I'm that sorry for what I said this mornin'. With Samuel—well, Violet always said as how it were only a matter of time afore somethin' like this happened."

"Annie—" He held out his hand to her. So much he wanted to say, so much he wanted her to understand, so much she needed to know. But how to start?

"No." She rose unsteadily and shook out her muslin skirts. "I got somethin' that needs sayin'. You've been kind, very kind, but my bein' so beholden to you— That ain't no way to go startin'—" She broke off. "I want to be free to make my own choices," she said, pronouncing each word with care. "Not do somethin' only on account of as how I'm obliged to. And not have someone else doin' it," she added, "because they feel sorry for me."

"Meaning," he said deliberately, "if I was to ask you to marry me, you'd never be certain I did it because I love you—or because I worry about you?"

She caught her lower lip between her teeth and nodded. "And you could never be sure I took you because I wanted to—or just jumped at the security you offered."

She had pride, his little Annie. Pride that had once driven her from the peace of a country estate to take her chances in London. And pride that still might drive her from the arms of the man who loved her.

Except he knew something she didn't.

"Annie," he said with quiet authority. "If you was to have two thousand pounds, what would you do with it?"

A shaky laugh set her shoulders trembling. "I'd take care of Violet and Rose," she said, "and I'd never be no burden to no one again."

Did that mean she'd rather live alone? He clenched his hands. He never realized just how hard it would be, letting her go, knowing she'd made the choice freely to live without him. He cleared his throat and forced himself to say the words that might take her from him forever. "You have it, you know. Templeton offered it as a reward to anyone who could bring the murderer of his uncle to book. And no one can doubt as how it's you as has done that."

"I—" She stared at him, taken aback. "T—two thousand pounds?"

"You can do anything you want. You're a woman of substance, now. Think, Annie. Any life you want." Only please, he silently prayed, let it include him. Though after all she'd been through, she'd probably use it to escape as far from him, as far from these memories, as she could get. He forced his voice to remain calm, betraying no trace of his yearnings, of his strained emotions. "I know a few people who can advise you, get it invested all safe and snug in the Funds so as how it can support you and Violet and

Rose for the rest of your lives. You won't never need to work again."

"Oh, yes I will." She still seemed stunned. "I—I could never be idle."

He looked up. "Annie, you're not going to refuse it, are you? It's not a blood price for your brother nor nothing like that. It's a reward, honestly offered and honestly earned. Oh, I'll admit as how Templeton never thought he'd have to pay it, but you deserve it, Annie. And the Templetons owe it to little Rose."

She gripped the railing. "Any life as I want?"

He nodded, fighting his sinking heart. He had nothing to offer her now, no inducement to keep her with him. At least she'd be happy and secure.

She came down a couple of steps, moving slowly as if numb. "We're even now, ain't we? I don't owe you nothin'?"

"Not a thing," he agreed, though he wished he could think of some massive debt that would tie her to him for just a little longer. Hell, for the rest of their lives.

She descended another stair. "And what is it as you want? As you *really* want?"

"Me?" Hope, that great betrayer, surged through him. "You know what, Annie. But we're not talking about me. This is your choice."

She drew in a quavering breath. "I—I couldn't never marry no Runner."

His hope faded, leaving his spirits lower than before. Still, he had to try. "How about a farmer? There should be a good bonus for this case, enough so's I could retire and buy a snug little cottage in a quiet village. Far from London."

Her eyes widened, and she came down three more steps before she said, tentatively: "Any man as took me would be gettin' himself a whole family."

Longing enveloped him, and for a moment it made it difficult for him to breathe. "I can't think of a nicer fate," he said when he could speak again.

"Can't you? If Rose won't have no father, she'll be needin' an uncle." She sounded uncertain. Almost afraid.

He forced in a deep breath, then another for good measure. "How do I apply for the position?"

Two more stairs. She stood only a little above him, now. Somehow, without realizing it, he'd crossed to the foot of the staircase.

"Are you sure you're wantin' to?" Her voice trembled.

He swallowed. "I already feel like an uncle to little Rose, and Violet has the makings of a first-rate sister-in-law."

"And—and me?"

He reached out, grasping her about her slight waist, and swung her down so she stood before him. He kept his hold tight, not quite daring to believe he might yet win. It was his whole life he staked on this next hand.

He brushed an errant curl from her eyes, his fingers lingering on her tear-stained cheek. "You, I need. Always. Life just don't seem to have no meaning any more, without you. If you're willing, we'll find ourselves a big cottage, with a fair bit of land to go with it. Little Rose will be needing cousins, and they'll be needing room. What do you say, Annie love?"

She pulled free, only to fling her arms about his neck. With one hand he caught her hair, tilting her head back until his mouth found hers. After a very long, very satisfying minute, he allowed his lips to stray across her cheek, then back to her mouth. "Well, love? Will you take one last desperate gamble on me?"

She shook her head, snuggling it against his chest, and her voice broke on a quavering sob. "This—this ain't no gamble. This here's the surest thing I've ever found."

TODAY'S HOTTEST READS
ARE TOMORROW'S SUPERSTARS

VICTORY'S WOMAN   (4484, $4.50)
by Gretchen Genet
Andrew—the carefree soldier who sought glory on the battlefield, and returned a shattered man . . . Niall—the legandary frontiersman and a former Shawnee captive, tormented by his past . . . Roger—the troubled youth, who would rise up to claim a shocking legacy . . . and Clarice—the passionate beauty bound by one man, and hopelessly in love with another. Set against the backdrop of the American revolution, three men fight for their heritage—and one woman is destined to change all their lives forever!

FORBIDDEN   (4488, $4.99)
by Jo Beverley
While fleeing from her brothers, who are attempting to sell her into a loveless marriage, Serena Riverton accepts a carriage ride from a stranger—who is the handsomest man she has ever seen. Lord Middlethorpe, himself, is actually contemplating marriage to a dull daughter of the aristocracy, when he encounters the breathtaking Serena. She arouses him as no woman ever has. And after a night of thrilling intimacy—a forbidden liaison—Serena must choose between a lady's place and a woman's passion!

WINDS OF DESTINY   (4489, $4.99)
by Victoria Thompson
Becky Tate is a half-breed outcast—branded by her Comanche heritage. Then she meets a rugged stranger who awakens her heart to the magic and mystery of passion. Hiding a desperate past, Texas Ranger Clint Masterson has ridden into cattle country to bring peace to a divided land. But a greater battle rages inside him when he dares to desire the beautiful Becky!

WILDEST HEART   (4456, $4.99)
by Virginia Brown
Maggie Malone had come to cattle country to forge her future as a healer. Now she was faced by Devon Conrad, an outlaw wounded body and soul by his shadowy past . . . whose eyes blazed with fury even as his burning caress sent her spiraling with desire. They came together in a Texas town about to explode in sin and scandal. Danger was their destiny—and there was nothing they wouldn't dare for love!

Available wherever paperbacks are sold, or order direct from the Publisher. Send cover price plus 50¢ per copy for mailing and handling to Penguin USA, P.O. Box 999, c/o Dept. 17109, Bergenfield, NJ 07621. Residents of New York and Tennessee must include sales tax. DO NOT SEND CASH.

Taylor—made Romance From Zebra Books